THE TROUBLE WITH BLACK CATS AND DEMONS

A CARY REDMOND NOVEL, BOOK 1

KAT SIMONS

T&D PUBLISHING

THE TROUBLE WITH BLACK CATS AND DEMONS

Published 2019 by T&D Publishing
Cover design: © 2019 Evernight Designs
Interior book design © 2019 T&D Publishing
ISBN-13: 978-1-944600-22-8 (Trade Paperback Edition)

First printing T&D Publishing edition: September 2019
For information, contact T&D Publishing www.tanddpublishing.com

For my mom, who helped me see a bigger picture.
For all the people who encouraged me to get this story published.
And for my whole family, for all the fun and pizza.

"Not again." Cary Redmond ducked as another fireball clipped over her head. "You don't think fireballs are a bit over the top," she shouted up at the ceiling then had to duck again as a dagger whispered past her ear.

Close. Her heart pounded. Way too close.

She needed to find the damned cat and get out of here. She scanned the apartment from her dubious cover behind a table piled high with unopened mail. Fireballs, daggers, gusts of preternatural wind, freezing hail and the occasional lightning bolt dropped around her, roaring through the living room in a bright cacophony of magical mayhem.

The lightning bolts flashing in the small confines were pretty spectacular. If they hadn't been trying to fry her, she might have enjoyed the show.

"Jaxer, I'm going to kill you for this."

Normally, this kind of thing was just part of her job. She was a Protector and literally got paid to run around keeping people safe, mostly from magical bad guys. Not that she'd asked for the job, but that was another story. It *was* her job, so she faced off against dangerous stuff because her bosses told her to.

Tonight, however, was not an official assignment. Tonight, she was doing a favor for her demented faery mentor. The bastard knew exactly how to get to her. All he had to do was mention a defenseless little black kitty cat and she was done for. How could she refuse to help a kitty? People did rotten things to black cats on Halloween.

Jaxer had forgotten to warn her about the fireballs.

She screeched through her teeth and dove behind the couch as one of the aforementioned fireballs barreled toward her. She cursed Jaxer as she took a quick look under the couch for the cat. Where the hell was it?

She'd called out to it when she'd first entered the apartment but hadn't gotten any irate kitty responses. After her lurching hunt of the living room and kitchen, the only place left was the bedroom.

She pulled in a deep breath as she contemplated the long space of unprotected ground between her hiding spot behind the couch and the bedroom door. Once she found the cat, this would be easier. When she was actively protecting something, very little of the magical dangers could get to her, and nothing deadly would touch her. She just had to *find* the cat first. And quickly. They had to be out of this cursed apartment before midnight. Before the wizard got home and all hell broke loose.

Again.

She ducked flying objects and ran to the bedroom, squealing when a lightning bolt hit the ground right behind her. Crossing her fingers there were no nasty spells waiting for her, she lunged through the half-open door and cringed in anticipation of magical repercussions as she fell onto a red-carpeted floor. She held perfectly still, waiting. When nothing happened, she pushed herself up onto her hands and knees and shook her head.

All this for a cat. That bastard Jaxer had a lot to answer for.

She rose to a crouch, trying to calm her racing pulse, and froze.

In front of her sat a huge bed, which she barely noticed because the naked man lying in the middle of the enormous mattress stopped her heart.

Holy hell.

He was absolutely magnificent. Tan skin, well-defined muscles, thick, black hair hanging down over his forehead. He was lying against a giant headboard with his head hanging forward so she couldn't get a good look at his face, but his golden eyes seemed to glow up at her from under his brows. Piercing and stunning and breath-stealing.

Cary swallowed. Hard. Because even the captivating gold of his eyes wasn't enough to keep her gaze from wandering over the breadth of his naked chest, the corded muscles of his shoulders and arms, the flat expanse of his stomach. It took a great deal of will power not to follow the line of dark hair arrowing down his abdomen…lower.

The man straightened and Cary heard the clink of chains at the same time as she got a look at his neck—and the thick, metal collar covering most of it.

What the hell had Jaxer gotten her into?

"Who're you?" she asked, breathless and embarrassed.

"Who are you?"

His voice carried a deep reverberation that made her spine tingle. Oh boy.

"I'm looking for a black cat," she said, knowing the explanation sounded inane. Jaxer had told her about Sheldon the wizard, but this? This was something else all together. What was this guy doing here? He wasn't Sheldon, she was sure of that, but then who was he? And where was the cat?

She blinked and a black leopard lay on the bed where the man had been. She sucked in a sharp breath, blinked again. And the man was back.

"Whoa." Cary swallowed. "*You're* the black cat I came to rescue?"

Oh, she really was going to kill Jaxer now. He hadn't said anything about a fully grown man who happened to be a leopard shapeshifter. He'd made sure she thought she was after a little, harmless kitty cat, not a deadly dangerous big cat who shifted into a beautiful, naked, very large man.

The faery was dead. Not that she knew how to kill him, but that was beside the point.

"Jaxer sent you?" The man's eyes narrowed and his features took on a dangerous edge. He hissed a curse under his breath and shook his head. "Stupid."

"Hey!" She stood, the better to face his gorgeous disgust. No one should look that good while insulting you. "You could have done worse, buddy."

She took a step toward the bed, wiping damp palms on her jeans. The chains she'd heard earlier linked the collar on his neck to the headboard, which was brass twisted into a scrawl of symbols she didn't recognize but looked like they might mean something if she stared at them long enough. He wasn't bound anywhere else that she dared peek, and the chains appeared flimsy enough. So the power keeping him confined must be in the collar.

"What is that?" She gestured with her head toward the thick band of metal.

"A binding ring," he said slowly, as if speaking to a child.

She frowned, both at his tone and the news. "But you just shifted."

"It's been designed to contain both my forms. Any other questions before you get me out of here?"

"Yeah, what crawled up your butt and put you in such a pissy mood?"

"Being held captive for sacrifice by a wizard and having a child sent to rescue me has dampened my day a bit," he said.

She grinned and enjoyed watching his eyes narrow suspiciously. "Child, huh? You know, at my age that's considered a compliment."

"How old could you be? Twenty?"

She shook her head. She'd actually turned thirty-two last April. But when she'd gotten tricked into becoming a Protector at twenty-six, she'd stopped aging at a normal rate. One of the few things about the job that didn't irritate her.

She took a quick moment to glance around the rest of the room. The red carpet wasn't the only gaudy element. Lots of black leather covered the walls and an animal skinned rug, which she was afraid to think about too closely given the captive on the overlarge bed, was tossed across the floor in front of what she thought might be a closet. A wood and metal trunk sat against one wall, red silk drapes covered the single window, and the overhead light was covered by thick, dark metal chains which gave the room strange shadows.

Fortunately, there were no nasty attack spells in here, which meant Sheldon didn't want his captive accidentally hurt by a stray lightning bolt. That worked in her favor, giving her time to solve the binding ring problem without being pelted by hail.

Though even if there had been spells in here, now that she was officially protecting someone, she could keep them both safe.

She did wonder why Sheldon would care if his shapeshifting captive got hurt before the midnight sacrifice. Obviously, he didn't want him killed too early. You couldn't sacrifice something that was already dead. But an additional warning spell in here probably wouldn't have killed his prisoner. Maybe. If Sheldon had enough control.

If he didn't, and was as powerful as Jaxer claimed, they really needed to get out of here. Fast.

She eased up to the bedside, still leery of traps, and leaned in close to the shifter, trying to ignore the yummy, stomach-fluttering male scent of him as she studied the binding ring. It was a thick band of silver and copper intertwined in a complex pattern of twists and folds. Over the silver, tiny runic symbols danced and shimmered so they were impossible to read.

"Oh good," she said, "a hard one."

The prisoner shivered, a low growl rising from his throat. The sound made Cary's heartbeat jump.

Speaking of hard ones.

She could feel his glare on the side of her face, but she resisted looking. She had other things to worry about at the moment.

Like how the hell she was going to get this damned spelled containment brace off his neck without alerting the entire mystical neighborhood.

"You did that on purpose," the man snarled.

"Huh?" She glanced at him. "What are you talking about?"

"Don't breathe on me again," he said.

She scowled. "What am I supposed to do? Hold my breath until I get your collar off? Just relax, big guy. You'll be out of here in a minute." To herself, she mumbled, "Wouldn't have gotten this much grief from a proper black cat."

"You some kind of witch?"

"No." After a moment, she sighed and shook her head. "Well, there's no help for it. I'm gonna have to use brute force. It'll take too long to get this off subtly."

"We don't have much time. It's nearly midnight now."

"Gee, really?"

He ignored her sarcasm. "Brute force?"

"Hold onto your valuable body parts," she said and tried not to think about his exposed valuable parts. Then she wrapped her hands around the collar, easing her fingers gently under so the backs pressed against his neck. His skin was warm and another shiver danced down her spine.

"Wait."

She met his gaze.

"What the hell are you doing? If I can't break that with my bare hands, you can't—"

He stopped short when she tugged and the collar came away with a quiet click.

"I'm not without some talent," she murmured.

"Who *are* you?"

"Come on. We have to get you out of here. I just made a lot of magical noise with that little stunt."

"Hold on."

He grabbed her hand. The feel of his warm palm wrapped around her fingers sent tiny sparks of electricity dancing over her skin. He dropped his hold, but she saw his eyes widen with the same shock she felt. He inhaled deeply, and against her will, she watched the strong muscles of his chest rise and fall.

"What's your name?" he asked.

"Cary."

"Cary. I'm Deacon."

"Nice to meet you." Did that sounded as stupid to him as it did to her given the circumstances?

He smiled, a slow, deadly grin that made her pulse race. "Nice to meet you, too."

She blinked and shook her head. "Come on, Deacon. We need to move."

As he slid to the edge of the mattress, Cary turned her back to avoid embarrassing them both—despite the temptation to look over every inch of him. The sound of material moving over skin behind her didn't help curb her less polite impulses, though, so she hurried to the door to see how the lightning bolts and fireballs were doing.

SLIPPING INTO HIS JEANS, DEACON WATCHED THE WOMAN AS SHE peeked around the edge of the doorframe toward the living room and the still popping spells Sheldon had set to keep help from reaching him.

She wasn't the rescue he'd been expecting. He'd expected the damned faery to come himself.

Jaxer had convinced him to let the wizard "capture" him, so they could find out *why* Sheldon was kidnapping shifters. They'd only found a few of Sheldon's victims—their bodies anyway. And they'd been little more than desiccated husks. The rest, even their bodies had vanished.

Wizards didn't go after shapeshifters for sacrifice very often. They were too hard to contain, and most of them didn't have the kind of magical energy an average human wizard could absorb through ceremonial magic. Shapeshifting wasn't typically magic. It was just biology.

Deacon knew none of the shifters killed so far had had any actual magic. He was a different case, but he wasn't sure Sheldon knew that. Jaxer did, which was why he'd come to Deacon in the first place, and Deacon had felt obliged to help even though none of the shifters taken so far had been leopards.

He suppressed an irritated growl. This was the last time he'd let the faery use him for bait. He'd been chained to that fucking bed all day with no sign of help. Then Jaxer went and made things worse by sending this…woman to rescue him instead of coming himself. How dare he endanger someone else when this crusade against Sheldon was his own personal business? Bad enough he dragged Deacon into it.

But as Deacon watched the woman straighten away from the doorframe when a lightning bolt flashed, he realized there *was* something about her. He couldn't deny the power she must have to break through the binding ring. Yet she looked and smelled like a normal human woman.

Her blond-brown hair hung in a long ponytail down her back over a battered brown leather jacket. She wore jeans, hiking boots, and a purple t-shirt with a glittery Happy Halloween emblazoned over a manically grinning jack-o-lantern. Her blue eyes had sparkled when he'd called her a child, then flashed with irritation when he'd insulted her.

And for reasons he couldn't quite understand, he'd found it hard to look away from her, especially when she'd knelt next to him on the bed.

Something about her…something about her scent tugged at his instincts.

Who the hell was she? *What* was she? She had to be more than human, but none of his senses picked up anything particularly preternatural about her. So where did all that power come from?

Jaxer had some explaining to do.

Deacon shook off his preoccupation and walked up behind her to stare at the living room over her head. Black scorch marks marred the hardwood floors, and a layer of frost covered one side table. The air was heavy with electricity and the smell of burning ozone.

Despite the multiple magical eruptions, the apartment was in remarkably good shape. As he watched, a dagger flew toward the bedroom, dropped harmlessly a foot from the doorway, and disappeared as if it hadn't existed.

Clever. Less clean up. And a testament to Sheldon's power.

He couldn't blame Jaxer for being worried about the little shit. But given a choice, Deacon would have taken a more…active approach to dealing with the wizard.

Unfortunately, and he was reluctant to admit this even to himself, his approach probably would have gotten him killed. The bastard was powerful. How Sheldon managed to be so powerful at his age was a mystery. But maybe that was the reason Jaxer was so obsessed with finding out the whys behind Sheldon's actions.

If Deacon got out of this apartment alive, he'd ask the faery. In the meantime, he and this very human woman had to navigate the bespelled living room and get away before Sheldon got back.

Deacon drew in a slow breath and was hit again by Cary's scent. Vanilla and cinnamon. And something else. Something that shot jolts of lust and need through his gut, making him lean closer to her just so he could feel the heat of her skin. He felt a possessive growl rising in his throat and swallowed it back, fisting his hands by his side to keep from reaching for her.

What the hell? He had more control that this. A lot more. He had to or people got killed. Resisting a woman, even one that smelled like heaven, had never been a problem before. With Cary, it took an effort to keep from pulling her close and burying his face in her neck to soak up her essence.

If he didn't know better, he'd think she was a witch casting a lust spell on him as some sort of sick joke. But she didn't smell like a witch.

His nostrils flared. That scent of hers…

It reached down inside him, calling to a deep instinct. As he breathed Cary in, his leopard whispered, *Mine.*

Out in the living room, wind-lashed hail whipped toward the bedroom without actually coming through the doorway. And behind that, a lightning bolt sizzled the floor.

"Sheldon didn't make this easy," he said, quirking a brow when she jumped at the sound of his voice.

"Are you dressed?" she asked without turning around.

He couldn't help smiling at the slight panic in her voice. "Yes."

"Okay. Stick close. Stay behind me and don't try to dodge around me. Got it? That's how we'll get out of here alive."

He frowned down at the top of her head. She must have some pretty powerful shields to get through that mess. But she wasn't a witch.

He grunted a noncommittal response, and she swung around to face him. The flash of heat in her eyes made his pulse kick.

"Listen, buddy," she said, her chin tucked back as she glared at him, "if you don't let me protect you, we're both dead. Okay? Don't go trying to be a hero. Just stay close and let me do what I came here to do."

She mumbled something unflattering under her breath as she turned back to the living room, and he had to fight a completely irrational urge to kiss her.

Over the course of the long day, with no sign of help from Jaxer, he'd had to face the possibility of his own death. His reaction to Cary might be a result of that, a need to reaffirm he was alive.

But as he breathed in the heady scent of her again, he wondered…

2

Cary reached back and grabbed Deacon's hand, trying to ignore the way her stomach clenched and her skin tingled. She eased through the bedroom door towing Deacon in her wake.

Focusing was difficult with her bare skin touching his, but damned if she knew why. She didn't react this way to men just because they were gorgeous. *Especially* if they were gorgeous. The only men she'd met that were as stunning as this particular black cat were guaranteed trouble with a capital T—and that included her mentor. Everything about Deacon screamed Trouble. Shapeshifter. Unnaturally handsome. Annoyingly arrogant. Smelled too damned good. Grin that could stop traffic. Voice like sin.

And he'd lied about being dressed. A pair of jeans with the top button left undone and nothing else covering that amazing body was not dressed. It was sexy as hell. But it did *not* qualify as being dressed.

With a scowl, she forced her thoughts to her current situation. She could ponder her irritating reaction to Deacon later. Now, she had to get them through this maze.

She heard his surprised gasp as daggers and fireballs swerved to avoid them. Hail flicked past in cold blasts but only a few, non-lethal ice balls touched her, and all of them missed Deacon completely.

Lightning struck close enough to make the hair on her arms stand up but always zigged away before hitting them.

She couldn't explain exactly how her Protector magic worked because she didn't know—neither her bosses nor Jaxer had seen fit to go into the details. She never even felt the "magic" powering up or flowing through her or whatever it did. She just knew that her bosses had invested her with it, and when she was standing between someone and danger, the magic happened.

After six years of jumping between bad guys and innocents, she could mostly ignored her fear that *this time* the magic wouldn't happen, the soul-crushing terror that this time she'd screw it all up and her charge would get killed. The magic hadn't failed her yet. So far, she'd managed to do exactly what she was supposed to do—protect people.

Still, she breathed a secret sigh of relief as the magical mayhem around her kept its distance.

But the closer they got to the front door, the more frantic the wizard's spells got. By the time they were halfway through the living room, they were trudging through a whirlwind of power so strong it was sucking the oxygen out of the air. She worked at controlling her heartbeat. This wasn't the first time she'd had to pit her magic against this much chaos. The Protector shield could take it. It had before.

She was going to need at least two shampoos to get the stench of scorched wood and burnt ozone out of her hair, though.

Jaxer owed her big time for this.

They were within a few feet of escape, Cary's anxiety just starting to ease, when a cracking sound alerted her an instant before the front door flew off its hinges, tumbling into the room right at them.

Despite knowing it wouldn't actual hit her, she still gasped and took a step back. It was really really hard to stare down a flying door without reacting.

Solid hands closed over her shoulders and strong arms cradled her against a rock hard chest. When she felt Deacon tense to move her out of the way, she planted her feet, holding her ground in front of him, and watched as the door defied the laws of physics by changing directions to move up and over their heads.

"How…?"

His voice whispered across the top of her hair and the heat of him seeped into her back. For a brief moment, Cary felt her eyes drifting shut from the sheer pleasure of having Deacon's hands on her.

Then a tall, skinny, pimple-faced teenager stepped through the smoking remains of the doorway. His dark hair hung in greasy strands across his forehead and sweat trickled down his temples. He wore a black silk shirt and black leather pants that only emphasized how painfully thin he was. He breathed hard as he faced them, but his watery brown eyes glowed with feral delight.

Sighing, she pulled reluctantly away from Deacon to confront the teenager. "Let me guess. You're Sheldon the wizard?"

"I am. And I will not allow you to leave with my leopard."

The boy's voice broke in the middle of his sentence and Cary's chest tightened. God, what else could go wrong tonight? What was she supposed to do with this *kid*? Jaxer, the bastard, hadn't warned her the wizard was this young. She could no more hurt a child than she could a helpless kitty.

At least the apartment had stopped firing hail and lightning at them. The spells must have deactivated when Sheldon came through the door. One less thing to worry about. And since the entire four-floor, twenty-unit apartment building was empty (she would have moved out if Sheldon was her neighbor, too), she didn't have to worry about protecting innocent bystanders. But the rest of this situation was a disaster.

How the hell did she get this skinny, awkward kid out of her way without anyone getting hurt?

"I'm pretty sure the leopard belongs to himself," she said as she tried to work out a plan. Plans weren't her strong suit. Jaxer usually handled those. She just got between good guys and bad guys and kept the good guys from getting killed. She was a walking, talking Kevlar vest, and Kevlar vests didn't do strategy.

"Not after tonight," Sheldon snarled in response to her distracted quip.

The hair on Cary's arms rose. Something truly evil flickered in the boy's leer. Shit. That wasn't good. She decided not to take his adolescent skin problems as a sign Sheldon would be easy to handle. He was obviously powerful enough to capture a leopard shifter and hold him. No telling what else the kid could do.

She just wished he wasn't so damned young. "I don't suppose you'll just get out of the way so we can leave?"

He lifted his lip in a painfully sad-looking snarl. "I'd like to know how you broke through the binding ring."

"Trade secret." She shrugged and stepped closer to him.

Maybe he'd be forced back by her magic if she and Deacon just walked out. This was the first time she'd been caught in an apartment with a demented teenager between her and escape. She'd rarely tried to bully her way past a bad guy before. They usually got fed up and went away when they couldn't get through her to their intended victim.

Sheldon didn't look like he'd give up easily, though. If she had to, she could stand here protecting Deacon all night. She just hoped it didn't come to that.

She took another step toward the wizard. To her surprise and horror, Deacon jerked her backward and moved in front of her. She shoved at his shoulder, but it was like pushing a brick wall.

"Damn it, Deacon, get behind me."

"You don't know what this little shit is capable of."

"It doesn't matter what he's—" She broke off as the little shit raised a hand to cast a spell. Desperate, she stepped away from Deacon and flung herself around him before he could stop her.

"What the hell are you doing?" he hissed.

"Just stay behind me, all right."

Sheldon studied them, his hand raised, his eyes narrowed. Why didn't he cast his spell? She was pretty sure he wasn't as concerned with her wellbeing as she was with his. So what held him back?

A low growl rose from behind her, reminding her Deacon wasn't going to passively listen to her orders. Damned arrogant leopard.

"I will not let an innocent woman stand between me and danger," he said.

She rolled her eyes. "Chauvinist. And I'm not all that innocent."

"We'll discuss *that* later."

The deep, husky promise in his voice made her toes curl, and she jumped when his hands dropped onto her shoulders again. But she was prepared for his tricky tactics this time. When he tried to move her, she held her ground.

"Listen," she hissed over her shoulder, "I'm the Protector here, okay? I'm the one doing…the…" She trailed off, biting her lip as Sheldon's eyes widened.

"I knew it! You're a Protector?" He bounced on his toes, grinning like a maniac.

"Damn," she muttered. This was so not good. So so not good. No wonder he'd been staring at them and not casting spells. He must have suspected what she was.

"A what?" Deacon asked.

"A Protector," Sheldon said with a triumphant little crow.

Their voices barely broke through her growing panic. Sheldon the wizard knew she was a Protector. She never told people exactly what she was for a reason. If Sheldon knew about Protectors, he might know how to get around her magic. It was tricky but not impossible. Which meant he'd know how to kill her.

Shit shit shit shit.

"This is perfect," Sheldon said. "Once I've taken the leopard's body and killed off this one—" he snarled down at his skinny form, "—then you, Protector, will keep me safe. With you as my personal bodyguard, nothing can harm me."

Her eyes widened as she realized what Sheldon had intended to do to Deacon. A body swap. Switching the essences of two people so that each inhabited the other's body. And killing off one of the bodies, along with the spirit trapped in it, would make the change permanent. He wanted to steal Deacon's body and keep it for himself. And he didn't care that doing that would require murdering Deacon.

Sheldon the wizard was starting to look less like a teenager and more like the evil bastard Jaxer said he was.

Then the rest of his little speech sunk in through her shock. He wasn't considering killing her. He only wanted her to protect him. Maybe he didn't know… Which meant she could still keep Deacon and herself alive.

"That's right," she stuttered to herself, relief making her a little giddy. "That's what I do. I protect."

"So you'd protect me if I looked like *him*?" Sheldon hissed.

"What?" She blinked, refocusing on the situation. "No. I wouldn't protect you willingly no matter what you looked like."

"And why's that?"

"Because you were going to kill a cat," she said simply.

Granted, it was that very philosophy that had gotten her into this Protector business in the first place, but that didn't change her basic worldview. If you could harm an animal, you didn't deserve her protection.

"He won't be a cat for long," Sheldon spat. "I'll be the cat when I'm finished taking his body. Then you'll *have* to protect me."

Deacon once again tried to move her out of the way. She stomped her foot and resisted. "Stop that," she snarled.

"No. Get behind me. He's insane."

"Really? I never noticed. You heard him. Protectors are good at protecting, so let me."

"I will not allow my mate to be hurt."

"I thought we… Your what?" she screeched. Her mouth dropped open as she glanced back at him. He could not be serious.

He used her shock to shove her aside, pushing her into the soft couch behind him. Then he spun.

And the leopard faced the wizard.

Sheldon screamed in triumph. The leopard growled, lowering its lean body into a crouch. Cary watched it all happening in slow-motion horror.

No!

She launched off the couch, hurling herself forward as Sheldon raised his hand to strike. Without thought, she leapt onto the leopard's back, high up near its head, just as the wizard's spell shot out from his fingertips. The energy bolt caught her in the side, flinging her back over the top of the leopard. She hit the ground hard on her shoulder and rolled, grunting when the base of the couch stopped her.

Ouch. Her vision blurred and a sharp stab of nausea clogged her throat. She felt the vibration of the residual power crawl over her skin before the pain took her full attention. She sucked in a breath and held it, choking back the rising bile.

The leopard's roar echoed in the small apartment. Cary's vision cleared enough for her to see Sheldon crumble to the ground just as the leopard jumped. She tried to shout at Deacon to stop, but her injury stole her voice.

The big black cat swatted at the wizard's inert form. And then Deacon stood in the open doorway, naked again and glaring. Cary groaned and closed her eyes so she wouldn't have to notice how good Deacon looked naked.

A moment later, she felt strong arms gathering her up against a warm chest. She hissed as more pain lanced her side.

"Where are you hurt?" he breathed against her hair.

"Ribs. Probably cracked a few. I hate that."

He cradled her closer, and Cary thought, *This feels nice. Right.* But that was too odd, too intimate a reaction to have with a stranger. What the hell was wrong with her?

She was too sore to move, so she stayed in his arms. She'd deal with this completely out of character response to Deacon after she got to a hospital. Or maybe a few days after that. Or maybe never. Especially if she never saw the man again. That would be easier.

"Why aren't you dead, you crazy woman?" he said against her temple.

"Crazy? That's rude after I just saved your life." She adjusted her position, trying to get more comfortable. "I'm not dead because I'm a Protector. That's how it works. So long as I'm protecting someone, all that magic stuff can't kill me. Which is why his spell ricocheted off me and rebounded on him." She took a few shallow breaths because deep breathing hurt. "It wasn't supposed to be a killing blow anyway. He was trying to incapacitate a leopard shifter, not kill one."

"But the spell would have killed a human woman."

"And it was strong enough, when it doubled back, to kill a human wizard."

"He was already dead when he collapsed," Deacon murmured in understanding.

"That's usually what happens." Damned stupid—possibly evil— kid. She really wished he hadn't been so young.

"Why are your ribs cracked?" Deacon asked.

"I still get hurt sometimes." She didn't laugh at the understatement only because laughing would feel awful right now. "It's like being shot while wearing a Kevlar vest—you still get bruised and sore. Except I'm more like the vest than the body inside the vest. And the vests do get damaged." Or so Jaxer had told her. The getting hurt part was one of the many things about her job she didn't like.

She was rambling, though, and rambling about things she wasn't supposed to be talking about, so she closed her mouth. Something was very wrong with her tonight. She decided to blame Jaxer. For all of it. Just because. It probably was his fault anyway.

"We'd better get you to a hospital," Deacon murmured.

He started to lift her, but a shot of pain through her side made her groan. "Wait." Sweat beaded on her brow. "Just give me a minute." She really hated when her ribs got broken.

He went back to cradling her.

"You're gonna want some clothes on before we go anywhere," she said, amazed how aware she was of his body despite her injuries. Typically pain robbed her of an awareness of naked flesh. But not Deacon's. Oh no. Deacon's naked body still managed to make her tingle in very private places even though the tingles were being outshone by her aching side. The fact that she was tingling at all was just weird.

"Sheldon's clothes won't fit me," he pointed out.

"Maybe he has a pair of sweats." She didn't much like the idea of other women seeing Deacon naked. Though why, she wasn't sure. More weirdness. Blame Jaxer, she thought. All his fault.

"I'll check in a minute."

"You should strip before shifting, you know. To avoid ruining your clothes." Cary rolled her eyes at herself. What a stupid thing to say. He was old enough to have figured that out by now.

"There's not always time," he said. "And I can always buy more clothes."

He gently kissed the top of her head, and her senses swam. So so not good. She had to stop reacting to this virtual stranger like this. He was going to figure out what he did to her soon and then she'd be in real trouble. She couldn't afford this kind of trouble. She had more than enough in her life already.

"How did you get to be a Protector? Were you born to it?"

Glad for his questions because they distracted her, she answered truthfully. "No." She snorted, but the movement hurt and she ended up wincing. "It's a long story. I was tricked into it."

"Tricked?"

"Well." She made a face, half embarrassed, half irritated. "That demon shouldn't have kicked the puppy." She scowled at Deacon's soft chuckle.

"You became a Protector because you tried to save a puppy from a demon?"

Her frown deepened. "I have a soft spot for animals," she muttered, amazed that her cheeks were heating with embarrassment. *This* embarrassed her? She should be feeling a little more ashamed of the fact that she was enjoying sitting in the arms of a very sexy, very naked man she didn't know. But no, that she was fine with. What a ninny.

"Good," he murmured and kissed her head again.

Gently, he swept her hair away from her neck and nuzzled her, his lips soft and seductive against her skin. She would have moaned if she weren't afraid it would hurt. She should probably put a stop to all this. Any minute now. Just had to gather her strength.

She was truly mortified by her disappointment when Deacon was the one to move away first.

"We need to get you to a hospital," he said again.

And before she could protest, he lifted her and set her on the couch. The movement hurt, but shock was dampening the pain. Finally. Then she made the mistake of looking at Deacon's naked back as he walked to the bedroom. Wow. She could get used to that view.

"By the way," she said when he returned wearing a pair of black sweat pants that were almost long enough for him but hugged his muscled body like a second skin. She swallowed and completely lost her train of thought. He might as well have been naked still. "You're gonna be cold like that."

"I have a naturally high body temperature."

"Oh good." She mentally shook her head and said, "What was all that about my being your mate? You said that just to get me out of the way, didn't you?"

He leaned over and lifted her into his arms. The fact that he could carry her so easily startled her as much as the tenderness in his touch.

"No," he said, heading toward the door.

"What do you mean?" She glanced down at Sheldon's body as the passed and sighed. Jaxer would have to clean up the mess. He usually did, but this time, the mess was clearly his fault, so she felt no guilt at all about passing him that responsibility.

"I mean," Deacon said, drawing her back to the conversation, "I didn't *just* say you were my mate to get you out of the way."

"I'm human," she felt the need to remind him.

"So."

"So…I'm not a leopard," she again pointed out the obvious.

As far as she knew, unlike their mundane animal counterparts, leopard shifters did form mate bonds. But only with other leopards. They might have affairs with humans, but she'd never read anywhere that leopards could actually bond with humans.

"Your scent." He nuzzled her neck again as he carried her to the elevator. "You're mine."

Cary's stomach tightened, dancing a crazy jig that did more to stop her breath than her cracked ribs. For a long moment, her brain refused to work. None of this made sense.

"We don't know anything about each other," she said lamely.

"What do you want to know?"

She asked the first thing that came to mind. "What do you do for a living?" She glanced up to see him smiling, a wealth of tenderness and humor in his golden eyes.

"I own and run animal sanctuaries around the country," he said.

Her eyes widened. "You protect animals?" she asked as the elevator doors opened.

He carried her in and pressed the button for the ground floor. "I do."

She stared up at his gorgeous face. He protected animals.

The elevator doors closed, and Cary turned to see her wide-eyed, pale reflection in the polished silver.

Oh boy.

3

*C*ary groaned as she eased down onto her couch. The painkillers she'd taken before leaving the hospital were wearing off and her ribs ached. The bruising didn't help. But at least she was home. She hated hospitals, no matter how often she had to avail of their services.

Thankfully, the doctor had been nice this time. He'd refrained from giving her that *look*—the one that said, "I suspect you're a battered woman given your medical records, and I want to help you so I might just have to call the police, and I'm definitely going to ask you a lot of awkward questions."

Leaning her head against the back of the couch, she closed her eyes. She probably did ask for the look. She'd amassed a horrendously long list of odd injuries over the last six years. And she'd never managed to find a doctor here in Portland that she could trust with the truth about her secret career.

Her bosses, who she'd nicknamed the Nags, were no help. They just told her to get hurt less. And every "medical" person Jaxer had tried to hook her up with had turned out to be a disaster for one reason or another. The California "healer" who turned out to be a vodun priestess ranked right up there as one of the worst. They had *not* gotten along.

Cary wasn't entirely sure why it was so hard to find a single doctor they could trust. She had a seamstress friend who made her bespelled clothes that kept her keys in her pockets when she had to jump around protecting people. A doctor used to supernatural injuries should have been easier to find than a seamstress.

But for six years, she'd come up empty. And so the ERs at the various hospitals around the greater Portland area had become her haunting grounds.

The worst part was that she always had to come up with lame excuses for the injuries. She couldn't just admit the truth to strange hospital personnel. That went against the rules and would put her in danger. Besides, who would believe her?

So that single serious bruise and the crack in one rib "came from falling on the edge of a blunt piece of pipe," even though she'd actually gotten the injury from jumping in front of a bullet.

The black eye? "I got that…falling down the stairs." Such an obvious excuse! But she couldn't very well say she got caught in the face by a wizard bolt aimed at a child without sounding insane. And to be fair, she should have turned so the shot hit her shoulder. She knew better than to dive in face first. But hindsight…

"I got the broken toe tripping over the end table." Actually, she'd gotten mad and kicked a kitten-biting vampire in the leg. Now that had been really embarrassing.

This trip to the hospital hadn't been any easier to explain. Though bruising along her side and several cracked ribs could come from any kind of a fall. But this time there were no awkward questions or looks. She supposed the man who'd taken her to the hospital might have had something to do with that. If she'd been the doctor, she'd have avoided giving the look anywhere near Deacon, too.

Her dogs picked that moment to start barking excitedly in the backyard, a welcome disruption in her train of thought. Sounded like Fred, her beloved mutt, had found a squirrel. She smiled, the comforting sounds distracting her from the ache in her side and unwanted musings about the man who'd kept her company at the hospital.

Then her doorbell ding-donged. She'd just managed to get comfortable, now she had to stand?

She rolled her head to stare at the door and considered ignoring whoever it was out there. But the visitor set a finger to the chime and didn't let up. She sighed and turned toward her good side, using the couch armrest to push herself to her feet. She only knew one person rude enough to abuse a doorbell that way when she was inside battered and bruised.

She opened the door a crack. "What do you want, Jaxer? I've earned the day off."

The impossibly beautiful blond man on her front stoop grinned—his most charming grin, she noticed sourly—and pushed into her little house. As she turned to tell him to get out, he took her face in his hands and kissed her on the mouth. Cary's eyes widened. For a split second, she couldn't react.

Then she shoved him away and scowled. "What the hell was that about, you crazy faery?"

Jaxer had never kissed her on the mouth before. Oh, he was flirty and charming and too touchy-feely as far as Cary was concerned. But she'd gotten used to him over the years. That was just the way he acted. And she was—for the most part—immune.

But a full on mouth kiss was new. And it sparked a serious level of suspicion. Jaxer did nothing without reason. He probably knew she was going to kill him as soon as her ribs healed, and he was trying to distract her.

"I'm just glad to see you're home and feeling better," he said.

His green-blue eyes warmed, sparkling with something she wasn't sure she liked. "Who said I'm feeling better? I feel rotten, thank you very much. And it's all your fault. I'd kill you now, but I hurt too much."

"Cary." He gave her an irritatingly elegant shrug. "You know you'd never kill me. You love me."

She snorted.

"Besides, I needed your help. I couldn't let Sheldon kill him. And you did rescue him, didn't you?"

"And got broken ribs for my troubles." She could have gotten a lot worse, too. "Sheldon knew about Protectors, you ass. The little shit could have killed me." She jabbed an accusing finger at Jaxer's perfectly muscled chest. "You said I was going after a black cat. You knew what I thought. You should have told me the black cat was a fully grown leopard shifter. And you should have warned me Sheldon was a teenager. And you sure as hell could have mentioned he *knew* what a Protector was."

"Would you have gone if I had?" He raised a brow. "Rescuing an adult man from a teenager?"

He knew her too well. Damn it. She always agreed to protect children, women, the elderly, and animals easily, no arguments. But she was less willing to put her physical wellbeing on the line for fully grown men. As far as Cary was concerned, grown men should be able to take care of themselves.

Though, as it turned out, this particular fully grown man really had needed her help. And the teenager *had* had a wicked streak of evil going. But still. That wasn't the point.

"It doesn't matter if I would have agreed or not," she countered, waving the hand on her uninjured side in a dismissive gesture as she turned back to the couch. She wasn't about to admit the truth now and lose the moral high ground. "The point is I went in without all the information. And..." She rounded, glaring at him again. "You didn't tell me you'd been after Sheldon for months. What the hell, Jaxer? You should have let me know the real situation."

In fact, she still didn't know the full story. Deacon had also been stingy with details when she brought the topic up at the hospital.

"I thought you'd get out of there before he got back to the apartment." Jaxer spread his hands, displaying his well-defined chest muscles through an open silk shirt.

Cary grimaced. It didn't matter that it was cold as a bear's butt outside. Jaxer always wore shirts that showed off his chest. He did, admittedly, have a nice chest to show off. A nice body in general. Along with a handsome face which she suspected wasn't nearly as stunning as his real visage. Behind the glamour all the Fae used with humans to appear less mystical, she suspected Jaxer was probably too beautiful for her mind to take. Though, in her more nasty moments, she pretended he was one of the really really ugly Fae, aspiring to be handsome.

"You got out just fine," he continued. "I don't see why you're so upset."

Her mouth actually dropped open. "You don't… What is wrong with you? Sheldon *knew* I was a Protector."

"And you were protecting someone, so you were safe." He closed the space between them and cupped her cheeks. "Cary, I would never send you into a situation I didn't think you would walk away from."

"Oh, right. That's what I've been doing for the last six years. All the easy stuff. This Protector gig is a real walk in the park. Why should I worry about getting killed?" She shook her head to dislodge his hold. "And what's with that kiss you landed on me when you came in?"

Jaxer, for all his irritating qualities, was her friend as well as her mentor. He'd stood by her from the beginning of this whole Protector business. She felt like he was changing the rules of their friendship with that kiss, and she didn't like it.

Jaxer grinned, his expression softening into something Cary could almost have mistaken for real emotion. Except the faery rarely expressed his true feelings outwardly.

"I'm relieved you're okay," he said. "And you looked so cute scowling at me through the door, I couldn't resist."

"In future, resist," said a deep voice from Cary's still open doorway.

Her heart tripped over itself to keep up with her suddenly rushing pulse. Exactly two hours had passed since she'd last seen Deacon at the hospital, when he'd put her in a taxi and sent her home. Though she'd secretly hoped to see him again, she hadn't really thought he'd show up at her door.

The fact that he could find her house at all was a testament to the fact that she did want to see him. Which would be embarrassing if he knew about the spell on her home and how it kept people she didn't want around from finding her sanctuary.

Unfortunately, she wasn't actually prepared to see him yet.

"Hi," she said, because the mere sight of him made her brain short circuit. No one should look that good this early in the morning.

"Hi," he said back.

The sound of his voice sent a giddy jolt of excitement through her entire body. Geez. Still? She still couldn't be around him without her body immediately overheating with lust? This was just so wrong. Something truly weird was going on with her.

He rescues animals.

The ridiculous thought kept spinning through her head, confusing years of well-honed instincts which kept her from trusting spectacularly handsome preternatural men. She'd met more than her fair share since becoming a Protector. Hell, she was mentored by one. But every one of them had been a grade A pain in her ass, and on more than one occasion, they'd tried to kill her. Not circumstances which encouraged trust. Out of self-preservation, she'd developed an immunity to charm and good looks.

But Deacon was…different. He rescued animals for a living. Last night, he'd gotten her yummy non-hospital coffee when she'd sighed at the prospect of the available sludge. He wasn't trying to kill her, which was a definite bonus. And he *rescued animals* for a living.

What the hell kind of preternatural sex god did that?

It took Jaxer's voice to pull her out of her thoughts. Which was really embarrassing.

"Deacon," he said, his tone overly cheerful. "Glad to see you safe and sound."

"Don't ever send me in as bait again," Deacon said without glancing away from Cary. "Next time, I'll take the wizard out without all the pretense."

"We had to know what he was doing with all the shifters," Jaxer said. "More could have died otherwise and you know it."

Deacon ignored him and asked Cary, "How are you feeling?"

She shrugged then winced. "The painkillers the doctor gave me are wearing off. What's all this about other shifters and Sheldon?" Deacon had told her the part about Jaxer looking into Sheldon for months. He hadn't mentioned "all the shifters" being killed.

Jaxer opened his mouth but Deacon cut him off, avoiding her question when he said, "You should be in bed if you're in pain."

"I was resting on the couch, gearing myself up for bed, when the doorbell rang." She glared at Jaxer who raised a guiltless eyebrow. "Now tell me more about what's happening with the shifters."

Deacon eased inside and closed the door. Like Jaxer, he didn't even have a jacket on. But his jeans and wool sweater were at least mildly more appropriate to the weather than Jaxer's silk shirt and linen trousers. Portland, Oregon wasn't exactly the tropics in November.

"You shouldn't have made her get up," Deacon scolded Jaxer.

The faery rolled his eyes and lounged against the wall, managing to look casually elegant and relaxed in her tiny living room.

"She recovers fast," Jaxer said, a note of annoyance in his voice. "No need to play the mother hen just because she saved your life."

"She needs to rest. Go home. Let her recover in peace."

"Stop talking about me like I'm not here," she said. "What's going on with the shifters?"

"Don't worry about it, sweetie," Jaxer said with a smile. "I'm taking care of it."

Sweetie? Maybe Jaxer had finally gone insane. Or she had. It was hard to tell at the moment. She really did need to rest.

She headed toward the couch, ignoring both men, hoping Jaxer would listen to Deacon. He never listened to her when she told him to go away. But this had been a night and a morning of firsts, so she could always hope.

She groaned as she settled on the cushions and closed her eyes, leaning her head back. "Don't answer my questions if you don't want to," she muttered. "Since Sheldon is dead, I don't suppose it matters anymore."

"He's dead?"

The surprise in Jaxer's voice had her opening her eyes. "You didn't go clean up?"

"I did. I didn't see Sheldon."

"We left his body in the doorway," Deacon said, frowning.

Cary sat up. "You swear you didn't see it?" she asked Jaxer.

"I'd hardly lie about that." But he was frowning too.

"Shit." She looked at Deacon. "He *was* dead, right?"

"You didn't check?" Jaxer had the audacity to sound annoyed.

She gave him a deadpan stare. "Broken ribs. Remember?"

"I didn't check closely, either," Deacon said. "I assumed, but was too worried about Cary to double check. I didn't hear a heartbeat or breathing, though."

"Oh, this can't be good," she said mostly to herself. That little shit knew what she was.

"I'll handle it," Jaxer assured, sitting on the couch next to her, casually dropping an arm around her shoulders.

She scowled at him but was too tired to shrug him off.

The sound of Deacon's growl raised the hairs on the back of her neck. She turned to see a scary dangerous glare hardening his handsome feature. Oh boy.

"Take your hands off my mate," he said to Jaxer.

"You're what?" Jaxer said, his voice deepening.

To her surprise, he actually did move his arm, but mostly to stand up and face off with Deacon.

She groaned. There was way too much testosterone poisoning in the room. She really didn't feel up to this. "Guys, guys. Dial it down or get out of my house. You're scaring the dogs." She could here Buck growling, and Pickles had started to howl.

Since Buck was a demon dog and Pickles a foo lion, upsetting them was not a good idea. Though she suspected Fred, the mundane mutt, would be the most dangerous one of the pack.

Jaxer let some of the tension ease from his body and smirked. Deacon remained ridged and glaring.

She rolled her eyes. "Maybe someone might want to go look into the missing wizard while I heal?" she suggested.

"Don't worry, sweetie, I'll handle him."

Sweetie from Jaxer again. What the hell was wrong with everyone today? She turned into a lust-crazed idiot around Deacon. Jaxer called her sweetie and kissed her on the mouth. Deacon had this bizarre idea she was his mate. Next thing she knew the Nags would stop…well, nagging.

Then she'd know for sure the End Times were upon them.

With a slight head shake, she relaxed back into the couch. She was too tired for all this. She needed to rest so her ribs would stitch back together. She might heal faster than a normal human, but it still took some time. After that, she'd work out the tangled strangeness. There had to be a reason for it all, she was just too achy to think clearly right now.

"Why are you here, Deacon?" Jaxer asked.

Couldn't they take a hint a go away? She opened her eyes. "Jaxer, let it go. Deacon, thanks for checking on me. Now, could the two of you please leave? I have sleep I need to get to."

Deacon lifted a bag in his hand she hadn't noticed before. "You forgot your prescription."

"Oh." Oops. She must be getting too used to pain that she'd completely forgotten the extra drugs. "Thanks."

He smiled as he set the bag down on the coffee table and Cary had to blink a few times. Wow. With a grin like that, he could rule the world.

Jaxer cleared his throat when the silence between her and Deacon carried on just a little too long for company. "Do you need anything else before we go, sweetie?"

"Yes. Stop calling me sweetie."

Jaxer gave her a heavy-lidded, crooked smile that had probably felled stronger women than her. Though why he was flashing that at her, she had no idea. Maybe it was just because Deacon was here. From the very quiet growl the shifter let out, she suspected that was the real reason behind Jaxer's suddenly flirty behavior.

"Back off, faery. She's mine."

She looked at Deacon, eyebrows raised. Oh really? She was about to comment aloud on his presumptuousness when a familiar shiver moved down her spine and dread settled in her gut.

"Oh no." She narrowed her eyes and rose slowly. "Not now."

4

$\mathcal{C}$ary glared at the two exquisitely stunning newcomers standing in the center of her living room. She flicked a quick glance at Jaxer who was leaning against the fireplace mantle, his gaze trained on the arrivals, his expression impossible to read. She knew her own was not so neutral as she faced her unwelcome visitors.

Mutinous was probably the most apt description.

Her bosses. The beings who'd tricked her into becoming a Protector more than six years ago.

They made only a minimal effort to appear human, but they were incredibly beautiful in a way she always found hard to describe. Like the beauty of nature itself, but turned up. They belonged to a species of Fae native to North America and had been known to different Native American tribes by different names. Her favorite came from the Passamaquoddy. They called them the Nagumwasuck, which Cary had taken great delight in shortening to the Nags. Since they were.

She had a real love-hate relationship with them. They tried to do good, and for that she admired them. But she wasn't all that happy with their sense of timing.

"No," she told them before either could say a word. "I'm hurt, I'm tired, and I'm not doing anything for at least forty-eight hours, so just go away and come back when my ribs have healed." She held their gazes, ignoring Deacon—with a great deal of effort—when she felt him move up behind her.

"Protector," Wisat said, in a patient tone that set her teeth on edge. He was all black and red, his skin a shade of red not typically found in nature, his robe and short hair black as midnight. His eyes were an unreal green that stood out like glowing glass against his skin. Two interwoven red halos covered in soft, velvet-like fuzz crowned his scalp. "Would we come to you if the need wasn't great?" he asked.

Yes, yes they would. "Wisat, I need time to recover."

"And whose fault is that?" Liruk said, her tone significantly less patient. She had long white hair, hanging to the ground like a veil against the shimmering pearl of her robe. Her skin was a deep, golden brown, her eyes the same green as Wisat's. Where Wisat had halos, Liruk had two little golden horns sticking out through the mass of her hair.

Liruk had never understood Cary's reluctance to fully embrace the job of Protector, so her intolerance for what she considered Cary's stubborn eccentricities colored most of their dealings. Occasionally, Cary could say she got along with Liruk. But she preferred Wisat.

Except at the moment. Right then, she didn't want to see either one of them. Not when they were pointing out—again!—that she wasn't good enough at her job to avoid injury. It was their fault she was doing this job. Telling her repeatedly that she sucked at it was not a good way to endear them to her.

"It's my fault Cary got hurt," Jaxer volunteered. "I didn't tell her everything I should have about Sheldon when I sent her in."

Cary glanced sharply at her mentor. He usually left her to take the heat from the Nags on her own. Having Jaxer come to her defense now was a surprise. But she hated being under-informed in front of the Nags. Liruk gave her enough grief as it was because Cary had spent the last six years studying and still didn't know everything she needed to know to do her job.

"And she saved my life," Deacon said from behind her. "While I was doing a favor for you and Jaxer. She deserves a rest. And she needs a lot more than forty-eight hours."

"She heals fast," Liruk said to Deacon, her tone matter-of-fact. "She will be better soon."

"We need her today," Wisat said. "There is someone who will require your protection, Cary."

"Today?" She let out a little sigh. What could she do? This was her job, Portland her territory.

Technically, she had to do what the Nags required of her. They were her bosses. Whether she'd actually applied for her current position or not was beside the point. Saying no when she could probably still manage to protect someone wasn't an option.

Which irritated the hell out of her.

"For the moment, we just need you to keep an eye on him," Wisat said with his usual patience.

"He isn't in immediate danger," Liruk added, her voice softening as well. "But we are sure he will be. Very soon."

"Fine." She blew out a resigned breath. "What do you know about him? Where do I find him?"

"I'll take care of the initial watch," Jaxer said, pushing away from the fireplace. "She won't be any good to you exhausted and hurt. I can look after this guy until she's healed."

Cary tilted her head to one side. For the first time since last night, she didn't feel like killing her mentor. "Jaxer. That's really nice of you."

He shrugged, a graceful lifting of the shoulders, and grinned with his usual charming arrogance. "I got you hurt sending you to rescue the leopard boy. I can watch one human for a day to pay you back."

She rolled her eyes at his leopard boy comment but was glad he'd finally apologized. Sort of. As much as Jaxer usually did. And since he was helping her, she let her murderous plans for his future ease back to something less final.

The Nags gave her a brief rundown on the person she needed to protect—a thirteen-year-old boy with a very interesting talent.

"He can speak with animals and call them to him? What a cool skill. Why is he in need of protection?" she asked.

Liruk and Wisat exchanged a look, and Cary frowned. That look didn't bode well for her.

"We aren't entirely sure where the danger is coming from," Wisat admitted after a moment. "Only that there is danger."

"The boy is innocent now," Liruk added. "His gift is neutral, neither good nor bad. He could still go either way."

"We wouldn't want him exposed to the wrong influences," Wisat said.

"At thirteen?" Cary snorted. "The entire world is a bad influence on a kid that age. Anything else I need to know?"

"The danger will be to the boy, not to others because of the boy. At first." Liruk frowned, a very slight expression that did nothing to mar her incredible beauty. "The omens have been vague on the exact nature of the danger."

That was the problem with omens and premonitions. They were frequently too vague to be useful. The Nags were very good at looking after humans and other magical beings. It's what they did. What they'd done for centuries. Cary had never fully understood why, but the fact that they tried counted for something.

They created the Protectors, who were mostly humans, and assigned them mentors, mostly from the magical races, who had experience in all aspects of the preternatural world. Her mentor was a faery. Another Protector's mentor could be a goblin, a leprechaun, an elf, a witch—any creature experienced with working in the mystical realms. She wasn't sure how they picked the mentors. Jaxer had never told her how he'd met the Nags nonetheless how he'd started working with them—even when she'd ask him point blank.

For their part, her bosses detected danger to other creatures through omens, premonitions, and sometimes a little old-fashioned research. Then they sent the Protectors in to save the day.

Obviously, the system wasn't flawless or there'd never be another child abuse case or murder in the world. They couldn't take care of everything, everywhere, all the time, for everyone. Often the signs of danger were so ephemeral they weren't able to pinpoint a person or place to send help. And there were a limited number of Protectors.

But the Nags tried. For what it was worth. And because they continued to do what they did century after century, Cary had always admired them. She wasn't too crazy about the way they'd tricked her into her current job, but that was another issue.

Wisat gave Jaxer the boy's address, a not great but not rotten neighborhood in the southwest part of the city. "If something happens, I'll contact Cary." Jaxer winked at her. "I could probably manage a little magic of my own in the meantime."

She snorted. Jaxer's best magic was glamour. He was better even than most other faeries at making people see and experience what he wanted them to. His illusions were so potent, they *felt* real. Through careful use of his talent, Jaxer could get almost anyone to do anything he wanted. For a short period of time anyway. A scary enough power all by itself. But he definitely had other tricks up his sleeve.

"The boy's name is Jonathon Webber," Wisat said, and started a short lecture on the proper ways to protect someone without revealing oneself. Jaxer cut him off with a rude comment and the official briefing came to an abrupt end as Liruk and Jaxer got into a word duel.

Once everyone was out of her house—Deacon, to her surprise, going with Jaxer to help watch the boy—Cary made sure the dogs were happy in the backyard, then went to bed. She slept for ten hours, got up long enough to eat a bowl of soup, kick a ball around in the yard with the dogs, carefully, so as not to hurt her ribs, took another painkiller, and went back to bed.

Sometime in the middle of the night, Deacon's scent invaded her dreams. Without opening her eyes, she could picture him in the dark, near her bedroom door, watching her. And because she was still asleep, she wasn't the least bit afraid. Why shouldn't Deacon be in her room in the middle of the night? He was her mate.

"What are you doing here?" she murmured.

"I wanted to make sure you were okay. Still breathing."

"That's nice." She felt the bed dip next to her.

"Are you?" he asked.

A feather touch glided across her cheek. "Am I what?"

"Okay?" Humor crept into his deep voice.

"Mmm… Yes. Sleepy. You smell nice."

"You do, too."

She felt the press of firm lips on her forehead, the wash of warm breath across her cheek. "Did you find Jonathon?" she murmured even as the feel of his lips made her hum in the back of her throat.

"We did. Jaxer is watching him tonight."

"You aren't with him?"

"I needed to check on you."

"Oh. I'm fine. Sleepy."

"I'll let you get back to sleep now."

"Stay. You're warm." She shifted closer to his heat, curling around his body where he sat on the bed next to her. She drifted for a moment, savoring the warmth. She couldn't feel her damaged ribs and her brain floated in a wash of contentment.

"I wish I could stay," he murmured into her hair. "But you need your rest. I'll come back in the morning. Should I bring you breakfast?"

"Yes. Bagels."

"With cream cheese and lox?"

"No fish. Cream cheese. Donuts."

"You want donuts, too?"

"Mmm… Donuts."

"Bagels and donuts it is, then."

Cary pressed her face into his heat, breathing deep to pull in his scent, and drifted into another dream.

When she finally woke, light streamed in through a crack in the curtains and the clock on her cellphone told her it was ten in the morning. She groaned, stretched, then sat up, testing her ribs and bruises. Better. Much better. Sleeping for most of a twenty-four hour period could do that for a girl.

Good dreams helped, too.

She stared at the sage green curtains covering her window. He was sneaking into her dreams already. She shook her head. She was in a world of trouble were that man was concerned. And she had no idea what to do about it or why it was even happening.

She'd hoped to wake up and miraculously understand why she reacted to him the way she did, why she wanted him around, why thoughts of him made her stomach tighten with anticipation. They'd met two nights ago. She knew nothing about him beyond his job, that he was a leopard shifter, and that he looked delicious naked. The mate business seemed too far-fetched. Some weird shifter pickup line maybe? But there *was* something different about Deacon and her reaction to him.

On the plus side, she'd be able to talk to him about her day. That was unique. There were only a handful of people she trusted with her secret identity. Even her parents didn't know what she really did. They thought she was a research assistant for one of her old college professors who was working on a series of popular science books. Her younger sister Valerie knew. And her three best friends knew. Jaxer, of course, though she wasn't sure he counted. Her computer guru Chris knew, but that was because Chris worked for the Nags, too.

But never a partner, never a man she could be completely open with.

She groaned and turned to stare up at the ceiling. She couldn't even find a good doctor. What made her think she'd be able to find a man to fit into her weird, chaotic life?

With a grunt of irritation, she swung out of bed and wandered into the bathroom, determined to put Deacon out of her mind for the morning. She had a job to do. That meant she had to be awake and focused.

Which meant coffee.

On her way to the kitchen, the dogs jumped from their beds in the living room under the big picture window that looked out into her backyard and follow her. All three sat patiently waiting to be let out as she crossed to the coffee machine.

"Be with you in just a sec, guys," she said as she got her required caffeine fix ready. "You all hungry?"

Fred the mutt, a cross between a collie and a terrier, barked and jumped up, his smallish size belying his large and energetic personality. Her basset hound who was actually a retired foo lion, Pickles, scratched her ear. Buck, the demon dog currently in the shape of a normal sized blond Labrador, thumped his tail on the floor twice. Chuckling, she flicked the coffeemaker on and went through the mudroom to the back door. She opened the screen, then screeched in shock.

Deacon stood with one hand raised as if to knock, the other hand holding a large paper bag. "Hi," he said.

The sight of him fried the synapses in her brain, making it impossible to speak. Her cheeks warmed for no good reason. And she had a completely irrational desire to run her fingers through her hair even though it was pulled back in a ponytail.

"Sorry I startled you." He grinned sheepishly and lowered his hand.

Cary decided there were few things in the world quite as charming as Deacon's grin. The dogs pushed past them both, eager to get out into the cold morning air, and their jostling broke her daze.

Shaking her head, she stared after her dogs. They hadn't paid the least bit of attention to Deacon, as if they'd expected him to be there. Weird.

"What are you doing here?" she asked. "And why at the back door?" Then the smell of whatever was in the bag hit her and her stomach growled. "What did you bring?"

"Donuts and bagels, as requested."

Cary's mouth fell open. "How did you...? That was a... That wasn't a dream?"

He tilted his head. "No. I thought you realized."

"How the hell did you get in? And past the dogs?" No one got past Pickles. In her previous incarnation, Pickles had guarded palaces!

And how had Cary slept through having a virtual stranger in her home? Physical attraction or not, she didn't know Deacon beyond some superficial stuff and the fact that he was a friend of Jaxer's. And really, what kind of recommendation was that, being one of Jaxer's friends? She'd met plenty of the faery's buddies, and she wouldn't want them in the same state as her, nonetheless in her house.

Her sense of vulnerability made her scowl, but inwardly she

cringed. Deacon wouldn't even be able to find her house if she didn't want him to, so she had only herself to blame.

Still. This was no time to admit it.

Deacon's brow creased with a slight frown. "You have a key under the mat." He nodded to the green rectangle under his feet. "That's not a very good idea, you know. Anyone could walk in here."

"That's what three dogs are for," she squeaked.

He laughed and the sound was like velvet on her spine. Oh, that was really, really unfair. He shouldn't be both gorgeous and have a laugh that made her toes curl. There had to be something wrong with him. For her sanity's sake, he had to have a flaw. Where was that grumpy bastard she'd rescued two nights ago? Him, she could deal with.

Except she'd been hot and bothered by Deacon even when he was being an ass.

"I sat down with the dogs when I came in and we came to an understanding ," he said with a shrug. "When I asked if I could go check on you, none of them protested."

She was going to have a talk with those three. No trusting random men just because they seemed nice and rescued animals for a living. This time she winced outwardly. She needed to follow her own admonishments before scolding the dogs.

"Why'd you come to the back door?" She needed to change the subject. Some Protector she was, leaving her home wide open to breaking and entering.

"I didn't want to wake you," he said. "If you were still asleep, I was going to drop the food inside and leave." He looked her over, taking in her t-shirt and flannel pajama pants. "Can I come inside? You have to be cold standing in the doorway dressed like that."

Once he mentioned it, she noticed the chill. Begrudgingly, she stepped aside. He had brought her breakfast after all. It would be rude to ignore donuts. She only wished his presence didn't feel so…natural. If she was nervous about having him in her house, she'd feel better. Saner. The fact that she *liked* having him there was bad.

"You want something to drink?" she asked out of perverse habit. Her mother would be so proud.

"Milk, please." He tossed her a sexy smile over his shoulder before setting the bag on the counter.

Milk? She resisted groaning, but only barely. Of course, the cat liked milk.

As she poured his drink and readied her cup of coffee, she considered, yet again, how little she knew about him. He'd been in her bedroom last night—which should scare the crap out of her. Why the hell wasn't she scared? Or at least more freaked out? Shouldn't she be enraged? Why was she pouring him milk instead of tossing him to the curb and revoking his permission to find her house?

"I don't even know your last name," she said in a bewildered tone, glancing up to see him staring at her. "You have seen me sleeping. I have seen you naked. And I don't know your last name."

"You never asked. It's Jones."

"Deacon Jones." She glanced at the paper bag. "What kind of donuts did you get?"

"Boston cream and coconut."

Her eyes widened. "Coconut is my favorite. How did you know?"

"I asked Jaxer."

"You found out my favorite donut?"

His expression softened. "You're my mate."

He said that as if it explained everything. Maybe to him it did.

He snatched the bag back off the counter and looked around. "Table?" He nodded to the small, two-seater against the wall in a little nook beside the fridge.

"I usually eat on the couch." The table was more for show so her mother thought she ate meals like a grownup.

Taking her hand without another word, he led her to the living room. The physical contact sent an involuntary shiver over her spine.

Oh boy. Capital T Trouble.

Before they could sit down, though, that familiar feeling swept over her. She cursed as Liruk materialized on the opposite side of the coffee table.

"You need to go to Jonathan," she said without preamble. "Now. There is no time to discuss this, Protector. Get dressed. You must leave immediately."

The urgency in Liruk's voice overrode Cary's irritation. She was halfway to the hall when she realized. "My car is still at Sheldon's apartment."

"I'll drive," Deacon said. "Get dressed."

5

On their third circle of the area, Cary started to worry. "This is where Liruk said he'd be?" she asked. Again.

"This is the block he lives on," Deacon said.

"What if we're too late? Liruk seemed really worried."

"How can you tell?"

Cary waved a hand absently, still scanning the sidewalks. "I've had to deal with her for six years. Hey, there's a kid. About the right height."

Deacon nodded. "That's him. But I'm gonna have to circle again to find a parking spot."

"I'll get out here."

He pulled near enough to the curb for her to jump out.

Jonathan was on the opposite side of the road and half a block ahead. She ran across the street, already going over her cover story if he spotted her following him. She was halfway through her excuse when a big, black Lincoln Towncar slid up to the sidewalk next to Jonathon, parked illegally, and two men in dark suits got out.

Shit. She picked up speed, walking so fast it would have been easier to jog. But jogging in hiking boots and a battered leather jacket would be too obvious.

Then one of the men grabbed Jonathan by the arm. The boy shouted and tried to pull away.

And Cary broke into a full run.

She reached the struggling pair as Jonathon jerked free of the man's grasp. Without pausing, she wrapped the kid in her arms and turned her back to the two men just as a stream of fire like a sun burst rushed over her and the boy.

Her magic parted the flames, bracketing them in walls of fire, but the searing heat never touched them.

She took a moment to look into the kid's huge, dark eyes. He was nearly her height. When he hit his growth spurt in a couple of years, he was going to be tall.

"Hot in here, huh?" she said with a crooked smile as sweat slid down her temples.

"Uh huh."

Given how pale and wide-eyed he was, Cary guessed that was the best he could do just then. She couldn't blame him. Not every day you got engulfed in bone-melting flames without getting singed.

At least, for the average person this was a unique experience.

The flames died and her skin tingled in reaction, like ants crawling over her. She hated that aftereffect of using her power. But the wash of cold November air felt good after the intense heat.

Cary winked at the boy. "Don't worry. Just stay behind me and you'll be safe." She turned to face the two men, blocking Jonathon with her body.

The one who had stood back from the initial tussle was gripping the first man by the arm. "What the hell are you doing, you idiot?" he snarled. "The boss wants him alive, not crispy fried."

Jon shuddered behind her, and Cary's heart squeezed tight. "It's okay, kid," she said over her shoulder. "You're safe now. When this is over, we'll go treat ourselves to an ice cream and chocolate pig out. What do you say?"

"I don't like sweets." His voice was shaky, but at least he could talk.

Cary frowned. "You don't like sweets?"

"No. I'd rather have fries."

She shrugged. "Okay. I'll get ice cream, you get French fries."

The calmer of the two men frowned. The less calm one, the one who'd grabbed Jon and shot fire at him, said, "Who the fuck are you, lady?"

"Just a concerned citizen. Kid didn't look like he wanted to go with you. Seems to me you two should go about your business. Now. Before we have to call the cops."

"We're friends of his mother," the calmer one said. "She asked us to pick him up. She's in the hospital."

Cary's eyebrows popped up and an involuntary laugh escaped. "Are you serious? Geez, kidnappers have been using that line on kids since the beginning of time. What, you couldn't come up with something more original? You might as well have said, 'You want some candy, little boy?'"

Mr. Calm scowled. Less Calm took an aggressive step toward her, but Calm stopped him with a sharp hand gesture.

"Miss," Mr. Calm said, calmly as it happened. "The truth is our boss just wants to talk to the kid. No big deal. He's got a job offer, is all. Hey, you can come along too if you're so worried. Make sure everything's on the up and up."

She rolled her eyes and half-turned to look over her shoulder. "Do I have 'Big Stupid White Chick' written on my forehead?" she asked Jonathan.

The question surprised a snort of amusement from him, and he shook his head.

"Yeah, I didn't think so." She faced Calm and Less Calm again, settling her gaze on Less Calm. "Those flames were yours, I take it. Nice work. Really hot. Fingertips or palm?"

Less Calm's expression turned stormy. He opened his mouth. Calm slapped a hand under his chin, forcing Less Calm's mouth shut. The gesture elicited a mumbled string of curses from Less Calm, words no teenage boy should be exposed to.

Cary lifted a brow as a puff of smoke from Less Calm's mouth accompanied the curses. Huh. Well, that was new. Over her shoulder, she said, "Were you serious about the chocolate?"

"Yeah. I've never liked sweets much," Jon said, his voice more steady now.

"Weird."

"Would you two shut up about the damned sweets," Calm said, some of his calm beginning to slip. He reached inside his jacket and pulled out a very big hand gun, its black finish giving it a muted, sinister aura.

"Ah hell," Cary muttered, straightening her shoulders. "I hate getting shot."

She wrapped her arms backward to keep Jon in place. If she didn't have to jump between him and a flying bullet, chances were excellent the bullet would have time to change trajectories before getting anywhere near her. When she had to jump into the path of an already moving bullet, that's when she got hurt.

Those pinpoint bruises and bone cracks were a bitch to explain to the emergency room staff.

"Listen," she said, "I'm sure we can..." She trailed off as Less Calm also pulled a big black gun from his jacket. She swallowed. "Like I was saying, the kid and I are just gonna go our way and you guys—"

"Shut up," Less Calm shouted. "You talk too damned much, bitch. Now, either you and the kid get in the car, or we're gonna shoot you and take the kid anyway."

She sighed. The worst part of this was there was no one else around to call the cops or interfere. No one looking out their windows. No one walking a dog. It was kind of eerie to be on a residential street in the middle of the day, surrounded by houses and apartment buildings, with two guns pointed at you, and know you could be shot dead without anyone so much as shouting an objection.

No wonder the Nags had created Protectors.

"I'm not letting the kid go with you," she said. "You're just gonna have to shoot me."

"No," Jon shouted.

He pushed at her bracketing arms, but she held him in place, keeping her body solidly between him and the two gunmen. Why did so many of her charges always struggle?

Less Calm stepped toward her, lifted his gun, and fingered the trigger. Jonathan struggled harder against her grip, so she half-turned to hold him in place. A surprising growl came from a direction Cary couldn't see, the sound so low and vicious it made the hair on her arms stand up. There was a flash of black, the sharp retort of a gun, and Less Calm screamed as a huge black leopard latched onto his gun arm.

Cary gasped as she recognized the animal. Shit!

Deacon had Less Calm's arm clamped in powerful jaws and his body pinned to the ground. Less Calm's gun had skidded across the sidewalk to land at her feet. She watched in horror as Calm turned his weapon on the leopard holding down his partner.

She'd never get between the bullet and the leopard in time. Even if she could, to do so would leave Jon vulnerable. She couldn't use her own body as a buffer for both leopard and boy while they were so far apart.

Protector instinct kicked in when her conscious brain panicked. She scooped up the gun at her feet and said to Calm, "Don't even think about it." She cringed a little at the clichéd line but too late to take it back.

Calm swung his weapon between Cary and the leopard, clearly unsure who was the greater threat.

"Don't," she said again. "I can put a bullet through your brain before you could get a shot off. The leopard's with me."

"Jesus Christ, lady, get it off him. I swear to god, call it off, or I'm gonna shoot it."

She glanced at Deacon. He was still holding Less Calm pinned with the thug's arm in his mouth, but he wasn't doing any more than keeping the man in place.

She turned back to Calm and said, "Lower your gun, and I'll call him off."

"How do I know you can? How do I know you can even fire that gun?"

She held the weapon steady in one hand, her free hand still on Jon, shifted her aim just slightly to the left, and shot out the side window of the Towncar.

"I can use the gun," she said as she pointed it at Calm again. She nearly called Deacon by name, then thought better of it. "Okay cat, I think he's learned his lesson. Come here, please."

She heard a growl and Less Calm whimper and curse, but she didn't dare take her eyes off Calm. She watched his rapidly flickering gaze, the set of his shoulders. Watched and waited, praying Deacon would do as she asked so she could protect him.

When she felt a gentle bump against her thigh, she nearly dropped the gun in relief. Now she could risk a glance down. Deacon sat next to her, seemingly relaxed, but she could practically feel the coiled energy waiting to pounce.

"You okay?" she asked. A low rumbling growl answered her.

She turned back to Calm. He was helping Less Calm to his feet with one hand, keeping the gun pointed at her with the other.

"You might want to get him to a hospital or something," she said. "That bite's going to need stitches."

"This isn't over, bitch," Less Calm hissed, his face red, his jaw clenched.

She glanced at his injured arm and was surprised to see the wound wasn't as bad as she'd thought. "Why do you guys always say stuff like that? 'This isn't over, bitch.' Of course it's over because I've got your gun and a vicious cat just waiting to rip your throat out. Go away. Now."

Calm flicked a look at Jon, then back to her. "The boss will be in touch."

"Uh huh." That didn't sound good. But what did she expect?

She held the gun steady until the two men had climbed back into their car and disappeared around the corner three blocks up. Then she let her shaking arm drop to her side.

After a moment, she looked away from the road to consider Jonathon and the leopard. Jon's eyes were huge but his expression looked suspiciously excited now. The kid had nearly been kidnapped, she'd almost had to take a bullet for him, and he had a huge black leopard sitting next to him. And he was excited.

Teenagers.

"Well. Now what?" she said aloud. "Are your parents home, kid?"

"My mom's at work. It's just mom and me."

"I can't let you go home alone. Those guys knew who you were. They're sure to know where you live. And if they don't know already, we don't want to risk leading them there. Probably should take you to the nearest police station. We can call your mom from there." She contemplated the gun in her hand.

Shuddering, she took out the clip, emptied the chamber, and stuck the clip and bullet into the pocket of her jeans. The gun she slipped into her jacket pocket. She hated guns. And no doubt this one had a history. The police would probably love to get their hands on it. But it had her prints all over it now. She'd have to take the thing home and let Jaxer get rid of it.

"Do we have to go to the cops?" Jonathan asked.

"Two men just tried to kidnap you. Why wouldn't you *want* to tell the police?"

In truth, she'd rather leave the cops out of this, too. They couldn't keep Jon safe. If they could, there'd be no need for her to protect him. But that fireball proved they were dealing with people who were not mundane and who were after a kid who could call animals. The cops weren't equipped to handle this kind of situation.

But normal, sane people usually wanted to report near kidnappings to the authorities.

Jon shrugged. "Don't want mom to find out."

"We're gonna have to tell your mother something."

The boy's expression turned stubborn, and just a little pouty.

She sighed and glanced around. "I don't like standing out in the open like this."

She had this odd feeling like they were being watched. Her Protector instincts weren't detecting a threat to her charges anymore. But still, the sense of being studied made the skin between her shoulder blades crawl. No one was obviously paying attention to them. The street was still empty.

Probably just someone peeking out of their window. Finally. She wondered if the cops were already on the way.

"I suppose we could go back to my place and call your mother from there?" she suggested. At least going to her home meant they'd be able to lose anyone following them.

Jon gave her a sideways look. "How do I know your place is safe?"

She pursed her lips. Kid had a point. He didn't know her any better than he'd known the men with the guns. "You want to wait somewhere public for your mother? You got a cellphone?"

Public wouldn't keep them safe from determined kidnappers. This was a public street after all. Still, Jon had been through enough in the last ten minutes. She didn't want to force him to go where he didn't feel comfortable.

"Phone battery's dead," he mutter. "Where's your cell?"

She grimaced. "I forgot it at home." She'd been in too big a hurry to get out of the house. "I suppose we could ask to use someone's phone. Or we could go to your mother's work."

"No," Jon said hurriedly, raising a hand. "She'd get really pissed if I showed up at the hospital." He shrugged and stared at his feet. "Your place'll be fine."

"You sure? I don't want you going somewhere you feel uncomfortable. A coffee shop will have a phone." More people to potentially have to protect, too. But she'd just have to deal with that.

Jon glanced at the leopard then back at his feet. Finally, he looked up and met her gaze. "I figure you're all right. Even if you do like sweets."

She laughed at his crooked smile. "Okay. My place it is then. And I promise not to force any chocolate on you."

"Thanks."

She looked around, realizing with some chagrin that she had no idea where Deacon's SUV was parked. She glanced down at the leopard and raised her eyebrows in silent question. The leopard bumped her hand with his head then started off down the sidewalk. She fell into step beside him, hoping it wasn't too obvious to Jon that she was following the lead of a wild animal—or what looked like a wild animal.

As Jonathon caught up to them, walking next to her on the opposite side from the leopard, she wondered if he could talk to Deacon in his animal form. Her curiosity nearly had her asking, but she wasn't supposed to know yet that Jon had a supernatural talent. She'd have to wait to find out. Maybe Deacon could tell her if he'd been able to communicate with the boy.

They got lucky, making it all the way to the car without being spotted or stopped. Funny how quiet the street was. But she wasn't about to argue with *good* luck, now that there was no one pointing a gun at her. Maybe Jaxer was doing some of his glamour mojo on the block. At least there were no siren-blaring cars screeching up to surround them.

Cary reached to open the car door, driver's side since Deacon obviously couldn't shift back to human at the moment, and was struck by yet another difficulty. No keys.

She could see Deacon hadn't taken the time to lock the doors, but without the keys, they weren't going anywhere. She glanced around and saw what looked like the ripped remains of Deacon's clothes— though in such small pieces it was hard to tell the scraps had once been cotton and wool. She surreptitiously hunted for keys amongst the debris.

The leopard bumped her hand again and then swatted at something near the curb. Metal jingled. She scooped up the key fob and hoped Jon thought she'd just dropped it.

Deacon jumped in the driver's side door and moved between the front seats to the back where he laid down, looking large, beautiful, terrifying, and anachronistic. She followed him in as Jon climbed in the passenger side. He glanced over his shoulder at the leopard, swallowed visibly, and settled at an angle in his seat facing Cary so he could keep an eye on the cat.

"He's safe enough," Cary said trying to reassure Jon as they both strapped on their seatbelts. "He won't hurt you."

Jon nodded but didn't change positions. In the back, Deacon yawned, displaying an impressive array of large, white teeth, blinked at the kid with his golden eyes, then turned to look out the window.

She started the car and pulled away from the curb, trying not to wince at Deacon's behavior. Men.

"What's his name?" Jon asked after they'd driven a few blocks.

She hesitated. She couldn't very well call him Deacon and then introduce Jon to the human Deacon. "I never call him by a name," she said, hedging. "If I have to call him anything, it's usually cat."

Jon nodded. "Where'd you get him?"

"He just sort of followed me home."

"From where? The zoo?"

Jonathon sounded incredulous, and she couldn't blame him. As far as explanations went, "he followed me home" was pretty damned ridiculous. Instead of answering, she tried to change the subject. "Speaking of names, I never got yours. My name is Cary. Cary Redmond."

"Jon."

"Any idea what those guys wanted with you, Jon?" She needed to find out how much the kid knew. Maybe he'd even give her an opening to ask about his talent.

"Don't know," he mumbled, glancing back at the leopard. "Said their boss wanted to offer me a job. Knew mom was having money trouble. But I didn't believe them."

"Probably good you didn't. Any idea what kind of job?"

He shrugged. "No. They never tried to explain before that one asshole grabbed me."

She winced at his curse. "Yeah. I saw that part."

"How come the fire didn't burn us?"

Cary sighed. She knew that question was due, but she'd hoped to be home before he asked. "It's a long story. I'll tell you all about it after we call your mother."

"Are you a witch or something?"

"No. Not a witch. But something."

"Cool."

She grinned crookedly. Kids these days.

6

*C*ary pulled into her driveway, up to the closed garage, and turned off the engine. Jon was out of the car before she'd opened her door.

"How many dogs do you have?" he asked, staring at the one story cottage she called home.

The dogs were out back barking their greeting. She smiled. "Three. And there's a cat around here somewhere, but Scratchy only deigns to visit when he feels like it."

"What do the dogs think of your leopard?"

"Actually," Cary said, looking at Deacon still sitting in the back seat of the SUV, "they get along."

The fact that he'd gotten into her house, came to an understanding of some kind with them, and then they'd let him wander back to her bedroom all without sounding an alert was a pretty good sign. Even if she wasn't entirely sure how to feel about that.

She started to follow Jon up the front walkway when the leopard growled. She glanced back. The big cat nudged a backpack on the seat next to him.

"Oh yeah, I guess you'll need some clothes," she murmured for Deacon's ears only.

The leopard made a noise that sounded suspiciously like a chuckle and jumped out of the car, sauntering toward the house without hurry. She grabbed the backpack and followed her guests, glancing around and hoping none of her neighbors noticed.

"Hey, aren't you worried those guys might have followed us?" Jonathon asked as she unlocked the front door.

"Not really." Not with the safety guard the Nags had put on her house.

If the bad guys tried to follow her, they'd just end up driving around the neighborhood, lost. The spell was a more advanced glamour than even Jaxer could perform. She still wasn't entirely sure how it worked, just that it did—a bit like her Protector magic.

She had to give someone permission to find her home. The Nags did the same sort of thing for all Protectors so they would have at least one safe place, one place *they* would be protected. It also provided a good safe house if she needed it for a charge, a fringe benefit she doubted was an accident.

But she couldn't very well tell Jonathon all that. No one except Jaxer knew. Like so much about her life, the fewer people who knew the specifics, the better.

So instead, she said, "I was watching the rearview mirror the whole time. No one followed us."

Inside, Deacon strolled directly to the hallway that led to the bedrooms, while Jonathon went the opposite direction toward the kitchen and the back door where the dogs were going wild trying to get in.

Cary hesitated in the entryway, watching boy and leopard making themselves at home. She sighed.

From the kitchen, she heard the dogs come pouring inside, all barks and yipping and one deep basset hound woof from Pickles. A sudden silence fell. Then Jonathon came out of the kitchen with three dogs trailing behind. Fred was grinning, Pickles was trotting to keep up, her tongue hanging out, and Buck lumbered along behind, dark eyes bright and attentive.

"They're really nice," Jonathon said, stopping to squat down and pet them. The dogs instantly surrounded him. "They like you a lot, too."

"Oh? How can you tell?" A perfect opening if the kid wanted to take it.

Jon shrugged. "They're really healthy and everything. And they all look happy."

Guess he didn't want to spill his guts yet. She was going to have to get him to admit to his gift, but she didn't want to scare him by admitting just how much she already knew. Maybe if she talked about the dogs more. Given the look on the boy's face and the enraptured dog grins, she was sure Jon was talking to them while he sat quietly petting them.

Without looking up, he asked, "Where'd the leopard go?"

"Oh." Oops, she'd nearly forgotten. Deacon had probably shifted back to human by now. He was sitting somewhere in the house, naked and waiting for his clothes, which she still carried in the backpack. "He's, uhm… He's in the bedroom. I'll be back in a sec. I just need to make sure he's, uh, settled. Make yourself at home. I've got milk and juice in the fridge."

"Got any coffee?"

"You're too young for coffee." She stumbled toward the hallway. The thought of Deacon naked made her cheeks warm.

The reality of Deacon standing naked in her bedroom was even more mind-spinning than the thought. She closed the door behind her and tried to keep her attention on his face. Which proved to be almost impossible. Against her will, her gaze traveled down to his broad shoulders, his thickly muscled chest covered lightly in dark hair, the flat expanse of his stomach. She swallowed and tried to drag her gaze up.

"You realize," Deacon said, "this is the second time in only a couple of days I've ruined a pair of jeans trying to save you."

"Stop trying to save me, then," she said, still unable to pull her gaze up to his face. All she could think was, wow.

She managed to keep her gaze from going below his waist, barely. But the longer he stood there, the weaker her willpower got. She should hand him his clothes. She really should. Any minute now. He needed to put his jeans on. Now, would be good.

But for some reason the bag still hung at her side, and her gaze still traveled over the impressive sight of his upper physique.

"I can't help trying to save you," he said. "You're my mate. It's what I'm supposed to do."

"Yeah, but I'm the Protector."

He took a few steps closer, and Cary sucked in a breath. She needed him dressed and she needed to get out of here. Why wasn't he dressed yet? Oh yeah, the backpack. Still hanging loosely in her fingers.

She thrust the bag at him, using it to keep some distance between them. "If you want to keep any of your jeans intact, you're going to need to learn not to…"

Her voice trailed off as Deacon stepped closer, ignoring the bag. He lowered his head close to hers. His breath washed hotly over her mouth.

"I don't really… This is not…"

"I know."

At least someone did because she couldn't think anymore.

He dropped his lips to hers, and Cary thought her head might explode.

He tasted perfect. His mouth was hot, his lips firm, his possession complete. His tongue swept into her mouth, tangled with hers, and his hands clenched on her waist. The tight ball of lust in her stomach twisted tighter. She pressed against him, trying to relieve some of the building pressure. His backpack dropped from her fingers, making a dull thump on the carpeted floor.

Somewhere, someone who sounded suspiciously like her conscious ordered her to stop kissing this man and step away. Yes, he kept trying to protect her, which was really pretty sweet and infinitely better than trying to kill her. And yes, he looked amazing naked. But that didn't mean she could just rush into this…this…whatever the hell this was.

Did it?

No, no, it didn't. She needed to get to know him better, and she wanted to understand why he thought a human could be his mate.

She raised her hands to his shoulders intending to push him away and ended up digging her fingers into the hard muscle to anchor herself closer.

It was the strangest sensation to be standing fully dressed while he was completely naked, his hard cock pressed against her stomach through her clothes. The feeling was more erotic and overwhelming than anything she'd ever experienced. So strong, her knees weakened. Deacon's grip tightened, holding her up. Then her senses spun and she realized he'd lifted her off the ground.

Whoa. She wasn't a small girl, but he seemed to carry her like she weighed nothing at all. Knowing he could was amazingly sexy.

He sat down on the edge of the bed with her in his lap and pulled back, finally breaking the kiss, to meet her gaze. Cary stared back, trying to catch her breath while she figured out what had gotten into her.

"Uh," she said after a minute.

He smiled. "My sentiments exactly."

"What the hell is this between us?" Her behavior scared the crap out of her. She was used to being in better control of herself. Hell, control of herself was just good common sense in her profession. So why couldn't she seem to control herself around him?

"It's what happens with mates." He set his forehead against hers and took a deep breath. "I wasn't going to kiss you until we'd spent more time together. But how am I supposed to resist you when you stare at me that way?"

Oh yeah right, this was all *her* fault. "Hard not to stare when you're naked."

His laugh sounded strained. "Glad you approve."

Not exactly what she meant, but since he was right, she couldn't really argue.

He lifted his head. "But since we still have a teenager in the other room, I think it best if we stop now. When we get to this part, I want to take my time with you."

Her eyes nearly rolled back in her head at the thought of Deacon "taking his time" with her. Then the first part of his sentence sunk in. "Oh my god. Jonathon." She started to climb to her feet, but he held her firmly in his lap.

"A few more minutes. Then I'll get dressed and go officially meet our guest."

She really didn't want to stay put. Actually, she wanted to stay where she was for a very long time, and since that was a bad idea, she really really needed to get up. But his hold was very convincing. Maybe just a few minutes. That couldn't hurt, right?

She was painfully aware of his still very erect cock pressing into her hip. Sitting on his lap made it difficult *not* to drift into fantasies. "We'd better talk about something."

"What?"

"Anything. Something distracting. Something that will make it easier for you to button your jeans in a few minutes."

He laughed, the sound deep and resonant. Cary grinned. He had a wonderful laugh.

"Well," he said. "This might help. I talked to my mother about you."

"What? You did? When? Why?" Her voice cracked on the last word.

"I wanted her advice. She always said I'd lose most of the control I've spent years honing when I finally found my mate. I never believed her. Then I met you, and all those years of hard won discipline went out the window. So I asked her about the jealousy thing."

"Jealousy thing? What jealousy thing?"

"The jealousy that overwhelms me when other men who are attracted to you are anywhere near you. Like Jaxer."

She waved that away. "Jaxer is not attracted to me."

"He is. And I want very much to rip his throat out for it."

She shivered a little because he sounded very serious. "Trust me, he's a flirt but there is nothing there. We've been working together for six years. If anything was ever going to happen between us, it would have already. I am not his type."

"I'm not sure how you could *not* be his type."

She opened her mouth to explain but he stopped her with a raised hand.

"Whether you believe it or not, it's true. And the jealousy is incredibly difficult for me to handle. I've never experienced this kind of control slip before. My mother said it was natural. And would only get worse until we'd made love a few times. Actually, a lot."

Her eyes widened. "You talked to your mother about having sex with me?"

"Not in specific detail," he said dryly. "But according to her, mates have to make love quite a few times before the male feels secure enough in his claim to…regain control of his baser emotions."

She just couldn't talk to him about having lots of sex while he was still naked. Especially not in the same conversation that involved his mother.

So she changed tack. "You still haven't explained to me *how* I can be your mate. Everything I know about leopard shifters says this isn't possible."

"I don't know how it's possible. She couldn't answer that."

Some emotion moved through his expression, raising more questions, but before she could ask what he was thinking, he patted her hip and said, "Anyway, it's happened. And I'm going to be dangerous until we've made love and I feel secure in my claim."

She shook her head. "We haven't even known each other for forty-eight hours. You're making a lot of assumptions here."

He frowned. "Do you… Is there someone else? Do you not want me?"

Because the last question was loaded—and the answer should have been self-evident given the last few minutes—she answered the first. "I'm not seeing anyone. That's not the problem. The problem is this shouldn't be happening between us. I'm not exactly feeling like myself either." She forced herself to meet his gaze as she admitted, "It's scary. Okay. I don't act this way with random men—"

"I'm glad to hear it."

She ignored that. "I usually have more control too. And I'm not sure how I feel about chemistry I can't understand affecting my feelings this way."

"Truthfully, I'm not sure how I feel either."

"Really?" For some reason, that made her feel better.

"I am never out of control. It's dangerous. I've spent my entire life ensuring my self-control is absolute, and in less than two days, hell in only a matter of minutes, you completely destroyed all that work."

"Not on purpose," she muttered, a little embarrassed because his comment actually pleased her.

He chuckled. "I know. But here we are." He hugged her a little closer. "I won't rush you, if I can help it. My instincts are pushing me to claim you. In fact my leopard is encouraging me to seduce you right now."

"Tell him down boy. We have company."

He smiled. "Don't worry. My more rational self understands your hesitance. I don't want to force anything on you. I can wait."

"You don't sound very confident of that."

He shrugged. "My leopard hasn't pushed me this hard in years, so it's not easy. But I will make an effort not to pressure you. I can't guarantee I won't try to seduce you. I'm not that noble."

She pressed her lips together so she wouldn't grin.

"But I'll make an effort to wait until you're ready." He patted her hip. "Now, I think I'm ready to button my jeans. You'd better get out there. I'll follow in a minute."

"Yeah. Good idea."

She scrambled away from temptation and stuffed her hands into the pockets of her jacket. The gun bumped against her fist. Damn. She took it and the clip in her pants' pocket and hurriedly buried them in the top of her closet, under a pile of sweaters, out of casual sight and reach.

When she finished, she faced Deacon again, only to realize he hadn't pulled on his jeans, or anything else for that matter. The sight of all that beautiful naked skin made her pulse pound.

Irritated with herself and the situation, she hurried from the room, ignoring his quiet chuckle.

She paused in the hallway and pressed a hand to her stomach to quiet the nervous butterflies dancing there. Whatever the hell was happening between her and Deacon was happening way too fast. She felt like she was on a runaway train with broken brakes heading right for a cliff that dropped into a bottomless pit. It was not a good feeling.

She took a couple of deep breaths. When she felt some semblance of control return, she straightened and headed into living room.

Enough. She had a kid to protect. This madness with Deacon would just have to wait.

7

———————

*J*onathon was on the couch with all three dogs sitting in front of him, staring intently. He didn't seem to be talking out loud, but his head was tilted as if in thought.

Cary cleared her throat to get his attention. "Sorry I took so long."

"It's okay. Me and the dogs were just talking."

"Talking?" Another opening. Now, she just needed to pull the truth out of him.

Instead of answering her question, he said, "I put on a pot of coffee. I thought you might want some."

She blinked. "How'd you know I needed a cup?"

"You have a lot of coffee in your freezer." He shrugged. "I figured you were as much of an addict as my mom."

She dropped onto the couch next to him and leaned forward to see inside his mug where it sat on the coffee table. Milk. She smiled. "I am a coffee addict. Thanks. That was very nice of you."

He shrugged again, grinning as he looked at the dogs.

"We have to talk," she said. "I need to know why those guys were after you. I know there's something you're not telling me."

He kept his gaze on the dogs. "You gonna call my mom."

"Yeah."

"Can we just tell her I'm working for you or something? Like an after-school job? I don't want her to know about that stuff earlier. She'd just freak out and get all weird."

"She's got a right to freak out. We need to tell her the truth. She has to understand that you need to be protected right now."

"I can take care of myself."

"Yeah. Can't we all. But you're going to have to humor me and your mother and deal with more protection than just your own wily skills. You're avoiding my question. Why were those men after you?"

Just then Deacon appeared from the hallway. He was fully dressed, shoes and all. But he still looked unfairly sexy.

"Who's that?" Jonathon asked.

His accusatory tone brought her roughly out of another Deacon-related fantasy. "Jon, this is Deacon. Deacon, Jon."

"Nice to meet you," Deacon said. "You're a friend of Cary's?"

"Yeah. What are you?"

Now aggression intertwined with Jonathon's accusatory tone. She frowned at him. Had all the men entering her life recently come from some strange twilight zone? What was with the instant dislike?

Deacon's friendly demeanor dropped. "I'm Cary's boyfriend."

She raised her eyebrows at that. Deacon ignored her expression.

"You live here?" Jon asked.

"No. I was waiting for her to come home."

"Speaking of home," Cary interrupted. "We need to call your mother, Jon. But before I do that, I need to know everything you know about what happened today."

"Does he have to be here?" He jutted his chin out at Deacon.

"Yeah. He does."

"I don't want to talk about it in front of him."

"He won't repeat anything you say. I promise."

Jonathon continued to frown at Deacon. After a moment, his shoulders hunched and he said, "I can talk to animals. Like really. Not like the way everyone pretends to. I understand them."

His voice was so quiet, she barely heard him. "You talk to animals?"

"Yeah. I'm not weird."

"I know you're not weird. Geez, after what happened earlier, you think I'd be shocked at something like talking to animals?"

He shrugged, but his mouth twisted into a reluctant grin. "I figured you'd understand. My mom knows, but she wants me to pretend I can't do it. She doesn't want anyone else to know."

"Does anyone else know?" Someone must. Otherwise, why would this mysterious "boss" pick Jon out of the crowd?

"I don't know. The kids at school think I'm weird, but they don't know why. I suppose a couple of people might have figured it out."

"But...why would those thugs want you if all you do is talk to animals. What good does that do them?"

Jonathon hunched a little deeper in the couch. "I can do more."

"Like?"

He looked up at Deacon then, his gaze focused and intent. Deacon's eyes widened and his face started to shimmer and twist. Black hair ran over his skin, and he convulsed once, taking a step back as if he'd been hit in the stomach.

Cary came half off the couch. "Deacon?"

He held up a hand and straightened to his full height. His features were normal again, the racing swaths of black fur gone. But his golden eyes burned with fury.

"Don't you ever, ever do that again, kid. I'm not someone to be toyed with."

Deacon's suppressed rage took Cary's breath away. She remained half-standing, half-crouched, unable to move. Not sure what to do. Or who she was going to have to protect from whom in the next few seconds.

What the hell had just happened? "What was that?" she murmured.

"I can call animals, too," Jonathon said. There was a touch of smugness in his voice but over it was a tremor of fear. "Mostly. I can call shapeshifters as well as ordinary animals."

"You can make them shift against their will?" Cary dropped back onto the couch.

"Some of them." He jutted his chin out. "Most of them."

"But not this one," Deacon said, his voice so deep it was more a growl. "I'm a lot stronger than you are, kid."

"For now maybe," Jonathon muttered, but he dropped his gaze, staring at his lap instead of Deacon.

Cary met Deacon's gaze. "You okay?" she mouthed. Which was really two questions. Had Jon's efforts caused any damage? And was Deacon going to lose his cool and go after the boy?

He nodded briefly then turned back to stare at Jonathon.

Cary didn't like that look on his face. She edged closer to the boy, just in case. "How did you know about Deacon?" She hoped the question would divert them both from this struggle of wills.

"I could tell when he came back out. I didn't know when he was the leopard cause he wouldn't talk to me when I tried. But I could tell when he came out like that he was also the leopard."

"Can you always tell a shifter in human form?"

"Mostly. I'm better at it than I used to be. I'm getting stronger every year." This he threw at Deacon like a challenge.

"So." She frowned. "So those thugs wanted you, their boss wanted you, because of this? Because you can call shifters?"

Jonathon shrugged. "Don't know. Why would they? Not much use, is it?"

She wasn't so sure about that. She'd be willing to bet someone could come up with a nefarious use for Jonathon's skills. "We need to call your mother."

"She won't understand. She'll freak out." There was a resigned promise in his tone. "You'd be better off telling her I'm working for you after school. Walking the dogs or something. She'll believe that."

"I'm not going to lie to her."

"Maybe you should," Deacon said. "She'll only worry if you tell her the truth."

His response surprised her, though she wasn't entirely sure why. "If she's not worried, she won't be careful." She frowned at both of them. "What's her number? We'll call her now."

"She's at work." Jon flung himself from the sofa and ambled into the kitchen. He was punching in the number on her cordless phone as he came back. "She's gonna be pissed we're interrupting her while she's working."

He held the phone to his ear a minute then thrust it at Cary. "Her name's Sally Webber."

Cary fumbled with the phone, getting it to her ear in time to hear, "Emergency room."

"Hi," Cary said, scowling at Jon. "Can I speak to Sally Webber, please?" When a new female voice answered, Cary said, "Mrs. Webber, my name is Cary Redmond."

"It's Ms. Should I know you?"

"No, you don't. Your son Jon and I are..." She hesitated a split second before saying, "Friends."

"Jon. Is he okay? What's going on? Who are you? Why hasn't he mentioned you? Are you from the school? A teacher? How old are you? Where's Jon? Let me speak to him."

The questions came so fast, and so loud, Cary had to pull the phone an inch from her ear. She blinked at Jon who only smirked in an "I told you so" way.

"Ms... Ms... Ms. Webber!" Cary finally shouted down the phone until the woman fell silent. "I'm not a teacher or from the school. Jon and I just met recently. There's a bit of a situation, and—"

"Situation! What situation? What the hell are you talking about? Where's Jon?"

"Jon's right here. He's safe for now."

"Oh my god! Who are you? What do you want? Don't hurt my son!"

Cary took a deep breath and tried again. "Ms. Webber, Jon is just fine. A couple of men tried to kidnap him and—"

"Kidnap!"

Cary jerked the phone back at the shriek.

"What do you want for him? Please, let my son go. I don't have much, but if it's money you want..."

"No. No. Ms. Webber, *I'm* not a kidnapper." This wasn't going as smoothly as Cary had hoped. Deacon lounged nearby, a suspicious quirk to his lips.

Jon made no effort to hide his own amusement. "I told you she wouldn't like this," he mouthed.

She made a face and tried to interrupt the stream of hysteria still spilling out of the phone. "Ms. Webber. Jon is fine. Strangers tried to take him. I stopped them. And he's now at my home where he is safe." She managed to get the full story out before another round of questions blasted out of the phone. She waited until Sally paused for a breath then said, "You need to come get Jon, and we need to talk. I think the men who tried to take him will try again."

"What? Don't let them hurt my baby, or I'll rip your throat out."

Cary swallowed, pretty sure Sally Webber meant that threat. "I have no intention of letting anyone hurt Jon. But you need to come over so we can discuss keeping him safe."

"How? Who are you? I'm his mother. I'll keep him safe. Where is he? Tell me now, or I'm calling the police."

Cary gave up with a sigh. She gave Sally her home address—which in turn implied Sally had permission to find the house without being affected by the glamour—and pulled the phone away again when the line went dead with a crash.

"I think your mother's on the way," she said to Jon.

"I warned you. You should have said you wanted to hire me to walk the dogs. She'd still call the cops on you but probably wouldn't be as crazy."

"She's going to call the cops?"

"Oh, yeah. And by the time she gets done telling the tale, the cops'll think I'm here being tortured with burning metal pokers."

Great. Just great. "Don't you dare laugh, Deacon Jones." She pointed a warning finger at him when his suspiciously quirked lips twitched.

"Wouldn't dream of it."

To save a lot of explaining, Cary mentally gave the cops permission to find her home, too. Better to welcome the whole frigging lot of them and be done with it. Then she went to the kitchen for a cup of coffee. She had a feeling she was going to need it.

8

―――――

*A*s Jon had predicted, when Cary opened the door twenty minutes later, two uniformed police officers and a hysterical woman stood on her doorstep. The woman was about 5'1", had dark hair similar to Jon's, and wore scrubs. But that was all Cary could discern as she pushed passed her and rushed to pull Jon into her arms. Jon rolled his eyes and griped about her overreacting while his mother patted him down, looking for injuries.

Cary stepped aside to let the two uniforms in. She was inexplicably nervous about having cops called to her house. She'd mostly managed to stay under police radar while doing her job, often thanks to Jaxer. She had no idea how she was going to explain all this to them without sounding deranged.

From across the living room, Cary heard Jon say, "I'm fine, mom. Cary saved me, okay. She's cool."

One of the two cops said, "Ms. Redmond? We were led to believe there was a kidnapping."

This cop was a big man, at least 6'3" and thickly muscled. He had a pleasant face, dark blond hair, and serious brown eyes.

She swallowed and shook her head. "No, no. I mean there was an attempt. But the two men ran away and left Jon alone when they saw me."

The second uniform looked her over with a critical, flat expression. He was only around her height but as thick as his partner. His hair was dark, his eyes brown, and his face a lot younger, though no less intimidating, than the first cop's.

"Why?" he said, after finishing his visual analysis.

"Cary's a lot more formidable than she looks," Deacon said, unexpectedly. He stepped out of the living room shadows, startling the second cop enough he put a hand to his sidearm.

The first cop had a completely different reaction. "Son of a bitch. Deacon Jones. What on earth are you doing here?"

The cop and Deacon exchanged that male hug that involved a lot of back patting.

"Hey, Trevor. It's been a long time. How's Sue Ann?"

"Great. She'll be thrilled when I tell her I bumped into you. You haven't been in town much lately."

Thrilled, huh? Cary tried not to scowl. Sue Ann better be Trevor's devoted wife.

She nearly rolled her eyes when she realized she was jealous. How stupid was that? This not-acting-like-herself stuff was starting to get old.

"How're the kids?" Deacon asked.

He'd repositioned himself so he could drop a negligent, casual arm across her shoulders. Her eyebrows rose at the possessive gesture. She was tempted to step away but was afraid of how the cops would interpret the move.

"Fine, fine," Trevor said. "Stand down, Bacon. This is an old friend of mine and Sue Ann's."

The second cop dropped his hand from his weapon, but his expression remained unfriendly as he stared at Deacon.

Trevor took in the comfortable drape of Deacon's arm around Cary and grinned. "Guess I don't need to ask what brings you here after all."

Deacon squeezed her shoulder and made formal introductions.

Officer Trevor McKinsey shook her hand, still grinning and said,

"It's a pleasure to meet you, ma'am. This is my partner, Officer Calvin Bacon."

Cary nodded a greeting to the still suspicious looking Officer Bacon. "I guess I should explain all this."

She told both the cops and Sally the story she and Jon had agreed on. The two men had tried to drag Jon into a car, Cary had pulled up behind them and got out shouting and screaming waving her cellphone, threatening to call the police, the two men dropped Jon and ran away, and Cary and Jon decided it'd be safer for him not to go directly to his own house but to hers so he could call his mother.

Bacon had questions, of course.

"Why didn't you call the police first, or at all? Why drive all the way here? Why not to the nearest police station? Why didn't Jon use the cellphone his mother said he has? Why didn't you use your phone to call the police, Ms. Redmond?"

She had answers to all of his questions worked out, but she was pretty sure Bacon didn't believe her. At least, not entirely. With Jon backing her story, though, Bacon couldn't find the cracks so he eventually had to relent. Cary intended to discuss the real story with Sally once the cops left. But none of them wanted to admit the more fantastical elements of the incident to police. Deacon's part in the whole thing was never mentioned. He was "at the house waiting for Cary to get back from the store."

Sally had more questions. Cary brewed a second pot of coffee which was half finished by the time Bacon and Sally were mollified. When the cops stood to leave, Sally stood to follow.

"Ms. Webber," Cary said, "I was hoping we could talk a little longer. About Jon's safety."

Officer Bacon stopped halfway to the door. "Would you like us to stay, ma'am?" he asked Sally.

Clearly, he didn't want to leave mother and son behind, despite Trevor's assurances that all seemed well. Sally looked at Jon. She had him clamped to her side by a fiercely protective grip on his waist. The thirteen-year-old was a good half a foot taller than his mother.

"We should stay, mom," Jon said, his voice low and quiet. He held her gaze, unspoken meaning passing between them.

After a moment, Sally nodded. "I could use another cup of coffee," she said finally.

From the doorway, Deacon released a breath. He needed Trevor and his partner to leave. Now. Before his instincts got any harder to control. Trevor wasn't causing the reaction—he was both happily married and a reasonable man. He was no threat to Cary, and he didn't spark any haze of jealousy.

His partner, Calvin Bacon, was another story. He wasn't sparking jealousy either. But he was dangerous. On some primitive, instinctive level, Deacon knew Bacon posed a threat to Cary.

Deacon had to exert a great deal of willpower not to show his internal struggle to Trevor, a man who knew him well enough to notice if something was wrong.

Trevor stood next to him, shaking his head at his still hesitating partner. "Bacon get out to the car so we can leave these fine people alone. I think everything's under control here."

Bacon left but not without a parting glare at Cary who was going to the kitchen for more coffee. Deacon managed not to growl at the retreating officer but just barely.

Trevor sighed and shrugged. "He's new. Fresh from the academy not a month ago."

"Uh huh," Deacon muttered, forcing some of his muscles to relax.

Trevor narrowed his eyes. "You okay? You sound a little hoarse."

Deacon cleared his throat. So much for keeping his emotions to himself. "Fine. Just had a busy couple of days."

"Fair enough. So…" Trevor grinned. "You been with Ms. Redmond long? First I've heard of you having more than a passing affair with a woman. Or is that all this is?"

"No," Deacon said, his gaze trained on Cary as she came back carrying a fresh cup of coffee for Sally. His pulse pounded hard and his leopard crawled closer to the surface, urging him to take what was his. He pulled in a deep breath which filled him with Cary's vanilla and cinnamon scent. Everything around him seemed both sharper and less distinct at the same time. Except for his mate. She was the one crystal clear thing, the one thing that seemed to settle him.

He'd never felt like this before, edgy and panicky when she wasn't in sight, irrationally delighted when she was nearby. He didn't much like the sensation. It felt too much like he was losing his mind. But it was too late now. He'd been a goner the minute she tumbled into Sheldon's bedroom. Once a leopard found his mate, he couldn't *stop* needing her. He couldn't turn away from her any more than he could stop eating and breathing.

"No," he repeated quietly, "this is a lot more than passing. I'm going to marry her." He caught his friend's shocked expression from the corner of his eye and faced him again. "Cary doesn't know yet."

Trevor's mouth hung open. He snapped it shut and glanced back at Cary. "Well. Then Sue Ann will be expecting you both over for dinner within the week. She's gonna want to meet this woman of yours."

"I'll see how Cary's schedule is. Might have to give us a few weeks."

"Just so you don't make Sue Ann wait too long. There'll be hell to pay if you do."

Deacon clapped Trevor on the shoulder as he stepped out the door.

But before leaving, Trevor turned back, his eyes cop flat. "That story of Cary's had a few holes. It was a pretty tale, but it didn't ring true."

"She's protecting me," Deacon said. Trevor was one of the few humans who knew about Deacon's true nature.

"You were there?" Trevor asked.

He didn't respond. He held Trevor's gaze, saw when suspicion became understanding. And then acceptance.

"Don't worry about our report," Trevor said, his crooked smile returning. "I'll make sure there's no follow up." He glanced at Cary. "We'll look forward to having you two around for dinner."

Deacon let his shoulders relax. "I'll be in touch." He waited until Trevor and Bacon had driven away before he closed the door and rejoined Cary.

9

"You're a bodyguard?" Sally's expression was dubious, her slight frown and raised brows indicating obvious disbelief. "You?"

Cary resisted the urge to roll her eyes. "It's what I do."

"She's awesome, mom. You should see her. She's like a superhero."

"Honey, I'm sure she's no such thing."

Cary pursed her lips. As with everything to do with Sally, this wasn't going exactly as she'd intended. The woman already knew about her son's talent, even if she didn't like to acknowledge it. Maybe she'd be able to accept one more supernatural skill.

Because Cary was going to have to prove to Sally that she should allow Cary to continue protecting Jon. There was still a threat out there to the boy. Cary knew she couldn't just walk away from him even if her bosses would have let her. But words alone weren't doing much to convince his mother.

As she considered her options, Sally's gaze suddenly sharpened and zeroed in on her in a way that made Cary want to squirm.

"I've seen you before. Recently."

"I don't think so…" Cary wracked her memory. Sally wasn't the sort of woman you forgot after meeting her.

"Yes. I have. In the emergency room. Just a couple of days ago. You were in for cracked ribs and bruising."

Damn. There was no way her injuries should be completely healed by now. Not if she was an ordinary woman. And as a nurse, Sally would be well aware of that.

If she hadn't already decided Sally would need to know something of her "bodyguard skills," this revelation would have left her with little choice.

Sally's gaze darted to Deacon. "You brought her in. Did you cause her cracked ribs?"

Deacon's brows snapped down and his mouth tightened. "Of course not," he growled.

The expression on his face made Cary jump into the conversation. "He had nothing to do with that, Ms. Webber. That was job related."

"Bodyguard? How are you now?"

"Fine."

Sally assessed her closer. "You had cracked ribs a few days ago. But you jumped out of a car and ran at two men to save Jon? That must have hurt."

Cary nibbled her bottom lip, still hesitant to show Sally her skills. She couldn't help having people see her magic at work—the people she protected pretty much had to see—but it wasn't the kind of thing she talked about. This was why Superman and Spiderman had alter egos. It made their lives easier.

"I heal fast," she told Sally.

"Handy in your job."

"Very. Ms. Webber, when Jon called me a superhero… Well, that's not exactly true, but it's not entirely wrong either."

"Cary?" Deacon said quietly.

She glanced at him "She won't trust me to keep him safe unless she knows."

"Knows what? What do I need to know?" Sally's gaze danced back and forth between them.

"Deacon, can you help me with a little demonstration?"

He nodded and motioned her to lead the way. She glanced around the room for something that might cause damage to a person but wouldn't break when thrown. She picked up one of her hardback novels.

"Stand over there." She positioned Deacon with a blank wall and the hallway behind him. "Ms. Webber. I want you to throw this at him." She handed Sally the book. "Try really hard to hit him with it. And try to cause damage."

"I don't want to hurt him."

"You won't. But you need to aim for him. Don't pull the throw. Intend to hit him with that book."

Sally shrugged and rose from the couch. Cary moved closer to Deacon but didn't stand directly in front of him. She needed Sally to aim for Deacon and not get distracted and aim for her by mistake.

"Okay, Ms. Webber, get ready to lob that book."

Deacon leaned close and whispered, "Are you going to get hurt doing this?"

"No." She paused. "Well, probably not. But it's just a book. It's not like jumping in front of a high velocity bullet."

"Your job gives me nightmares."

She snorted. "Ready, Ms. Webber?"

Sally stood a few yards away, weighing the book, frowning. Then she looked at Deacon and her frown deepened. "I don't want to hurt him. I'm a nurse. It goes against my nature."

Cary decided not to remind Sally that she'd threatened to rip Cary's throat out if Jon got hurt. Unfortunately, this wouldn't work if Sally didn't *try* to hit Deacon.

"Jon, do you think you could hit Deacon with a book?"

The kid flashed a suspiciously gleeful grin. "Oh, yeah. Here, mom, give me the book."

Deacon's eyebrows popped up, but he didn't comment.

"Okay," she said to Jon. "I need you to try really hard to hit Deacon. Aim for his chest."

"That's your neck and sternum level," Deacon murmured.

"Do you want him aiming at your groin?"

"Fair point. But maybe for my stomach?"

"Fine. Jon aim for Deacon's stomach. And no lower!"

Jon chuckled, pulled back and threw the book as hard as his skinny arm allowed. Which was pretty hard and fast. Cary waited until the book left Jon's hands then stepped in front of Deacon. The book jerked a foot in front of her and turned sideways, hitting the wall beside Deacon and falling harmlessly to the floor.

Sally's eyes widened. "How did you do that? I didn't even see your hands move."

"That's because I didn't use my hands."

"But how…? How did that…?"

"See, I told you she was a superhero," Jon said.

"And I noticed you aimed pretty low, kid," Cary said.

He grinned, a real shit-eater grin. She shook her head. "Ms. Webber, as you can see, I'm very well equipped for taking care of Jon."

"But how? How do you do that? Are you a witch or something?"

"No. Not a witch." Funny how everyone asked the same question. "I'm just really good at protecting people."

"What about bullets? What about…speeding cars?"

She spent the next ten minutes explaining her "skills" as best she could, down to how she did sometimes get hurt but never too badly. After a thorough grilling, Sally dropped onto the couch and stared at the coffee table for a long moment.

Finally, she looked up. "You think Jonathon needs to be protected longer. You really don't think this was a crime of opportunity?"

"No."

"Why?"

Cary met Jon's gaze.

He shrugged. "Might as well tell her. She won't let you help, otherwise."

"It's because of his talent, Ms. Webber. His ability to speak with animals. The men claimed their boss wanted to offer Jon a job and didn't want Jon hurt."

"Why would you believe they didn't want to hurt Jon when they tried to drag him into a car?"

"That's what one of the guys said to the other," Jon answered, "when the other tried to fry us with a fireball."

"What?" Sally lurched up from the couch again.

Cary glared at Jonathon. They'd left the fireball out of the earlier discussion. And she'd never intended to mention it. "Don't worry about that, Ms. Webber. We weren't in any danger."

"He was a dragon shifter," Jon said, ignoring Cary's glare. "It was pretty awesome. Well, it was hot. But still, it was pretty cool. The fire just sort of wrapped around us and…"

"Jon! Enough. Your mother doesn't need to…" Then she registered what he'd said. "A dragon shifter? Wow. I've never met one before. They're pretty rare. How did you know?"

He shrugged. "Same as with…" He flicked a glare at Deacon, then said, "Same as with any other shifters. It's just the way my talent works."

Sally's eyes widened with each sentence. "Jonathon…"

Her voice was such a quiet whisper Cary could barely hear her. It was the first time she'd seen the woman unable to screech, which was worrying.

"Mom. You know I talk to animals. You just don't want to admit it. I'm different, okay. I'm not normal."

"But… But animals are one thing. What you're talking about isn't possible. There aren't dragons or werewolves or anything else."

"Deacon's one."

"Jon, damn it," Cary hissed. "That wasn't your information to give out."

Deacon dropped a gentle hand onto her shoulders. "It's okay. I doubt Ms. Webber will turn me over to the authorities."

"You're a werewolf?" Sally looked about to pass out.

"No," he assured her. "Not a wolf."

"He's a leopard," Jon supplied, ignoring Cary's outraged hushing noise.

"Leopard?"

Deacon half shrugged, half nodded.

"I don't believe any of this." Sally leaned back against the couch and closed her eyes.

"I know this is a little overwhelming. I wouldn't have told you all of this at once." She scowled at Jon again. "But it's important for you to know that Jon is in trouble from the kind of people… It would be almost impossible for the police or a regular bodyguard to protect him from these people. I can."

"For how long? And how much will it cost?"

"For as long as it takes. And no charge."

"Everything costs something."

"I don't need to be paid. I have an alternate source of income."

"You're rich?"

"No. But there won't be any money involved. Ms. Webber this is what I do. And I want to keep your son safe. It'll be easier if you cooperate."

"If I don't?"

"Then I'll follow him anyway and stay near enough to get between him and danger when and if it happens."

"That's stalking. I could have you arrested."

"But you won't."

"If I agree, how will that change things?"

"I can go into Jon's classrooms with him if I have your permission to be there. I can stay much closer than I'd be able to otherwise."

"You'd go to school with me? Cool." Jonathon bounced on the couch. Then he launched himself up. "I'm gonna go check on the dogs." They'd been locked in the backyard before the cops and Sally had arrived.

Once he'd disappeared into the kitchen, Sally asked, "What would you tell the school?"

"That I'm a bodyguard and Jonathon is under threat of kidnapping. The details of the case can't be discussed, but I need to be able to keep him in sight."

"You think they'll believe you?"

"I think they'll believe you."

Sally fell quiet and laid her head on the couch back, staring up at the ceiling. After a moment, she said, "I've always known about his… That he was different. Even when he was too young to talk properly he had an affinity with animals that wasn't quite…normal. He's more comfortable around animals than people."

She sighed and closed her eyes. "I've been so afraid. Afraid someone would find out and throw him into some laboratory to study like a rat. Afraid he'd never fit in. Afraid he'd just leave one day and never come back. He's done that before. I mean, he's always come back. But sometimes, when things get hard for him at school, he runs to the woods and stays there for days. Terrifies me every time."

Cary was starting to understand why Sally was so protective of her son. Keeping him safe from himself was hard enough, nonetheless protecting him from all the dangers of the outside world.

"I worry about how he'll use this thing of his. He's getting stronger the older he gets. Leaps and bounds since he hit puberty. He never mentioned werewolves before, but… But he can make animals do things now. He couldn't do that before. Only talk to them. Now, he can… I don't know. He doesn't force them. That's what he says anyway. He never forces them. But he…he talks them into doing things for him. I'm not always sure if they want to. I just keep hoping… I keep hoping he's a good enough boy not to do anything bad. He's still so young. And boys are hard. You can screw them up so easily. I have to work such long hours. He's alone a lot. I don't know what to do, don't know how to help him. I do the best I can. I tried to raise him to be a good boy. I love him so much."

Cary considered her next words carefully. "Ms. Webber…"

"Sally," she said on a tired sigh without opening her eyes.

"Sally. Jon is at a delicate age. And he is a good boy. My dogs loved him instantly, and they have very good instincts." The fact that they also liked Deacon quickly nudged at her conscious, but she didn't have time to think about that.

She sat on the couch, and Sally rolled her head to look at her. Her eyes were dark circled and held a weary wisdom that made Cary tired just looking at her.

"But if his powers are growing as much as you think," she said, "this is a dangerous time. And it would be best to keep him with the positive influence of his loving mother and his friends."

"Are you counting yourself among those friends?"

"I'd like to be. I'd like to make sure he survives to be the strong, upstanding man I know he can be."

"So would I," Sally whispered. "So would I."

10

ary sighed as she stepped into another classroom and walked up to yet another teacher to introduce herself. Jonathon was thoroughly enjoying strutting around with a bodyguard, and he played it for everything he could.

To be fair to the kid, she'd played it up a bit, too. She was decked out in all black. Black jeans, black turtle neck, black jacket, black boots. She had her hair in a tight braided, and she spent her time standing at the back of the room looking serious and mean. She could hardly blame the kid for enjoying the performance.

She felt a little silly—the full black thing was pretty clichéd. But the outfit gave off just the right impression. She needed to look capable and dangerous, but she didn't want to look like an FBI agent in a suit. This gave her a more gritty appearance. At least, that's what she was going for. Whether it was working or not was anyone's guess.

The principal had seemed impressed. She'd spent the better part of twenty minutes grilling Cary about her job. Cary suspected Mrs. Lieberman had been a bodyguard in another life. Either that or she considered the life of a bodyguard easier than being a school principal.

This was Jon's last class of the day, thankfully. Cary had spent the entire day remembering why she'd never liked high school. College had been great. But high school…

Forcing a professional smile, she shook hands with Jon's biology teacher, Mr. David Young. He was the only teacher about which Jon had anything good to say.

David Young fit his name. He was probably the youngest of Jon's teachers, in his early thirties at a guess. He was tall, well built, and handsome enough she would have daydreamed her way through biology if he'd been her teacher. His dark, curly hair was cut close to his head, his dark eyes sparkled with good humor. He dressed neatly, in trousers and a button down shirt with the sleeves rolled up over his forearms.

"I'll just stand quietly at the back," she assured him. "You won't even know I'm here."

"Oh believe me, Ms. Redmond, I'll know you're there," he said with a grin.

Well. If she didn't know better, she'd think Mr. David Young was flirting with her.

She leaned against the wall as the class started and tried not to let the lulling drawl of a lecture put her to sleep. Not that Mr. Young wasn't a good teacher, even an entertaining one. She just had a Pavlovian response to lectures. They sent her to sleep. She'd been fighting the drowsiness all day.

Her exhaustion didn't stem entirely from her sleep response to lectures, though. It had taken her hours, a pizza, a lot of coffee, and a promise that Deacon wouldn't spend the night while Jon was there—a moment of sheer, horrified embarrassment for Cary given she barely knew Deacon but Sally thought he was her boyfriend—before she'd talked Sally into moving herself and her son into Cary's house.

In the last six years, Cary had only needed to use her own home a couple of times to protect someone, but thanks to the secret glamour, it was an awful lot safer than Sally's apartment. Which meant that while they were in the house, Cary wouldn't have to be on constant guard. Since she couldn't tell Sally about the glamour, she'd had to jump through a lot of hoops to convince the woman to trust her.

Even after they'd agreed to the arrangement, they still had to go to Sally's place so they could pack bags, then they'd swung past Sheldon's apartment to pick up Cary's car.

While there, Cary had had another one of those "being watched" feelings, like she'd had that morning standing on the street after saving Jon. She couldn't see anything, but she was seriously creeped out by the sensation. It felt intense and…personal. Not like someone was just casually curious, looking at them from a window. Her skin crawled with the sensation and her every instinct went on alert.

The fact that Sheldon's body had gone missing still bothered her. She only hoped Jaxer was looking into it since she couldn't until things with Jon were settled. But worry followed her out of the parking lot.

By the time they got back to her house, had everyone settled, and she'd said goodnight to Deacon, she'd been exhausted. She'd dropped into bed and slept like a log, waking with the sure knowledge that she could sleep for several more hours.

Which made staying awake while acting like a big bad bodyguard a lot harder. Maybe she'd take a nap while Jon did his homework. Did Jon have homework? She'd been too dopey during his past classes to remember if he'd been assigned any. Some ace bodyguard she was.

She was watching the clock, counting the minutes left until the end of the period, when Deacon stepped through the door. She pulled away from the wall, trying not to look too shocked. He nodded to the teacher then motioned her into the hall.

She waved an apology to Mr. Young on her way out.

Mr. Young smiled and went back to teaching as soon as the door closed behind her.

The next thing she knew, Deacon's arms were around her, his mouth on hers, and he was kissing her like he'd never be able to get enough. After the initial shock, followed by the rather terrifying thought that this was the best thing she'd experienced all day, she pulled back and scowled up at him.

"What was that?" She wanted to curse at the sound of her own voice, all breathy and soft. She was supposed to be irritated and annoyed, not turned on. Right?

"Desperation," he said after a moment.

She raised her brows, but she had a feeling if she asked him more they'd get into a conversation she didn't want to have in the middle of the school corridor.

She eased back, ensuring there was some space between them. Then shoved her hands into her jacket pockets for good measure. "What are you doing here?"

"I've been thinking about kissing you all day, and I couldn't wait any longer."

She stared at him, waiting.

"Also, Jaxer sent me."

"Ah. You have a message for me."

"Yes. But my primary reason for coming was to kiss you." His voice was deep and husky, rougher than usual, the sound insanely sexy.

Lovely, she thought with more panic creeping in. "It's the middle of the day. Don't you have a job? Why aren't you there?"

"I was too distracted."

"By?"

"You."

She frowned. "I don't want that. You do important work."

"Don't worry, the work is still getting done. I wouldn't be a very good boss if I didn't hire people competent enough to keep things running while I'm away from my desk for a few days."

"Yeah, but—"

"Plus," he interrupted, "my sister is back in town, and I've left her in charge. She's better at fundraising than I am anyway, which is the most important part of the job."

"Your sister? I didn't know you had a sister."

"I have several. The animal rescue shelters are a family business."

"Oh." Yet another thing she didn't know about him.

"She's looking forward to meeting you," he said.

Cary's eyes widened. "You told your sister about me? I haven't even talked to my mom since we met and already your mother *and* your sister know about me?"

"I imagine most of the family knows about you by now."

"Big family?"

"Pretty big."

"Oh boy." She blinked and shook her head. "Maybe you should tell me what Jaxer wants."

"Mr. Young has a thing for you."

She scowled at the non sequitur. The edge in his tone, the faint growl in his words, made the hairs on her arms stand up. "I'm positive that isn't what Jaxer sent you here to tell me."

"He wants you."

"Jaxer?"

"Him, too. But I was talking about the teacher."

"How do you…?"

He tapped his nose. "I could tell the minute I stepped into the room." There was a definite growl now. And his voice had dropped an octave. "I won't be able to go back in when you do. It's going to be hard enough to let *you* go back."

"Let me?" He better not think he suddenly had the right to tell her what she could and couldn't do just because he thought she was his mate. That wasn't going to happen in this lifetime.

"I know I can't stop you. But that jealous streak I warned you about is just begging me to rip his throat out."

She gaped at him. "You wouldn't, though, right?"

His jaw muscles flexed. "I'm doing my best to keep that part of my nature under control. But it's not easy. In fact, it's a lot harder than I could have imagined."

She opened her mouth to say something, realized she had no idea how to deal with this, and turned the conversation to a safer topic. "Why did Jaxer send you?"

Deacon's golden eyes narrowed. He glanced toward the classroom and it crossed Cary's mind that she might have to protect Mr. Young from him. Oh, that wasn't good.

She studied Deacon warily, trying not to make any sudden moves. After a moment of hard staring, he blinked a few times and shook his head, like he was pulling out of a daze. Fisting his hands, his jaw tight, he sucked in a couple of deep breaths through his nose.

Finally, he faced her. The faint yellow glow in his eyes proved just how close to the surface his animal was. Her pulse kicked at that show of preternatural spookiness. As she watched, the glow slowly faded, but there was still an aura of wild danger surrounding him.

"Jaxer wanted me to tell you," he said with deliberate calm, "we've tracked down the boss of the men who tried to kidnap Jon."

That was enough to shock her out of her wariness. "Already? That was quick."

"Jaxer's been working on it since yesterday. And I put out a few inquiries myself."

"So. Who is it?"

"He's a ghost."

"A real ghost?" Her voice squeaked. She hated ghosts. Ghosts were scary. Even scarier than clowns. And clowns were terrifying.

Deacon shook his head. "I just mean we haven't been able to track down his real identity, just his presence."

"Ah." She tried not to sound too relieved.

A teacher passed them, glancing over her shoulder with a disapproving frown. Cary scowled back. They were just talking. Geez. Not like they were making out. Anymore.

"So what do you know about him?" she asked once the teacher rounded a corner.

"He has an agenda of some kind and has been working in the paranormal community, gathering specific types of powers to him for the last year. We haven't found out much more yet, but he's reputed to be very dangerous, with extensive resources at his disposal to get what he wants. Whoever or whatever he is, he makes Jaxer nervous."

"Oh good." This just kept getting worse. She ran a hand over her hair and tried not to sigh too obviously.

"Jaxer seems to think your house will be safe enough, but he's worried about the times when you're away from the house. That's why he insisted I talk to you before you left the school. He's afraid this Boss will try to snatch Jon again sooner rather than later."

"Well, hell."

"Jaxer suspects he's a sorcerer."

"And you?"

"I'd have to get close enough to get his scent before I'd know. I don't want to guess before I have all the facts."

"You don't like to plan for a sorcerer, get a necromancer, and end up fucked. Is that the idea?"

He chuckled. "Exactly."

He reached for her, but she resisted, putting a hand on his chest to keep some space between them. The hall was going to fill with students at any minute. She'd be mortified if all those teenagers caught her and Deacon in a clinch when she was supposed to be this tough bodyguard.

She backed toward the classroom door. "The final bell is due to ring soon. I need to get back inside."

He nodded, then he cocked his head to one side and frowned a little. "Can I ask you something?"

"Sure."

"You've known Jaxer a long time? He was adamant that I come to the school to give you this message. He refused to come himself, but he insisted you needed to know about the Boss before you left. Why wouldn't he come?"

"Oh that. You know how his greatest talent is with glamour? Well, a lot of kids can see through Fae glamour, even with someone as skilled as Jaxer. He might be able to fool one or two children at a time. In fact, he's so good, he could probably fool four or five at once. But a whole school full of them? Never. One would spot him as a faery and raise the alarm. It only takes one to set off a sort of chain reaction and soon all of them can see past his disguise. So he avoids little kids like the plague."

"Ah. What would he have done if I wasn't around?"

"He would have found someone else I know and trust to deliver the message. He usually asks my friend Angie. She's a green witch who works from home, so it's easier for her to get away in the middle of the day."

"I'm glad he tapped me this time. If he hadn't, I probably would have invented some other excuse to come see you."

She tried not to feel pleased. Really she did. "What are you going to do now?"

"Wait for you and Jon to finish. Then follow you home so you'll have some extra help if anything happens."

"You don't have to—"

He raised a hand to still her protest. "Yes, I do."

"I guess I'll see you back at my house then?" She heard the anticipation and hope in her voice and groaned inwardly. That was so embarrassing.

"I'll come in for a while. Before I have to get to the hospital."

Sally wouldn't know Deacon was shadowing her home. But Cary and Deacon both decided taking the precaution made sense. It would be entirely too easy for this mystery bad guy to use Sally against Jon. No point in giving him any extra leverage.

"Thanks for doing that," she said.

"It's my pleasure. I like Sally. She's…formidable."

Cary couldn't agree more.

She returned to the classroom, trying not to cause any more disturbance than necessary. Despite her efforts, her reentry turned every eye toward her. Jonathon gave her a little finger wave. Then Mr. Young called the students' attention back to the lesson. Minutes later, the final bell rang and the class erupted into cheerful noise.

She grabbed Jon by the collar as he tried to rush out the door and reeled him back. "Wait. We'll leave when it's less crowded."

"Why?"

"Because," she said in a low voice so only he could hear, "then I'll only have to protect you if there's someone out there waiting for you. If we get caught out in a crowd, I'm gonna have to try to protect a lot of people all at once, and that's harder to do."

"Can my friend Will come back to your place with us to hang out?"

"Don't you have homework?"

"I got it done already."

She raised her eyebrows. "Mr. Young just gave you an assignment. When did you get a chance to do that?"

"I can do it later. In the morning."

"And your mother would say?"

"She'd say yes."

"Really? Okay, let's give her a call and check."

Jon grabbed her hand as she raised her cellphone. "Okay, fine." He folded his arms over his chest and stared out the door. "Can't have any fun," he grumbled under his breath.

Cary had to work hard not to laugh. Teenagers were a funny species. Had she ever been that pouty? Probably.

When the noise from the hallway died down, she led Jon out of the class. Deacon was nowhere to be seen, so she assumed he'd gone back to his car. She checked the hall, waved goodbye to Mr. Young, and walked Jon to his locker.

They made it to the parking lot and were almost to her car when a kid in a long black coat stepped out from behind a van.

*L*ong black coat? Great. Cary really didn't want to know what was beneath all that material. Although, she had a pretty good idea.

She put Jon behind her. "Hi," she said to the black coat.

The kid was probably only sixteen years old, tall and well built, but with skin much too white, so pale it was almost translucent. It was not a good look. His long, blond hair seemed clean and well-taken care of, but there was a manic fire in his pale blue eyes that didn't bode well.

What was it with all the teenage bad guys this week? Black Coat looked even younger than Sheldon the wizard.

"Can we help you with something?" she asked him.

"I'm here for the kid." His voice was deeper than she'd expected. "Don't give me any trouble, lady."

She shook her head. They always said stuff like that. Why did the bad guys *always* say such predictable crap? Maybe there was a school someplace where bad guys went to learn acceptable bad-guy-banter.

"Listen, lady," Black Coat said, his voice rising, "I'm not gonna hurt the kid. I hear you're a bodyguard, right? Well, there's nothing you need to guard him from. Guy just wants to talk to him."

"Yeah. I know. The Boss. But my friend here doesn't want to talk to the Boss. So you can send him our best, and we'll be on our way."

And then, like clockwork, the shotgun appeared in Black Coat's unfortunately capable-looking grip.

"You're not going anywhere," he said. "Okay. Webber is coming with me. He's gotta okay."

Cary frowned. Behind her, she'd heard Jon suck in a breath at the gun. He moved an inch closer to her and touched her coat.

She reached back and patted his arm, frowning. Not at the gun—though she felt sorry for the surrounding cars—but something Black Coat had said… "Why does Jon have to go with you?"

"Because. It's the only way. They won't let me in otherwise. I can't do enough. I don't have anything. But if I bring him, then they'll have to let me in."

Well shit. This kid was trying to find his way into the Boss's gang. That meant he'd be rash and desperate and stupid.

"Listen," she said, "there's probably a very good reason why you want to be part of this group, but you're not going to do it by taking Jon. Sorry. You'll have to find another way. Or better yet, don't bother. I'd be willing to bet you'd be happier, and live longer, if you stayed away from the Boss and his people."

"What the fuck do you know, lady? Just shut up and hand Webber over, or I will shoot you."

Cary shrugged. "Go ahead. You're not getting Jon."

"Don't mess with me, lady." He raised the shotgun but the barrel shook.

"Kid, have you ever even fired that gun before? Have you ever seen anyone shot? It's ugly. Especially shotgun wounds. Big holes. Lots of blood. Very gross."

"Cary," Jon hissed.

"Don't call me kid," Black Coat shouted.

She opened her mouth but someone else spoke before she could comment.

"You might want to put that gun away." Deacon stepped from behind a pickup truck and leaned casually against the front bumper.

"Who're you?" The point of the gun swung toward Deacon.

Cary scowled. He was really going to have to stop doing this.

"My name is Deacon. And you are?"

"What do you want? Stay out of this, mister. This doesn't have anything to do with you."

"I'm afraid it does. You were pointing a gun at my lady."

"Yeah? Well tell your lady to hand Webber over now. Or I'll shoot her."

"No, you won't," Cary said. She glared at Deacon, trying to warn him with her eyes not to talk again. "You won't shoot anybody. You're barely old enough to hold a gun."

"Shut up, lady."

To her relief the gun swung back toward her.

"Just shut up!" the kid said again, his gun wavering. "I will shoot you."

"If you shoot me, that man behind you is going to jump you. And if you shoot him, I'm going to kill you."

It wasn't a hollow threat. Somewhere deep inside, some part of her knew she would kill if Deacon got hurt. She wasn't sure how she'd do it because when she wasn't protecting someone, her fighting skills left a lot to be desired—despite her friend Lucy's best efforts. That didn't seem to matter to the part of her that knew she'd follow through with her threat.

She was going to be pretty worried about that part of her once this was done.

The kid must have seen something in her expression because he lifted the gun higher and fingered the trigger. "You wouldn't. You can't."

"Put the gun down and no one gets hurt," Deacon said.

"He's right, kid."

"Don't call me kid!"

Deacon pulled away from the truck and took a step closer to Black Coat.

"All right, then," she said, bracing herself in front of Jon. "If you're so keen on shooting someone, shoot me." Better she got shot at and Deacon took the kid down than the kid shooting Deacon.

"Cary?" Jon's voice was a quiet whisper now.

"It's okay. Mr. Big Gun here probably can't aim that thing anyway, can you? Kid?"

"I said—"

"Yeah, yeah. Don't call you kid. Except you are. You're just a kid. A kid without the guts to fire that gun."

"Shut up. Just shut up!"

"No. You're so big and bad? You want to play with the Boss's gang of thugs? Then shoot me."

"I will."

"Do it. Shoot me."

"Shut up or I will."

"Do it! Come on! Shoot me."

The gun went off with a crack that made Cary's ears ring.

The buckshot scattered but slowed almost instantly after leaving the barrel. All of the tiny pellets curved to the right like a flock of birds, still moving fast enough to hurt if they hit someone, and plowed solidly into the side of a blue corvette leaving a hole the size of a dinner plate.

Someone was going to be pissed. She stared at the hole. A hole created after the buckshot had slowed down. Ouch.

The sound of metal clattering on tarmac pulled her attention from the hole in the car. The shotgun settled harmlessly on the parking lot cement. A very angry looking Deacon had wrenched the kid's hands behind his back. Fortunately, despite the gleam of fury in Deacon's golden eyes, the rest of him appeared in control. The boy was disabled but didn't seem to be in severe pain. He didn't look comfortable but at least he wasn't screaming in agony.

"That was so cool," Jonathon said, stepping from behind Cary. "The way he knocked the gun away from Paul."

"Who's Paul?" she asked.

"The guy who tried to shoot you. Deacon totally took him down."

Cary stared at Jon, her eyebrows raised.

"What? Oh, yeah, thanks. What you did was cool, too."

"Uh huh." Nice. Fickle teenagers. Yesterday, he couldn't wait to throw a book at Deacon. Today, Deacon was the big hero even though she was the one willing to get shot.

"Are you okay?" Deacon asked.

"We're fine," Jon answered. "Cary's indestructible."

"Uh, no…" she started.

Jon ignored her. "Hey, Paul." He edged closer to the struggling gunman. "You want to get me, you gotta go through my friends."

"Don't taunt him." Cary stepped close to Paul and made him look her in the eyes. "As you can see, trying to get at Jonathon is a mistake. Take my advice. Forget about joining the Boss. You will live a lot longer."

"What do you know about it?" Paul snarled, still trying to act tough despite the awkward position Deacon had him in.

"I know that this kind of work will get you killed."

"How'd you do that? You're a witch, aren't you?"

"No. You're just a bad shot. But the guy who owns the corvette is going to be really ticked off about the hole in his car."

"You want to call the police?" Deacon asked.

"No! No, don't." Paul started to shake in Deacon's grip.

"You know you really shouldn't try to shoot people if you aren't prepared to go to jail for it," Cary said, still in Paul's face.

"You don't understand. They'll kill me. I tried and failed. They'll kill me."

"Who?"

"You know who, bitch!"

"Watch it," Deacon murmured, wrenching Paul's arms a little higher. The kid winced and dropped his gaze.

"Great," Cary said. Just great. Now she had to protect the kid that had just tried to shoot her. How the hell was she going to do that and still keep Jon safe? "I don't suppose you had a backup plan? A place to run away to in case you failed?"

"Cary? What are you doing?" Deacon's voice dropped half an octave, adding to the air of menace already surrounding him.

"Well, I can't just turn him over to people who might kill him."

"He tried to shoot you."

"Yeah, but I did kind of provoke him."

"She did," Jonathon agreed.

"He brought a shotgun to this little kidnapping attempt," Deacon said. "He intended to use it."

Paul shrank under the weight of Deacon's voice, looking younger and more scared by the second.

"He's just a kid." She glared at Paul when he opened his mouth. "Yes, you are. You're what, sixteen years old? You're a kid. And you should never have picked up that damned gun. No, don't speak unless it's to tell me you have somewhere to hide for a while."

"Yeah, I guess," Paul muttered. "I've got a brother lives in—"

"Don't tell me," she interrupted, raising her palms to stop him. "Don't tell anyone where you're going except your parents. Just hide." She got closer and put her nose to his. "But if I ever see you again with a gun in your hand, if I even so much as hear of you threatening the life of someone, I'm coming after you myself. I will track you down. And you will wish the Boss's men had found you first. Do I make myself clear?"

Paul nodded, wisely choosing not to speak.

Cary straightened. "Fine. Then get out of here. Leave the gun. You won't be needing it."

"But it's my dad's."

"Tell him it was stolen."

Deacon reluctantly let Paul go and the kid tore off across the parking lot, disappearing at the far end into the trees surrounding the school.

"Was that a good idea?" Deacon asked, scooping up the fallen shotgun.

"I have no idea."

Deacon turned to stare at her, his eyebrow quirked. "That was a pretty scary threat. Did you mean it?"

She shrugged. "I was bluffing. I hope he believed me, but I wouldn't know how to begin tracking him. And I'm not sure I could hurt a kid anyway—not on purpose." She turned to look at Deacon. "But I know people who could if it became necessary."

"You think I could?"

There was no expression in his face, in his voice. But she could tell by the tension thrumming through his body that her answer was important to him.

"You think I would?" he said quietly.

"I think you'd hurt someone who tried to hurt me." He'd made that much abundantly clear.

"True."

"But I don't think you'd purposefully hunt that kid down and kill him now," she said. "People who rescue animals for a living don't do things like that."

At least, she was pretty sure they didn't. She was sure Deacon could be deadly if the occasion called for it. But she didn't sense in him the kind of killer it would take to hunt down and murder a sixteen-year-old.

His expression never changed. "Don't be so sure. If he turns into the thug he's promising to be, if he crosses my path again and threatens people close to me, I won't be as gentle as I was this time."

She held his gaze, though it wasn't easy to do, and nodded. "That doesn't make you a cold-blooded killer. Dangerous, yes. But not cold-blooded. It makes you like me."

That got a reaction. His eyebrows shot up. "Like you?"

"A protector."

12

The next morning Cary drove Jonathon to school while Deacon discretely followed Sally to work. Sally left with orders that, "They had to eat something besides pizza and donuts for dinner that night," and asked Cary to pick up the groceries.

Cary glanced at Jon, then back at the road. What did you feed a growing thirteen-year-old boy besides pizza?

When she was his age, she'd already been dieting, so she'd lived off of microwave chicken and canned green beans. She still couldn't look at a green bean without her stomach rebelling. It was only after she'd screwed up her system with constant dieting and spent years getting her metabolism back in order that she decided eating properly did not have to involve denying oneself pizza occasionally.

Or more than occasionally if the situation called for it.

But none of that helped with figuring out what *Sally* considered a "healthy" dinner for Jon. He looked like he needed more than soggy green beans and dry chicken.

She pulled into the parking lot at his school a minute before the first bell. When Jon started to open his door, she said, "Wait. We'll go in after everyone's settled."

"Go in late?"

"I warned your first period teacher. It's safer this way."

"Cool. How late can we be?"

"Don't get your hopes up. I told her we'd sneak in five minutes after the bell."

Jon rolled his eyes and mumbled, "Hardly worth it."

Chuckling, she searched the lot. When she couldn't see any potentially innocent bystanders, she stepped out into the cool November morning air.

She'd parked as close as she could get to the school entrance but that still left them with half the parking lot to cross. The principle wasn't fascinated enough by Cary's job to risk the wrath of the faculty by asking one of them to give up their parking spot for her, so Cary had to take her chances. As they made their way toward the main building, she kept her gaze moving, checking for shifting shadows, listening closely for a hint of sound. She let her senses open so she was aware of the area all around her.

And still the three witches managed to surround her and Jon before Cary knew they were there.

The spine tingles she got when danger was near hit her at almost the same instant as the witches made themselves visible. Cary shook her head. That was some impressive trick. Her Protector instincts usually reacted faster than that. Which meant the three women were very dangerous.

She pulled Jon close, wrapping her arms around him and keeping him in front of her. With the witches circling them, it felt safer to wrap herself around him rather than pushing him behind her, even though it didn't make a practical difference to her ability to keep him shielded. She had a momentary twinge, the ever-present-but-mostly-suppressed fear that she might fail this time, that Jon would get hurt because she wasn't a good enough Protector. She forced it down. No time for doubt now.

Facing the witch in her line of sight, she said, "What can I do for you ladies?"

The woman was around Cary's age, maybe in her late twenties, early thirties, with the bleached blond hair, blue eyes, and deep tan

Cary associated with Californians. She was wearing black leather pants, a cropped blue t-shirt that matched the color of her eyes and showed off impressive abs, and a long black sweater that brushed the ground. When she smiled, she revealed a row of blindingly white teeth.

"You know what we want," the blonde said.

"The boy will not be harmed," a second witch said.

Cary glanced to her right. This one was black: her skin, her short hair, her eyes, even her sexy, stylish trouser suit—which she worn without a top under the jacket as only a small breasted woman could get away with. The only break in color was the ruby red of her full lips. She looked young, a bit younger than the blonde, but something about her eyes hinted at an age beyond the evidence of her flawless skin.

"You've no reason to keep him from the master," the third witch said.

This one's voice was so deep it vibrated through Cary's bones. She turned to her left. The third witch had skin the color of rich mahogany, brown-red hair down to her narrow hips, and hazel green eyes surrounded by lashes so long Cary couldn't help but feel a little envious. The witch wore an ankle-length, fitted black skirt and a snug green sweater under a cropped black coat. This one was even more beautiful than the others, and looked even younger, twenty at the oldest.

Cary frowned. That one was the leader. The most dangerous one. The one with the strongest power.

She turned, with Jon still safely circled in her arms, to face this third witch. "You call your employer 'master'? I thought everyone just called him the Boss."

"He is more than merely our employer," the red-haired witch said. Her gaze flicked to Jon. "He's good to work for, child. He can provide you with anything you might ever wish."

"Like a long life that doesn't involve evil and breaking the law?" Cary asked before Jon could speak.

"Who said we break the law?" the blonde asked.

"I notice you're skirting the whole evil issue," Cary said.

"You waste your energy, sister," the black-haired witch said, ignoring Cary's comment. "There's no need."

"And alone," the leader said, "you cannot hold your shields against the power of three."

Cary raised her brows. Did the witch realize she'd just referenced an old TV show with that line?

Three witches working together *was* a powerful alliance. There was an innate balance to three spellcasters which increased their effectiveness exponentially. But that was true of seven witches as well, so the "power of three" comment seemed overly dramatic.

The fact that, like so many others, they thought Cary was a witch was also a little strange. *Actual* witches should know better. Her friend Angie could tell the difference. Cary wasn't going to enlighten them, though.

"Sorry, ladies," she said, with a quick glance back at the school entrance, "but Jon's going to be late for class. No time to talk. You'll just have to tell your 'master' we're not interested."

"You're very arrogant," blonde said.

"And troublesome," black-hair said.

"And involved in a situation you shouldn't be," leader said.

Cary grinned. "Yeah, that's me. Now, if you'll excuse us."

But she could already feel their powers building and swirling in the air. They began to chant in unison, low and in an ancient, magical language Cary hadn't learned fully yet.

So much still to learn and never enough time. She sighed.

A breeze lifted dirt and pebbles from the tarmac, churning the dust in an ever-increasing cyclone around her and Jon. The wind tugged at Cary's braid and a few stinging chunks of dust prickled the back of her neck. The witches lifted their arms and threw their heads back to face the sky. Their chanting grew louder as they invoked some unnamed spirit or god to join with them and power their incantation.

Cary watched in mild fascination. She hadn't had a chance to witness a lot of tri-witch magic in person. Jaxer would want her to study their techniques and pay attention to the spells they used. But after a few minutes of trying to decipher a language she wasn't familiar enough with, her head started to hurt. She grunted and turned her attention to the more important problem at hand.

"What do you think your mom meant by a 'healthy dinner'?" she asked Jon. "What does she usually feed you?"

He looked over his shoulder at her with wide eyes. "Huh?"

"Dinner, you know. Your mom told me I had to pick up something 'healthy' for dinner. What do you think we should have?"

He shrugged, his tight muscles relaxing a little with the gesture. She could still feel the fine tremor in his narrow shoulders, but he tilted his head as if really considering her question, determined not to pay attention to the chaos around them. She smiled and hugged him.

"Mom likes chicken and brown rice," he said.

"What kind of chicken?"

"I don't know. I just eat it. I don't make it."

"Well, that's no help. What use are you if you can't even tell me what I'm supposed to feed you?"

Jon laughed, the sound hard to hear past the rising cacophony of magic and debris circling them. She leaned forward so her ear was close to his cheek.

"We could have pizza again," he said. "Or maybe Chinese take-away."

"Yeah, I'm sure your mom would consider that really healthy." Cary grimaced. "Besides, she specifically said no more pizza."

"Hamburgers and fries? Fries are a vegetable."

"In what universe?"

"They're potatoes. Potatoes are a vegetable. Technically."

"Deep frying robs them of their nutritional value. But at least you're thinking vegetables. Try something that won't give your mother heart palpitations."

The chanting grew in volume, competing with a deep rumbling sound. The ground beneath them seemed to roll in a gentle wave. Cary adjusted her stance to keep her balance.

Jon turned to speak into her ear so she could hear him over all the noise. "We could get barbecue chicken and mash potatoes. I like those. They're almost as good as fries."

"Okay. This is good. We can do that. What about greens? Your mother will want some non-potato vegetables."

"Yeah," Jon said.

Cary felt the breath of his resigned sigh on her cheek.

"Maybe she'll let us get away with corn," he suggested. "She likes green beans, but I hate them."

Since Cary hadn't been able to face green beans in fifteen years, she couldn't agree more. "Corn it is, then. And maybe a fresh salad? That sounds like a pretty healthy dinner. Okay. Great. Problem solved."

"Uh, Cary?"

"Yeah?"

"What about the witches?"

She glanced up at the three women. Their arms had fallen to their sides and the blonde had dropped to one knee. Their shoulders sagged, but they were still chanting. A tug on Cary's skin gave away the power being thrown at her. A lot of power. She could almost feel the intent of the spell, something she couldn't decipher from their chant. It felt like it would be binding and painful. Fortunately, her own magic kept theirs at bay. She was pretty sure she didn't want to know what they were trying to do to her.

"They'll wear themselves out soon," she told Jon. "Then we'll have to hurry to class. Mrs. Zuckerman is going to be ticked off at us for arriving so late."

The chanting started to sound so hoarse Cary thought the witches might lose their voices before they clued in enough to stop. They were churning up so much magic, if she'd been an ordinary human, that power would have probably torn her to pieces by now. She suppressed a shudder at the thought, afraid Jon might misinterpret the gesture and start to worry again.

Finally, when the black-haired witch dropped to her knees, the chanting stopped. All three panted, sweat streaked their flawless skin and dotted their smooth brows.

"What are you?" the redhead asked in a voice so roughened by her efforts, the already deep tenor hit a base register that was almost masculine.

"Not a person to be messed with," Cary said. "Listen, just tell this master of yours to save himself a lot of trouble and leave us alone. The kid isn't interested." She grinned without humor. "And I'm really hard to get through."

"We won't be the last, sister. Guard yourself well. He'll kill you for this insult."

"Thanks for the warning." She shrugged. "Not the first time someone's wanted to kill me, though."

The redhead actually laughed. "Under different circumstances, I would have liked a longer conversation with you. You strange woman." She motioned to the others. "Come."

The other two rose to their feet, the blonde stumbling a little, and they followed their leader. When the blonde passed behind Cary, she hissed, "Bitch."

Cary turned to smile at her, showing a lot of teeth. The blonde's eyes narrowed, and Cary winked. The witch snarled, turned her back with a dramatic swirl of her long black sweater coat, and followed the others out of the parking lot.

"That was a fun start to the day," Cary said. "That witch's sweater was very cool, wasn't it? I wonder where she got it." Cary took a deep breath as the post-protection tingling along her skin settled, a lot of tingling this time around, like a swarm of ants crawling all over her. Ick. Then she patted Jon on the shoulder. "Come on, let's get to class before you miss the entire first period."

"I wouldn't mind," he said. His voice was a little hoarse too, from having to talk so loud, but he sounded calm.

Cary snorted and pushed him in front of her toward the doors. She glanced over her shoulder one last time, but the witches had disappeared.

1 3

Given the way the day had started, Cary wasn't the least surprised to find a leprechaun waiting by her car that afternoon. What was surprising was that she knew the leprechaun.

"Tom," she greeted with a crooked smile.

He was decked out in a natty gray suit with a crisp white shirt and a green tie decorated with little shamrocks. She rolled her eyes at the shamrocks. Tom was only four foot tall, but he took advantage of every inch to show off his perfectly proportioned physique. His dark brown hair was pulled back in a low tail that helped highlight the strong cut of his cheekbones and slight upward tilt of his green eyes.

"You're looking good," she said.

He grinned and tipped an invisible hat. "Very kind of you to say."

"What are you doing here?"

"Sure, I suspect you know already, Cary."

She sighed. "Yeah. But I was hoping you'd tell me I was wrong."

Tom was an…associate of Jaxer's. Or at least he had been, off and on, in the past. Jaxer claimed faeries and leprechauns rarely got along, especially when the faery had links with both the Irish and English Courts (though what those links were, Jaxer had never deigned to tell her). And as it turned out, Jaxer and Tom hated each other with a passion. But they'd been able to work together a few times. When money was involved. And blackmail.

Cary had always liked the leprechaun. She especially loved the way he could ruffle Jaxer's feathers. Knowing he was here working for the bad guy was both disappointing and sad.

"I think we've been pretty clear on the point," she said. "The kid doesn't want anything to do with this Boss of yours."

"Well and that's why I'm here. To see if I can talk some sense into you. He means the boy no harm."

"And that's why we've had dragon shifters blowing fire at us, witches casting spells, various sorcerers and shifters trying to follow us…"

"What?" Jon squeaked. "How'd you know? Why didn't you tell me about the sorcerers?"

Cary glanced over her shoulder. She'd instinctively put Jon behind her when they approached Tom, and to the kid's credit, he hadn't protested. His dark eyes were huge and round as he stared at the leprechaun, though Cary couldn't tell if it was Tom or the mention of sorcerers that had Jon so scared. Maybe both. She noticed he didn't mention the shifters trying to follow them home. Given Jon's talents, he probably knew about those already.

"I didn't want to worry you," she said.

"You've some powerful protection spells working for you, Cary," Tom said, drawing her attention back to him. "But it won't be enough."

Tom didn't know she was a Protector. Jaxer didn't trust him enough to reveal that piece of information, thankfully. The leprechaun thought she was a sorceress, slightly inept but powerful and being trained by Jaxer.

"If the Boss means Jon no harm," Cary said, "then why do we feel under constant threat?"

Tom let slip a big, charming smile. "Because you're a clever woman."

"So, he is a threat?" Cary said.

"Oh, he certainly could be. Which is why I'm trying to talk some sense into you. I've always liked you, Cary, despite the company you keep. This isn't to do with you. Let the kid meet with the Boss. He can always turn down the offer."

"What is this guy, anyway?" she asked. "Wizard, demon, vampire, shifter?"

"What he is is rich, powerful, and scary." Tom pushed away from her car and tucked his hands neatly into the pockets of his pants. "And you're putting yerself on his bad side for no good reason."

He straightened his suit jacket and tipped his invisible hat her way again, as if preparing to leave.

Cary raised a brow. "What, no attempt to get around me to Jon?" she asked.

Tom grinned crookedly and nodded behind her. Three leprechauns she didn't know were pulling themselves up from the tarmac, shaking their heads or rubbing their backsides. They'd obviously tried to get at Jon from behind and ended up tossed away by her magic. Once under her protection, the actual direction of an attack didn't mattered. You couldn't just sneak up on a Protector to get to their charge. Cary rolled her eyes and looked back at Tom, shaking her head.

"Can't blame the lads for trying," he said. "I warned 'em it wouldn't work."

She hadn't even felt a tug or bounce against her shields. Not that she always felt a reverberation from an attack. Especially if the attack wasn't much of a threat. But she usually knew when an attempted attack was *taking place*.

Sneaky little devils, those leprechauns.

"I'm sure we'll be talking again soon, love," Tom said. "In the meantime, keep your back well guarded. And mind yerself. It'd be a shame to see you killed over such a minor thing."

"Gee, thanks," she said to his retreating back. "Hey, Tom." When he turned, she said, "If I were you, I'd resign from this job."

"Ah, but I never could resist a pot of gold." He winked and ducked behind a tree.

She groaned at the very bad joke. Glancing back, she made sure the other three leprechauns left, too.

"Cary?" Jon's voice was quiet in the still, chilled afternoon air. "This Boss. He couldn't really kill you. Could he?"

"He'd have a hard time doing it, Jon. Don't worry." She clapped him gently on the shoulder. "I'm pretty tough to kill. And I guarantee I'll keep you safe."

Her deepest fear raised its head again. What if this time she failed? What if this bad guy was too strong for her? But she didn't let any of her inner uncertainty show. Jonathon trusted her to keep him alive and that's what she intended to do.

She turned him toward her car. "So I noticed you weren't surprised to hear a few shifters have tried to follow us home?"

He shrugged. "I knew they were there. Don't know how. Never noticed before."

"Your survival instincts are kicking in," she said.

"Yeah? That's cool, huh?"

"Kind of. I guess."

Cool that Jon was being hunted so his instincts were forced to heighten? She didn't think so.

A shiver danced across her shoulders, awareness that made her frown. She glanced around. That sense of being watched crept over her, tightening in her stomach. She wasn't getting a Protector warning, yet she felt danger lurking. She searched the lot, scanning for the new threat. Nothing. And a moment later, the sensation vanished. She blinked. No more spark of danger in the air, no more sense of menace. Just a normal autumn afternoon, the air sharply cool and scented by the surrounding trees.

Still frowning, Cary slid into the car.

"Why can't they track us?" Jon asked, continuing their conversation. "There've been two wolves, a lion, a bear, and a cougar. But I think Deacon scared the cougar away."

"That is some talent you have there, kid." She fastened her seatbelt. "I couldn't tell what kind of shifters they were." They'd been in human form when she'd spotted them. The only reason she could tell they were shifters was because of the way they'd tracked her.

"But why can't they follow us all the way to your house?" Jon said. "They get lost."

Cary shrugged and concentrated on merging with street traffic.

"You've got a spell or something on the house! I knew you did."

"If you say so." She was happy to let him think he'd stumbled on the right answer. He was too close for her comfort anyway.

"How come Deacon didn't meet us today?" Jon asked. He turned in his seat so he could face her.

"Your belt on?" She glanced over to check.

"Yeah, yeah." He pulled the shoulder strap out a little so she could see. "So, Deacon?"

"He has a regular job, you know. He had to work."

"But he's the boss."

"Which means he's got most of the responsibility."

"You think he'd give me a job? I could help with the animals."

"That's a good idea." She grinned at Jon before focusing on traffic again. "When you hit sixteen, I bet he could find something useful for you to do. You might not make a mint, but it'd be really worthy work."

"Deacon has lots of money," Jon said.

"What makes you say that?" She wasn't sure herself. He didn't seem to be struggling. And his top of the line hybrid SUV wasn't a cheap vehicle. But his family ran animal shelters and depended on donations and grants to make the business work.

"He said he's got a house," Jon said.

"Yeah, well I have a house, and I'm sure not rich." Just decently paid.

"But you don't want my mom to pay you to protect me? Why not if you're not rich?"

Great. Just the question she didn't want to answer. "I got paid enough on my last job to not need any payment this time around. I'll be more mercenary with the next smart ass kid I have to protect."

"My mom would have fits if she heard you call me a smart ass."

"Better than a dumb ass, right?" This comment caused a peal of laughter that made Cary smile.

"Can I tell mom that?"

"I will deny any knowledge of this conversation if you repeat any of it."

He kept chuckling. "Smart ass is better than a dumb ass. That's so true."

Cary tried not to laugh with him. At least he'd been distracted from her source of pay.

"But Deacon's house is in Nobhill," Jon continued. "He'd have to have money for that, wouldn't he?"

So much for distraction. Now, if she could just avoid showing her own surprise. She'd had no idea where Deacon lived. Which was a little embarrassing to admit since Jon and Sally thought he was her boyfriend.

"Why all this concern with our finances all the sudden?" she said to avoid revealing her ignorance.

Jon shrugged and looked out the window. "Mom said she'd like a house one day."

"Ah. Well, houses are nice. But she'd make you mow the lawn."

Jon grinned. "I wouldn't mind."

"Really? So you want to mow my lawn, then?"

"No," he drawled. "Unless you pay me."

Cary chuckled as she turned down her street.

"Hey, don't we have to go to the store?" Jon frowned, then his eyebrows rose. "Or have you decided to go over mom's head and get pizza?"

"Go over *your* mother's head? Not in this lifetime." She pulled into her little one car garage and cut the engine. "We were being followed. Safer to come home and lose them. We'll go back out in an hour after they give up looking for us."

Jon's eyes widened. "Who was it this time? Not shifters."

She shrugged, then heaved herself out of the car. "Couldn't tell."

She let Jon proceed her into the house, down the narrow hall, past her little laundry room—which she studiously avoided looking at since she hadn't done laundry in a couple of weeks—and into the living room. Jon went straight to the kitchen after dropping his backpack in the middle of the floor. Cary picked it up and set it closer to the wall, then followed him into the kitchen.

The dogs were already jumping on him and bouncing around his legs in greeting. It took a full minute before they even noticed her and came over to say a quick doggie hello before scampering back to Jon. They followed him into the pantry when he went to get them treats.

She shook her head. "Nice to see you guys, too." Fred ran back, bounced off her thigh, then hurried after Jon again. "Well, thanks for the extra attention, Fred." She snorted and went to hang up her coat.

Jon had a pot of coffee started by the time she got back. "You're spoiling me, kid. I'm not going to want to let you leave if you keep making me coffee all the time."

Jon flashed her a smug grin. "I'm still not gonna mow your lawn for free."

"You distract the dogs. That's pretty handy, too."

"They're good dogs."

"Yeah." She scratched Buck behind the ear.

"Cary?"

"Hmm?"

"How come you didn't know who was following us? You knew sorcerers had tried. And shifters."

"Shifters and sorcerers have…tells, like in poker. They have ways of trying to follow you that, over the years, I've come to recognize. The van that tried to follow us today…" She shrugged. "I couldn't tell."

"Then how'd you know they were following us?"

Six years of experience and the tingling along her spine that happened when danger was near. But Jon knew too much about her powers already, so she just said, "Skill, kid. Skill."

He frowned at the answer. She grinned then changed the subject to homework and the weekend.

The weekend would be tricky. She preferred to keep Jon in the house where she knew none of the bad guys would find them. But how did you keep a thirteen-year-old house-bound all weekend?

After two cups of coffee and an hour of discussing that in vague terms, they headed back out to the grocery store.

Cary let her instincts open, waiting for the tell-tale tingle. She let out a quiet sigh of relief when nothing happened. In fact, they were out of the car and on their way into the store before the tingle bubbled along her spine. She pulled Jon close and scanned the parking lot. What was it with parking lots today?

Nothing happened, and she couldn't spot any suspicious bad guys. Not that she'd been having much luck lately spotting the bad guys before they stepped in front of her.

The sense of lurking danger followed her into the store, through the aisles, and while she stood at the checkout counter. She kept Jon next to her the entire time. He stood tense and wary, no doubt picking up her nervousness. They only talked enough to get the shopping done, and as her own gaze tracked the other shoppers, she caught Jon glancing furtively around.

"Don't worry, kid," she murmured. "You're safe with me."

"I know."

But he didn't relax.

They were loading the groceries into the trunk, when the first stray rock bounced off her car. Scowling, she put Jon behind her and looked around. Nothing. She waited, watched. Still nothing.

But the tingles were getting worse. Now it was like tiny needles poking her spine.

After a quiet moment, and a few strange looks from other shoppers, Cary turned to close the trunk. And a carton of milk burst from the bag, flew a few feet from the rear bumper, and splattered across the tarmac.

"Holy shit," Jon screeched. "What happened?"

Cary pursed her lips. She wasn't sure, but a list of possibilities scrolled through her mind. Pixies—a lot of them. A sorcerer with an invisibility spell—though if he posed a danger to Jon, she should be able to see him despite the spell. A telekinetic. A clever demon of diminutive size or one who could move at hyper fast speeds. A ghost— she shivered at the mere thought. Jon would probably know if it was a shifter of some kind.

She studied the spilled milk, tried not to groan out loud at the dumb puns running through her head, and concluded the milk was real. So the flying canister wasn't part of an illusion.

Suddenly, a hail of pebbles rained onto them. One rock reamed her in the shoulder before her protector shields deflected the brutal assault. She tucked Jon as far under her as she could manage and bent her head. She hissed in a breath at the sharp sting of the single hit, chalking up another bruise.

When a six-inch high circle of rocks and debris surrounded them, the assault stopped. Raising her head cautiously, she darted a gaze around the lot. She still couldn't see anyone. But the lot was suspiciously empty now.

Eyes narrowed, she closed the trunk with one hand and kept Jon close with the other. She could feel the tremor running through his body and heard the raspy pant of his breathing.

"Okay, Jon," she said. "We're going to climb into the car and drive away. We'll be safe as soon as we get back to the house."

"What's going on?"

"Not sure yet. But it's okay. I won't let anyone hurt you." She walked him to her side of the car and held the door for him while he climbed in and slid across to his seat.

She was just turning to get into the car when a knife flew at her face. She stood her ground but squealed in surprise. Fortunately, having that deer-caught-in-the-headlights reaction to a surprise attack worked for Protectors, so long as they were protecting someone. The knife stopped inches from her eye, hovered for a beat, the metal of the blade vibrating. Then it clattered to the ground. Cary released a slow breath.

When the knife rose into the air again, she cringed. "Shit."

She watched it slash in the empty space around her, seeking a way closer. She followed it with her gaze, afraid to look away long enough to find the attacker. After what felt like a very long time, the blade abruptly changed directions, cutting the air to explode through a car window. The sound of shattering glass made Cary wince.

She took the moment's reprieve to turn back to the open car door.

She intended to dive in but the sound of Jon's sharp hiss straightened her. Easily eight to ten knifes of various sizes hovered in the air on the right side of the car. So much for facing the attack.

She threw herself into the driver's seat as the knives trembled against her shield. Just like with the leprechauns, bad guys couldn't get around her just by sneaking up on her to get at her charge. Still, seeing those knifes hovering beside Jon's side of the car made her stomach roll with fear.

She started the engine, feeling only mildly safer inside the metal and glass frame. "Okay, I think we should leave. What do you think?"

"Yeah," Jon said. His gaze still focused on the hovering blades.

He finally looked away when Cary reversed sharply out of the parking spot and swung the car toward the exit. She slammed on the breaks when the ground in front of them started to buckle and heave upward.

"Shit!" She reversed, turning to watch where she was going. She jerked the wheel to one side, throwing the rear of the car into an empty spot, changed gears and drove toward the second exit. The car jumped and bounced beneath her as the tarmac continued to crumble. It felt like driving in an earthquake.

Gritting her teeth, she floored the gas petal and drove right over the top of the bucking pavement. If she had a Hummer instead of a Prius, the off-roading might not have seemed so impossible. As it was, she felt certain her car was going to make her pay for doing this to it.

To her horror, a huge slab of concrete rose up in front of them, blocking the second exit. Jon screamed. Cary spun the car to the right, wincing when her side mirror brushed the slab. She floored the gas again, and they jumped forward just as the slab tipped toward them.

"Fuck." She jerked in her seat at the sound of concrete slamming into the ground behind her.

Thanking whatever benevolent forces were keeping the lot free of innocent bystanders, she headed back toward the first exit. But before she reached it, she turned early, went through an empty parking space, jumped the curb, barreled over the sidewalk—barely missing a street light—and screeched onto the main road in front of a pick-up truck. The truck's horn blared.

She glanced in the rearview mirror. The truck's driver was mouthing something she was sure was rude.

And the parking lot was mending itself, the buckled tarmac settling back into place with only a series of cracks to show for its little dance. She didn't pause long enough to watch the repair job or see how thorough it would be.

They were four blocks away when she realized she'd never even glimpsed the source of all that chaos.

"Damn strong telekinesis skill," she muttered.

She winced as the pain in her shoulder started to throb, not helped by the fear and after-effects of her powers making her nerves overly sensitive.

"You hurt, Jon?" she asked.

When he didn't answer, she glanced at him. His right hand gripped the door handle so hard his skin was blotchy white and red. He was breathing fast and his free hand fisted and unfisted in this lap.

"Hey, Jon?" She waited until he looked at her then caught his gaze for a second before facing the road again. "Are you hurt?"

"N-no. Fine." His voice trembled.

Yeah, right. Fine. "Sorry about the driving," she said, keeping her voice calm and casual. "Guess I need an SUV like Deacon's, huh?"

She glanced over in time to catch his brief, shaky attempt at a grin.

They said very little the rest of the way home.

1 4

"**I**was thinking we'd stay in this weekend," Cary said over dinner that night. She noticed Deacon's narrow-eyed look but didn't respond. She hadn't had a chance to tell him about the three attacks as he'd arrived five minutes after Sally—as planned since he'd followed her back.

"Why stay in all weekend?" Sally asked.

They were sitting in the living room, eating off the coffee table as usual because Cary's kitchen table only sat two. Cary and Jon exchanged a look. By mutual consent, they'd decided to tell Sally about the witches and the leprechauns but not the telekinetic attack. Jon hadn't wanted to tell her any of it, but Sally needed to know the threat was ongoing and real. They decided to leave the last attack out of the discussion because it was the attack that had scared them both the most. And if Cary was shaken, Sally would be hysterical.

"We had a few…things happen today," Cary said. "And I think it'd be safer."

Sally's eyes widened. "Things? What things?"

Cary told the tale, taking intermediate breaks to calm Sally. Jon ended up pulled onto his mother's lap so she could hug him and make sure he wasn't hurt. He voiced the standard protests but there wasn't much conviction in them.

Deacon leaned close. "You're okay?" he asked.

"Yeah, yeah. Fine."

"There's more, though?" He spoke too quietly for Sally to hear.

Cary met his gaze and said, "Later."

He nodded, leaned away, and squeezed her shoulder. She was pretty sure the gesture was meant to be comforting, but he'd inadvertently gripped her bruise, and she hissed at the sharp sting before she could stop herself.

Deacon's eyes narrowed. "You're not fine. You're hurt. What happened? How bad is it?"

"It's nothing. Just a bruise." She tried to wave away his concern, but his comments caught Jon and Sally's attention.

"You're hurt?" Sally said. "Where? Let me see."

"It's nothing really," Cary insisted. "Just a little bruise. It'll be gone by tomorrow. Bumped my shoulder on the air dryer in the bathroom at the school today. Didn't want to mention it because it's a little embarrassing."

Sally stared at her, and Cary knew the woman didn't believe her. From Deacon's expression, he didn't either. But they weren't the reason she'd told the lie. She'd done it to erase the panicked fear from Jon's gaze. The last thing the kid needed was a guilt complex because she'd gotten hurt protecting him.

"Don't worry," Cary told Jon. "I'm fine."

Jon nodded, but his gaze flicked to his mom and back to Cary a few times.

"You sure you don't want me to take a look?" Sally asked.

"No. Thanks. It's just a little bruise."

Actually, her whole left shoulder could be black and blue for all she knew. She hadn't looked herself yet. Sometimes she preferred not to see the damage.

Later, when Deacon got up to leave, Sally took Jon and disappeared into the bedrooms. To get out of the way Cary suspected, though Sally was a genius at coming up with plausible-sounding excuses.

"You going to tell me what really happened today?" Deacon asked, as they stood by the front door. He leaned in close, keeping his voice low.

The feel of his heat was surprisingly comforting after the day she'd had. "The witches and leprechauns happened just the way I said," she told him. "Well, okay, the witches were a lot more powerful than I let on. And I knew one of the leprechauns. If you see Jaxer before I do, tell him Tom is working for the Boss. It'll probably make his century to be able to stick Tom in the 'bad guy' category."

"So what haven't you told us?" Deacon asked.

She sighed. "There was a third attack, outside the grocery store. I never saw the attacker, but he was one of the most powerful telekinetic talents I've ever witnessed. He had chunks of tarmac rising up to block our way."

"That when you got hurt?"

"I don't want Jon to know," she said, pointing a finger at Deacon to emphasize her point. "That attack scared him more than the others." She shrugged. "Scared me, too."

Deacon sucked in a sharp breath through his nose. She watched his jaw muscles flex, as if he was holding back what he wanted to say. She readied herself for an argument about her job. Then he cupped her cheek in one hand and rubbed his thumb over her skin, the gentle touch robbing her of thought. His arm muscles bunched and his jaw still looked tight with suppressed emotion, but his hand was warm, the sweep of his finger soothing. Some irrational part of her wanted to rub her cheek against him, savoring the contact.

She had to keep reminding herself Deacon was a virtual stranger still. Hell, she'd only found out where he lived because Jon mentioned it. She knew nothing about this man standing in her doorway. How could his simple physical contact make her feel safe and cared for?

He leaned down and set his forehead against hers. She thought for a moment he might kiss her and was embarrassed to realize she wouldn't have objected.

Instead, he said, "I'm going to meet you at the school from now on. Follow you home. Stay with you until I go to follow Sally."

"Deacon, you can't. You have your own life, your own job. We'll be—"

He cut her off with harsh hiss, his hand on her cheek moving to the back of her neck. "I need to do this, Cary. I have to." He swallowed hard. "I won't be able to concentrate if I think you're in danger and I'm not there to help."

She shook her head. Though, she had to admit, his offer was kind of sweet. "It's not necessary." When he opened his mouth to speak, she said, "But you're a grown man, and I can't stop you. Just do me a favor and don't complicate things for me. Stay where I can protect you, too."

He smiled, slow and dangerously. "It's also a good excuse to spend more time with you," he said, straightening enough to meet her gaze.

Her stomach danced at the look in his eyes, all heat and desire. His gaze dropped to her lips and she could practically feel the look like a touch. Her heart hammered, all thoughts of her job and the scary bad guys she'd faced that day forgotten. She pulled in a deep breath, taking in his yummy warm scent, leaning in a little closer before she could catch herself.

Oops.

She pulled back. "You'd better go before I forget I have house guests."

He glanced toward the hall leading to the bedrooms. "We have a few more minutes of privacy. Sally's making Jon look over his homework."

"You can hear them?" Cary asked.

He nodded once, then pulled her into his arms.

She considered objecting. She had a lot of very good reasons for wanting to take things more slowly with him. They hadn't even had time for a proper date yet. He wasn't actually her boyfriend. She barely knew him.

But when he lowered his mouth to hers, all the excuses faded into a background hum, less important than the feel of his lips against hers, the taste of him, the heat of him surrounding her. His arms flexed, pulling her flush against his chest and she sighed.

Later, she'd be worried about how right this felt, having Deacon's hands on her, kissing him like they'd been kissing for years. But after her day, she just couldn't seem to care.

She let her head loll to one side as he nudged the edge of her shirt aside to nibble the place where her neck and shoulder met. Liquid heat seeped through her veins. His mouth was so drugging, she barely noticed he'd moved to her uninjured shoulder. When he nipped her skin, she jumped, yelped, and moaned all at the same time.

"You probably ought to…to go." Gee, that sounded convincing, she thought with an inner wince.

"Okay," he said.

But he didn't stop kissing her neck or nuzzling aside her shirt. The hands she moved to his shoulders to push him away tugged him closer.

"I'm serious," she said, her voice breathy and patently *not* serious.

"You're right. I'll go now." His mouth found hers again.

Cary's stomach quivered, her toes curled, her blood boiled. Every lustful cliché she could think of played out inside her. Deacon kissed so damned good, she forgot everything. And that instant of living just for the moment was sheer bliss.

In the end, he was the one to stop the kissing and stroking, though he looked as pained by the effort as she felt.

"I'll see you in the morning," he murmured.

Saturday morning, and a weekend ahead of them with nothing to do but hide in the house.

"You're going to be bored," she warned. "We'll probably spend the day watching movies and playing with the dogs."

"I'll bring a few of my favorite DVDs. Donuts or bagels?"

"I'm serious, Deacon."

"About donuts or bagels? I know."

She laughed despite herself. "I meant about you being bored."

"I'll be with you. How could I possibly be bored?"

After closing the front door behind him, she bounced her head lightly off the wood. She could get addicted to that man very quickly. For more than just his kisses.

15

---

ary was out of bed early Saturday morning. Her night had been haunted by lusty Deacon dreams. Sweaty sheets, hard muscles, the slide of a clever tongue over her heated skin. The feel of him beneath her fingertips, the taste of him in her mouth.

When she woke, her sheets were a twisted tangle around her body, and she imagined she could smell him in her room.

Groaning, she headed out to the kitchen. If she wasn't going to sleep, she was going to drink coffee. Once the pot was on, she wandered out the back door with the dogs. The air was crisp and damp, cold enough to see her breath. The clouds were a dark gray, threatening a downpour later.

She walked around her small backyard as the dogs bounced around doing their business. When she reached the back fence, the tom cat, Scratchy, jumped down from a tree branch to land at her feet. She squatted next to him and scratched behind his ears. Her efforts earned her a rough, growling purr.

Fred came racing up to them, barking aggressively at the cat. He slammed into Scratchy when the cat didn't move, fell a step back, and then stared with a slightly confused look on his face. Fred was all about the chase. He had no idea what to do with anything if he actually caught it. Since Scratchy wasn't inclined to run, Fred was at a loss for what to do next. After the two animals stared at each other for a heartbeat, Fred barked once and sped away to the opposite side of the yard where he barreled over the top of a prone Pickles.

Cary chuckled at the antics. "Not very bright, is he, Scratchy?"

Scratchy licked a paw.

In that moment, she envied Jon his talent. She'd love to know what her animals were saying. To her, to each other. Did the dogs and the cat actually communicate in some way or were their languages as incomprehensible to each other as they were to her?

She wandered back to the kitchen, nearly tripping over Fred as he followed, eager for breakfast.

"Watch it," she told him. "You make me break my leg and who will feed you?"

Fred's mouth hung open in what looked suspiciously like a grin. Buck nudged her hand when she got to the back door, and she gave him a rub under the chin. He leaned into the scratch. Such a big bad demon dog, she thought fondly.

Once inside, she shed her coat, dumped food into the dogs' bowls and opened a can of cat food for Scratchy, which she left out on the back porch since the tom never deigned to come inside. Then she poured herself a cup of coffee. It was nice, having the house to herself for a few minutes. Jon and Sally were usually up before her.

When the dogs were finished eating and she'd finished her coffee, she wandered back into the living room. She glanced up at her ceiling. Her secret library was in the attic. All her books, encyclopedias, her secured computer system, everything she needed to study and learn what she needed to know to be a good Protector was stored up there so casual visitors to her house wouldn't be suspicious. Particularly her parents. They wouldn't understand why her work for the zoology professor required her to have an extensive collection of literature on the occult, psychic phenomenon, demonology, current thinking in the mystical sciences, not to mention her books on the phylogenies of all supernatural creatures currently known on the planet.

She did have two things in common with other superheroes—very few people knew what she really did, and she had a secret "bat cave." Only hers was a bat attic.

She looked toward the hallway. With Jon and Sally still asleep, she could probably sneak up there. She wanted to research this mysterious Boss a little on her own. Jaxer was her most reliable source of information, but he wasn't her only source.

Did she dare?

The dogs would probably tell Jon where she was if he woke up before she came back down. That wouldn't be good. Jaxer and her computer guru Chris were the only people who knew about that space. She sure as hell didn't want her temporary house guests to know.

Unless the dogs had already told Jon.

She scowled down at the tribe sitting in a half circle around her feet. "Did you tell Jon my secret?" she whispered. "Huh? Did you guys give me away already?"

Pickles flopped her tail on the floor and let loose a low woof.

"Shh." Cary glanced down the hall, but there was no movement or sound of restless people being woken up by dogs. She looked at her pack. "Maybe we should go back into the kitchen."

The dogs followed, tails wagging.

Once in the relative privacy of the kitchen, Cary hunkered down on the floor and gave Pickles a hug. This started a scramble for attention from the other dogs which resulted in a lot of face-licking and near-silent squealing by Cary.

"Ew, gross, dog germs."

Her false protests only encouraged them, and soon she was sprawled on her back with all three dogs vying to lick her face and make her squeal and laugh.

A soft male chuckle from the back door made her pause in mid-wrestle. She glanced sideways. Deacon was leaning against the door frame, a paper bag in one hand, his other hand tucked into the pocket of his jeans. His grin and raised eyebrows brought heat to her cheeks.

Scrambling up from the floor, she brushed dog hair off her sweats and grimaced. "We were playing."

"So I see. I didn't mean to interrupt. Please, continue."

"No, no. That's okay." She couldn't quite meet his gaze when he chuckled again. She looked at three grinning dog faces and said, "See what you guys got me into."

Deacon dropped the bag on the counter, standing too close for her comfort. And there was that scent again. Wow, he smelled good. Did she smell like that to him? Probably not at the moment since she likely smelled like dogs. She couldn't even pinpoint what it was about Deacon's scent. No one else seemed to notice. Maybe it was some sort of pheromone only his mate picked up? She tried not to grimace. She really had to stop worrying about the mate thing. There were other things to worry about right now.

"I like the way you play with the dogs," he said. "Looks like fun."

"Yeah, well if you keep coming around, you will see that display more than once."

"Good. Can I join in?"

Because he was smiling, she grinned back. Jaxer always made her feel like a child for getting on the floor and wrestling with the dogs. Deacon wanted to join the fun. That said a lot about him. And their potential future together. Except she wasn't supposed to be thinking about that.

He ran a finger over her cheek and tapped her chin. A slight frown replaced his smile. "You have circles under your eyes. Didn't you sleep?"

"Not well. Dreams."

"Bad dreams?"

Her cheeks heated. "No."

He raised his eyebrows. "Good dreams?"

Was it possible to spontaneously combust from embarrassment? Probably not. She wasn't that lucky. "Stop gloating," she said.

"I didn't realize I had reason to gloat."

But she could tell by the gleam in his eyes and the slight quirk of his mouth, he knew damned well what her dreams had been about and that he'd been the star.

"You better have brought me something good for breakfast," she said. "I've only had one cup of coffee. That's not nearly enough to put up with this degree of embarrassment."

"Where's Sally and Jon?" he asked.

"Still asleep."

"Ah." He eased his backside against the counter and pulled her into the v of his legs, wrapping his arms around her waist so she was forced to lean into him. "So for a few minutes anyway, we have some privacy?" He dropped his head close to hers, close enough for her to feel the heat of his breath against her mouth.

"Kind of," she said, momentarily distracted by the sensation of having her breasts flattened against the wall of muscle that was his chest. She exerted a great deal of willpower to keep from rubbing against him. "If you don't count the doggie audience."

"Give us some privacy, guys," he said to the dogs.

To her utter amazement, they left the kitchen, tails still wagging. "How'd you do that?" she asked.

"Secret leopard trick."

She dropped her chin and narrowed her eyes at him.

"Why don't we talk about these dreams of yours?" he said.

"Oh no. Very bad idea."

His lips skimmed over her cheek to her ear. "That good were they?" Then he nibbled her lobe.

"Deacon." But her resistance was crumbling. "What kind of soap do you use?" she asked.

"Why?"

"Because you smell really good."

"So do you?" He pushed her hair to one side and nibbled his way along her jaw. "You taste good, too."

"There's still…" She trailed off when his mouth moved to the sensitive skin beneath her ear. Groaning, she wrapped her arms around his neck.

"I'm waiting to hear about these dreams."

"Oh no you don't." Was she really panting? Oh god. "Sally and Jon…" Her breath hitched.

He angled her head up and kissed her on the lips, ending any sort of conversation they might have attempted. Not that she was really coherent anymore. Her dreams had left her restless and needy. She squeezed tighter against his torso, trying to relieve the building ache. The feel of his hardening cock against her abdomen sent little shivers of pleasure down her spine. She ground her stomach against his erection and he groaned.

"I want you so bad I can barely think," he growled, then captured her mouth again.

The sound of nails on tile and the feel of something butting against her thigh pulled her out of her haze. She glanced down to see Buck sitting patiently beside them, staring.

"Okay, that's a little weird," she said. Then she heard the noise in the other room. "Oops. Sounds like Jon's up." She started to ease away from Deacon, but he locked his arms around her waist. "I don't think it's a good idea for Jon to find us in a clench," she said.

"Worse if he found me in my current state without you to shield the evidence."

She squeezed her eyes shut. "You're right. That would probably be more embarrassing."

He brushed a hand over her cheek, tucking her hair behind her ear. She opened her eyes. His gaze moved over her face, settling on her lips for a moment, then back to her eyes.

She raised a brow. "I can't imagine my standing here like this is going to help the state of things either." She glanced down between their fused bodies. He was still rock hard against her. But he made no move to put space between them.

She tried easing back again, but one of his arms kept her in place. "Deacon?" she asked.

Something in his expression worried her. He looked determined, but that wasn't the problem. There was an edge there, a wildness she didn't always see. The flex of his muscles, the tension in his arms, the line of his jaw... He looked like a man barely holding on to his control.

That couldn't be good.

"I'm not ready to let you go yet," he said. "I need a few more minutes before I can pretend that being around you and not touching you is bearable."

"Why do you come over if it's so hard to be around me?" she asked.

"Because not being around you is worse."

Noise from the living room got louder as Jon started talking out loud to Fred and Pickles. She suspected he'd sent Buck into the kitchen to make sure it was safe to come in. The kid was a little too smart for his own good.

Deacon looked toward the living room. Then, with obvious reluctance, he put her at arm's length. "I'm not sure if it's good or bad Jon can send a spy in here to see what we're doing." He glanced at Buck, who was still patiently staring up at them. "But at least he gave us some warning."

"I just hope Buck doesn't understand enough about…kissing to rat us out."

Deacon dropped his hands from her shoulders. "When was he fixed?"

She tried not to wince when Buck growled. "He's not fixed."

Deacon frowned. "Why not?"

She looked at Buck, considering. This was really his secret more than hers, and she was still a little unsure of Deacon. "He didn't want to be," she answered lamely. "Don't," she added when Deacon looked like he might launch into a lecture. As the owner of animal shelters, she had no doubt how he felt about the necessity of fixing pets not destined to be breeders. She actually felt the same way.

But Buck wasn't a typical dog. And he was definitely a lot more than a pet. "It's no big deal," she added. "He's not…interested in that kind of thing."

Deacon's frown turned into a confused scowl.

"It's a long story," she said. "I'll explain someday." Maybe.

He looked like he wanted to argue but shrugged it off and instead asked, "How many men have you kissed in front of him?"

Her turn to scowl. "That's a very sneaky way to find out about my dating history."

"Since I can't ask the dogs the way Jon does…"

"You could have just asked me," she said. "As for what Buck has seen, probably only a couple of kisses."

"Then I think we're safe. Why has he only seen a couple of kisses?"

"Because I don't let him into the bedroom to see anything else."

Deacon's gaze darkened. His low growl made Buck whine and scurry from the room. Which was impressive given Buck's pedigree.

She crossed her arms over her chest. She wasn't afraid of Deacon's mood change, to her surprise. She wasn't afraid of Deacon doing her physical harm. But the fact that he'd scared her dog pissed her off.

"Mind telling me why you've gone all spooky and run Buck off?" she asked.

"How many men have you had here?" he said, through clenched teeth.

"Not your business."

"Cary…"

"Deacon. Pull in that growling jealousy thing. We're not nearly to a place where we have to talk about our romantic pasts. We haven't even been on a date yet. Right now, it's none of your damned business who I have and have not slept with. And it won't be your business until I decide otherwise. Besides, have I once asked about the number of other women you've had in your house?" She changed stances to face him more fully. "And speaking of which, why didn't I know you had a house in Nobhill? Learning that fact from Jon was embarrassing since he thinks I'm your girlfriend."

"The subject hasn't come up."

Highlighting—*again*—how very little she knew about him. After a silent moment, she said, "Well. Is it a big house?"

"My family owns it. I use it while I'm in Portland."

That didn't exactly answer her question, but it sparked another more urgent one. "How often are you not in Portland?" Her stomach did a funny twist that felt suspiciously like panic.

"I used to travel a lot for business," he said.

"Used to?"

"I don't intend to do as much now. My sister can take over that part of the job. She's better at the people schmoozing than I am, anyway."

Cary tiled her head to one side and studied him. "Why don't you intend to travel anymore?"

"Because of you." He said it so simply, so matter-of-factly.

She opened her mouth. Closed it. Sighed. "I think I need more coffee. Are there donuts in that bag?"

He nodded.

She refilled the cup she'd abandoned earlier then faced him. "Okay. If this is going to continue, if you really mean this mate stuff and you want to be in my life, we need to get to know each other better."

He crossed his arms, a move that highlighted the breadth of his chest and the solid muscles of his arms and shoulders. Cary turned back to fixing her coffee.

"Fine," he said. "What do you want to know?"

"What's your sister's name?"

"Which one?"

"Better question then would be how many sisters do you have?" She settled her hip against the counter and cradled her coffee cup in her palms.

"Six. And eight brothers. I have a twin brother and sister, Michael and Jocelyn. But I was born first of the three, so I'm the acknowledged oldest."

"You have a twin brother?" The idea of two men who looked as incredibly yummy as Deacon Jones walking around on the same planet boggled the mind. "Identical?"

"No," he said. "And you won't be meeting Michael anytime soon."

"Why not?"

"I don't trust him around my mate."

That was interesting. She was dying to quiz him further on the subject of his twin brother but given the flexing muscle in his jaw, switching to a topic less potentially volatile seemed like a good idea.

"So who's the sister working with you here in Portland?" she asked.

"Caitlin. She's ten years younger." Now a ghost of a smile twitched across his mouth. "But infinitely wiser in many ways."

Cary's muscles relaxed. "Then I'm looking forward to meeting her." She paused. "I think. How much have you told her about me?"

"Enough."

"Oh good."

Maybe meeting Caitlin could wait. She opened her mouth to ask another question, since Deacon was being so talkative, but stopped when she heard Jon and Sally nearing the kitchen. They were bickering over homework as they came in, Jon pulling that pouty face only teenager's seemed capable of achieving.

Whatever she'd intended to ask would have to wait. Sally and Jon thought she and Deacon were a couple. She was supposed to know the answers to most of these questions already.

She sighed. She needed a donut. Donuts always helped.

WHEN SHE WALKED DEACON TO THE DOOR THAT NIGHT, HE PULLED HER into his arms as soon as they were out of sight. "I'm not going to apologize for my reaction this morning," he said. "The idea of another man's hands on you makes me crazy."

"Deacon, I'm no virgin. And neither are you. Deal with it."

"I can't think beyond you anymore. I don't want to 'deal with' the fact that other men have been in your bed. I…" He shook his head. "My instincts are riding me hard."

She wondered if it would help matters or make them worse if he knew she'd slept with exactly two men in the last six years. Being a Protector tended to eat into her dating time. And most of the men she met these days, she met through Jaxer, which was a pretty sure-fired way to guarantee they were no good for her.

The irony of the fact that she'd met Deacon through Jaxer as well was not lost on her.

She cupped his face in her palms. "Neither of us can go back in time and change our histories, even if we wanted to. Which I don't. So you're just going to have to get over it."

"I already told you, I'm not going to. You're going to have to deal with that."

She opened her mouth to object, but he pulled her close and stopped all discussion with a kiss.

Cary sank into the feel of him and ignored her uncertainties. When she came up for air, she said, "At least I know a little more about your family now." A very little. But it was a start.

"I'll tell you anything you want to know," he said. "You just have to ask."

She frowned. What if she didn't know what to ask?

He ran a thumb over her brow, smoothing creases. "Donuts again tomorrow?"

Groaning, she dropped her forehead to his chest. "I shouldn't. You've found my weakness."

"I thought pizza was your weakness."

"That too." She raised her head. "Sally would want us to have something healthy and nutritious."

"I'll bring orange juice. That's healthy."

"So this means you weren't too bored today?" Cary asked. "With the endless round of teenager-friendly movies and lousy computer games? And dogs? And teenage boy questions?"

"How could I possibly be bored with all that?"

He kissed her one last time, deep and hard enough to guarantee she wouldn't sleep well again. Then he left.

As Cary headed back to the living room, her gaze strayed to the ceiling. Jaxer hadn't sent her any news today. But she still couldn't risk a trip to her secret battick. No doubt Jaxer would send her some information tomorrow. He'd know she couldn't do any research on her own. He'd make sure to get her news.

But Sunday passed, another cloudy, relaxed day in the house, without any messages from him. As she went to bed that night, she assured herself he'd send word Monday. After all, this mysterious Boss was pretty elusive. Gathering useful information on him probably just took more time than normal. No reason to worry.

So long as the attacks didn't get worse.

16

To Cary's surprise, the attacks didn't get worse on Monday. In fact, they stopped all together.

The beginning of the week passed without incident. Cary took Jon to school. Deacon met them after the final bell and followed them home. When the time came, Deacon drove to the hospital to shadow Sally home.

Everything went to schedule without any supernatural dangers.

Cary wasn't sure whether to be relieved or worried about that. She leaned toward worry when they reached Wednesday without any word from Jaxer.

She did get a call from her friend Lucy on Wednesday night, though. Cary hid in the bedroom to take the call, though given Deacon's hearing, she wasn't sure a closed door really gave her much privacy.

"You missed training this week," Lucy said, without preamble. "Again."

Her soft, whispery voice was almost childlike, despite Lucy being a thirty-five year old woman. The first time Cary had heard her speak, she'd thought Lucy was purposefully affecting that tone, but it was just the way she sounded. And her voice, combined with her petite size, curly red hair, and freckles, frequently gave people who didn't know her the wrong idea about her capabilities.

Because Lucy Evans-Nakada was also a multiple-black belt martial artist. After seeing her in a fight for the first time, kicking the ass of four full grown men with ease, Cary had never taken Lucy's voice or her petite size as a sign that she was vulnerable.

"I know," Cary admitted with a sigh. "I'm working."

She normally trained in self-defense technics with Lucy on Tuesday nights. She didn't actually have to know how to fight because her Protector powers kicked in and gave her the skills she needed when she needed them, so long as she was protecting someone. Lucy—one of the few people who knew about Cary's real job—insisted Cary needed the training, though, because when Cary wasn't protecting someone, she was as vulnerable to attacks as any normal human woman.

"You're never going to get better if you don't keep up regular training," Lucy scolded.

"I know. I know." They'd had this discussion before. A lot. But Cary's job had to take precedence. "Couldn't be helped this time. I swear."

"Long term job?" Lucy asked, sympathy in her tone.

"Longer than I was anticipating." Cary flopped onto her bed and stared up at the ceiling. "Looks like I'll miss girls' night this Friday, too."

"Ah, we'll miss you. Marianne, Angie, and I are dying to grill you about this Deacon fellow."

Cary closed her eyes and groaned. "How did you hear about him?"

"So it's true? You have a boyfriend you haven't told us—your best friends—about yet?"

"First, not my boyfriend. Only known him for a little over a week." Saying that out loud made Cary blink. Wow, not even two weeks yet? Scary. "Second," she went on so Lucy wouldn't notice the pause, "I have been working this new job since I met Deacon. I haven't had a chance to call you guys and tell you about him yet."

"We are going to need a girls' night soon. You have a lot to explain."

She winced. How the hell did she explain Deacon to her best friends when she didn't really understand what was happening between them herself? "How did you even hear about him?"

"Jaxer."

Cary sat up. "Wait, you've talked to Jaxer? When?"

"He called Angie over the weekend, checking up on something. He mentioned you had a new 'annoying man' in your life."

"He called Deacon annoying?" She snorted. "That's one way to look at it."

"How do *you* look at it?"

Cary sighed. "I have no idea what to think. He's a leopard shifter. And he claims I'm his mate."

There was a long pause. Then in a whisper that made Lucy's child-like voice sound even more childlike, she said, "Are you?"

"I have no idea," Cary admitted. "It shouldn't even be possible, right?"

"I'm not the paranormal expert. You'll have to ask Angie and Marianne."

"It's not supposed to be possible," Cary said more definitively. "Leopards only bond long term with other leopards. I thought."

"You think he's trying to trick you just to get into your pants."

"He wouldn't need to trick me for that. Wait till you see him."

"Better looking than Jaxer?"

Cary considered that. "Different. Same unnaturally gorgeous but… I don't know. Earthier."

"Wow. How did you meet him?"

"I rescued him from a demented teenage sorcerer."

"Sounds about right for you."

Cary laughed. She did tend to meet most of the people in her life through her job. She'd gone under a bridge to "save" Lucy from her attackers when they'd first met—only to realize as she watched that Lucy didn't need any help.

"Do you want him to be your mate?" Lucy asked, getting to the heart of the matter as only Lucy could.

Cary opened her mouth to answer with all her uncertainty, only to remember that Deacon was probably hearing all this—at least Cary's half of the conversation. She closed her eyes. "I don't know yet," she admitted. "And I can't worry about it yet. What did Jaxer need from Angie?"

"She didn't say. Why?"

"Because I haven't heard from Jaxer in more than a week, and I'm waiting on him for some information to do with this job."

"I'm sure he'll get what you need to you. Jaxer's always good at helping you."

"He's also good at getting me into trouble," Cary pointed out, thinking about Deacon again. With a sigh, she said, "I'd better go. I have a house full of people. Sorry about missing training. I promise as soon as this current job is finished I'll make it up."

"I'm more concerned with hearing about this mate of yours. Keep us updated."

Cary stayed hidden in her room for a bit longer after ending the call, too many different worries making her gut hurt. Where was Jaxer? Why hadn't he sent her a message or any information yet? What had he been asking Angie about and did it even have to do with Jon and the Boss? Why hadn't the Boss sent anyone after them yet this week? What did she feel for Deacon? Did she even want a man in her life right now? Did she have time? How long would she have to keep Jon and Sally here? How much longer would Sally stay?

Rubbing her hands over her face, she groaned into her palms. Too many questions. Too many dangerous possibilities.

And her without any real answers.

∽

THEY REACHED FRIDAY NIGHT STILL WITHOUT ANY ATTACKS, AND Cary's nerves were drawn tight with all the waiting. Another weekend stretched out in front of her, one that proved more of a protecting challenge because keeping a teenager tucked away in a house for two weekends in a row without video games or a collection of violent movies wasn't easy.

Cary did have some good action films in her collection but not near enough and apparently not the right ones. Plus, he'd watched them all already. Twice. And she only had boring computer games, nothing even resembling a proper gaming console.

Thankfully, the dogs kept Jon occupied playing catch in the backyard for most of Saturday morning or the complaints would have started much earlier.

Deacon arrived with bagels and donuts, enough to feed everyone, to Jon's enthusiasm and Sally's scowl. Though Sally did eat two donuts, so obviously her objection was more of a moral stand against excess sugar for her teenage boy. A couple of hours later, Cary understood why.

Sugar gave already active teenage boys *way* too much energy. And after a very quiet week with no more attacks, fear no longer burned up all that energy. Jon managed to wear out Pickles and Buck in an hour. Fred could chase the ball for days, so there was no hope of wearing him out, but Jon eventually lost interest. The dogs curled up to take their requisite morning nap while Jon went to find the cat. Scratchy had decided to make his presence known the night before by leaving a dead bird at the back door.

Scratchy and Jon seemed to have a very animated conversation while the dogs slept peacefully a few feet away. There was so much mewing and hissing by the cat, Fred raised his head once to see what was going on. He saw the cat, dropped his little head back onto his front paws and closed his eyes.

Cary, watching all this, couldn't help but grin. She was also very curious what that cat had to say.

That distraction only lasted another hour, though, and then Jon was in the house complaining of being bored. Again.

"Can't I go over to Will's house?" he said. "No one will bother me there. Will's dad has this big Glock in the closet."

Sally's eyebrows rose to her hairline. "You are never going to Will's house again."

"Mom," he drawled in that pained teenager way. "We know not to play with it. Mr. Borosky keeps it in a locked box anyway."

"Mm hmm. Well, I'll be having a little chat with Mrs. Borosky before I let you spend the day at Will's."

"But I'm booored."

"Yes, yes," Sally said with a long suffering sigh, "you're always bored. You are also still in danger."

She looked to Cary for confirmation, and Cary nodded.

Something was coming. Cary could feel it in her bones. It was only a matter of when.

"We could go to the park," Deacon suggested. "Take the dogs. Maybe bring a picnic. We aren't due any rain all day."

"Can we play football?" Jon launched off the couch and stood staring up at Deacon. "I bet you play football."

Jon's change from suspicion to hero worship was nothing short of miraculous. Cary wasn't entirely sure how to feel about the switch in attitude, but as long as they weren't at each other's throats, she could live with it.

"There aren't enough of us to play much of a game," Deacon said, "but we can toss a ball around if you like. You got a ball?"

"No." Jonathon dropped his head. "Guess you don't either?"

"Not yet. We'll stop and get one."

"Really? Cool. You're the best, Deacon."

"Thanks, kid. Put in a good word with Cary for me, would you?"

Jonathon laughed and swatted playfully at Deacon's significantly thicker arm.

Seeing the two men, so different in size, playfully punching at each other made her smile. Deacon looked up and caught her grin. He winked, then turned his attention back to Jon.

So beyond being supremely sexy and having a job that involved saving animals, Deacon was also good with kids.

She was doomed.

Sally was working that afternoon and most of the night, so they packed up Deacon's SUV with food, the dogs, and some blankets, followed Sally to the hospital—with her knowledge this time—made a quick stop at a sports store to pick up a football, and headed to a park not far from Cary's house where the off-leash area could be used all day.

They let the dogs loose first so they could run and, hopefully, wear themselves out a little. Fred, though the smallest of the three and the only one who didn't possess any supernatural qualities, still managed to nearly pull Deacon off his feet in his hurry to get to the other dogs. Fred was the social one in the group. Pickles liked other dogs, but she was more laid back about meeting them. Buck usually hung back by Cary, preferring to watch the antics.

Other dogs never seemed to notice that there was something different about Buck and Pickles either. Fortunately. Because she'd hate to keep Fred from all the socializing.

Jon laughed and jogged after Fred. In a matter of minutes, the teenager was surrounding by every single dog in the area, all of them vying for his attention.

"That kid's got some talent," Cary commented, watching a dog that looked like it could devour Fred in one gulp pushing his head into Jon's hand for a scratch. "I wonder what they're all talking about."

"Food or football probably," Deacon said. He pulled her close, his arm across her shoulders. "And speaking of food, I'm starving."

"Yeah, I could eat. Give the dogs a few more minutes, then we'll go out to the grass and tether them. Pickles and Buck will be ready for a nap soon."

"And Fred?"

"After we've finished eating and he's finished begging, he'll nap."

Cary turned her face up to the sun. It was a mild day, cold enough for a jacket, but the sky was clear and bright and the park filled with people taking advantage of the unseasonably nice weather. There was no telling how much longer it would last before full winter set in.

When they could tear Jon and the dogs away from the fun, they found a grassy spot to sit and eat their lunch of sandwiches, potato chips, egg salad, and soft drinks. Sally insisted they bring some apples, and because Deacon could eat as much as three men, he ate two. Since his hero didn't object to the fruit, Jon ate an apple, too. Cary had a candy bar.

"Hey," she said to Jon's accusing frown, "just because you're weird and don't like sweets doesn't mean I have to sacrifice good taste."

After lunch, they threw the football around, and Cary proved how uncoordinated she could be when not protecting someone—despite Lucy's best efforts. To Cary's humiliation, both Deacon and Jon spent a half hour trying to teach her how to catch better. They gave the effort up as a lost cause sometime around three in the afternoon and let her go sit with the dogs. She was better at watching anyway.

They were on their way back to Deacon's SUV when three large men and two equally large women blocked their path.

1 7

Cary immediately moved Jonathon behind her. "Five against two?" she said. "I suppose it could be worse."

"For you or for us?" a deep voice commented from behind the wall of people.

The voice held a distinctly English accent and sounded both amused and indulgent. From between the barricade of thugs, a man stepped forward. He was medium height, medium build, with gray hair, pale eyes, and a nose that could only be called distinguished. He wasn't unattractive, though she wouldn't call him handsome. Cary decided the word "character" best described his face. And a certain… power. He was probably in his early sixties, but he moved with the grace and ease of a young man.

At odds with standing in the middle of a public park, the man wore a dark gray suit, white shirt, and blood red tie, all covered by a long, dark coat. The outfit gave him an air of distinction. The suit was obviously well tailored and expensive, the tie made of silk, the coat heavy wool. The cufflinks winking at his wrists were diamonds.

She knew without asking who stood before her. Though the fact that he'd come in person, instead of sending more messengers, made her gut clench. She hadn't expected him to make a personal appearance. At least, not yet.

"Good afternoon, Ms. Redmond," the man said, his mouth tilting in the barest of smiles. "It's a pleasure to finally make your acquaintance." He looked beyond her to Jon. "Jonathon Webber. I've been trying to arrange a meeting with you for the better part of two weeks now."

"Who are you?" Cary asked mainly to pull the man's gaze away from Jon.

"You know who I am, Ms. Redmond."

"True. But it's impolite not to make proper introductions. Especially when you already seem to know who we are."

He smiled. "Holland. Oliver Holland."

Bond. James Bond. She gave him a mental raspberry. "What can we do for you, Mr. Holland?"

"As I said, I've been attempting to speak with Jonathon for several weeks now. A meeting you've been preventing for some odd reason."

"Yeah, I'm a little weird that way. Trying to drag a kid into a car for a 'meeting' is perfectly normal behavior. Why would I want to prevent that?"

"A simple misunderstanding, I assure you."

"And the witches, the telekinetic, the leprechauns, the shifters and wizards trying to follow us? All a mistake?" She raised her brows, giving him an expectant look designed to irritate. Irritated bad guys tended to talk longer.

"Poor communication and a lack of good judgment," he said easily. "We mean the boy no harm."

"Then what do you want with him?"

"To offer him a job. You have a unique talent, Jonathon. I wish to discuss employing you."

"Why the hell would you want to offer me a job?" Jon spat.

He was holding all three dog leashes, and the animals sat quietly and still in a half circle in front of him. Cary didn't need to be able to talk with the dogs to see that all three were vibrating with unease. Buck released a low sound, half whine, half growl, then fell silent again.

"So you can use that talent of yours to our mutual benefit," Holland said, answering Jon's question. "I pay very well for skills such as yours."

Cary shifted positions to further block Jon from view and bring Holland's gaze back to her. "Mr. Holland. I've heard quite a bit about you. Or should I say, I haven't heard nearly enough?"

That slight smile again. "I'm a very private man."

"Aren't we all?" she said. "But I do have one question for you."

He spread his hands in a gesture indicating she should ask.

"What are you?"

"I'm a businessman."

"No." She leaned in a little closer. "I mean, *what* are you?"

"You're an interesting woman, Ms. Redmond."

"Gee, thanks. Are you avoiding my question?"

"I find you quite fascinating."

"I'm flattered." She hated when bad guys avoided questions by changing the subject. It was rude. Just tell her it was none of her damned business and leave it at that. Don't try these interrogation tactics.

She conveniently chose to ignore the fact that she did the same thing herself sometimes. Maybe more than sometimes.

"Like that." Holland mirrored her gesture and leaned a little closer. "You're taunting me. You have no idea what I might do, what true danger I pose, but you taunt me with sarcasm. And believe me, I know sarcasm when I hear it. I'm British."

"So you like my sarcasm? Good. I've got lots of it."

"You show no fear." He shook his head, his gaze steady. "And then there's your job. A bodyguard. Such an interesting job—"

"If you finish that sentence with 'for a woman,'" she said, "I will be required by law to hurt you."

He laughed. "I was going to say for someone with no discernable training. You don't even own a gun. You don't practice firing a gun at any range, ever. You've never been in the military, the FBI, the secret service, the police. You've minimal martial arts training that only started after you took up as a 'bodyguard'—and honestly, a class every other month can't qualify as real training."

She winced at that. Lucy kept telling her the same thing.

"You've taken no classes in tactics at university," Holland continued. "You've never even taken a theatre course to learn stage combat. And up to six years ago, you were no one special."

"Hey," she said. "I resent that. I've been special since the day I was born." She was more than a little disconcerted by his knowledge of her background, but she hated for the bad guys to see her sweat. And this was one mother of a bad guy. The hair on her arms rose the nearer she got to him.

"Yes," Holland said, "well I imagine your mother told you that. They all do, you know, but it's rarely true. Then there's the fact that you don't age—"

"Now, that's not true. I age." Just slowly.

"You are thirty-two years old. But you don't look a day over twenty. Significantly younger than you are."

"Good genes," Cary said with a shrug. "My mother always looked young for her age too. And I do age. Ask my doctor. Or doctors." She muttered the last.

"Ah yes," Holland said, his gaze narrowing. "Your medical history. That was interesting reading. Strange bruising, cracked bones, dislocated joints."

"Guess I'm not so good at my job after all, without all that military training."

"And yet you withstood the full force of a dragon shifter's fire." He paused, leaning even closer. "So I ask, Ms. Redmond, what exactly are *you*?"

"Cool under fire. Get it? Dragon shifter fire." She waggled her eyebrows and grinned.

"Fascinating. Such bravado."

Her grin dropped. "Don't condescend to me, Holland."

"Wouldn't dream of it. I do find you very interesting, Ms. Redmond. It would be a shame to kill you."

"Yes, it would. I suggest you don't try."

He smiled.

Deacon growled and stepped closer to Cary's side. "It would be better for you if you didn't try," he said.

Holland's gaze shifted to Deacon. "The leopard. He belongs to you, Ms. Redmond?"

"Why do people ask me that?" she said. "He belongs to himself. But he likes me."

"I've no doubt," Holland said. "And I can understand why. Well, I wouldn't like to anger a leopard. Especially this particular one." He tilted his head in a mocking bow.

"No," Deacon said, "you wouldn't."

"What does that mean?" Cary asked, glancing between the two men. "'This particular one'?"

"She doesn't know?" Holland raised a brow at Deacon. "That will be an interesting conversation. Oh to be a fly on the wall."

"Is there a point to all this word play, Holland?" Cary said, trying hard not to snarl. She didn't like that Holland knew something about Deacon that she didn't. She really didn't like that Deacon had a secret big enough to give Holland that gleam in his pale eyes. But that was a conversation for later.

"Enjoyment, perhaps?" Holland said. Despite Deacon's looming menace, Holland leaned even closer and put his face an inch from hers. His breath smelled like peppermint. "I've never met anyone quite like you, Ms. Redmond."

"I'm unique," she agreed.

"Yes. You are. And I have a taste for unique things. I'd very much like to get to know you better. Understand more of that uniqueness."

"You better not be hinting at what I think you're hinting at, Holland. You're too old for me."

"So is he." Holland nodded at Deacon.

Cary slanted a glance at the man beside her. "No, he's not." She looked back at Holland. "But we like to pretend he is." And she winked.

Holland threw his head back and laughed, straightening away from her as he did. She swallowed her relief and slowly straightened as well. They still had to get away from this…whatever he was.

"I'll look forward to further conversations with you, Ms. Redmond," Holland said, still smiling. "I'd like to continue our discussion as to what you are." He looked between her and Deacon, then to Jon. "And you, Jonathon. Think about my offer. I pay very well. Ask anybody."

Without another word, and with absolutely no sign of discomfort, Oliver Holland walked around her small group and headed to the opposite side of the park, his thugs in tow.

Cary let out a breath that ruffled the small hairs teasing around her forehead, escapees from her ponytail. Though she held steady for Jon's sake, her knees felt rubbery. "That was interesting."

"What kind of job do you think he wants me to do?" Jonathon asked.

"Nothing you'd be able to do and still look your mother in the eyes afterward," Cary snapped, harsher than she intended.

"I was just asking. Geez. What's your problem?"

"I get antsy when strange men accost me in the park and know that much about me," she said. Then sighed. "Well, we knew he had resources." She watched the place where Holland had disappeared into the trees with his five thugs. "But I thought my background was a little harder to get at than that."

She turned to Deacon. "He knew about you. That can't be good." She still wanted to ask what Holland had meant by "this particular leopard," but that part would have to wait until they were safe in her house.

Deacon was also staring after Holland. "It's not unexpected, given he's a demon."

"He's a what?" she said, her voice rising before she could control it. "How come I couldn't tell? I should've been able to tell. I can usually spot a freed demon."

"He's old," Deacon said. "He's very strong. And he's very smart. He's been untethered for centuries, if my nose is any judge."

"Great," she said with a groan. "I hate dealing with demons. There are so many different kinds. I still get them all mixed up, and I've been studying this stuff for years." She put her hands against her head and squeezed to relieve the building pressure. "Too much to learn and never enough time to learn it all," she muttered to herself. "Where's a good demon hunter when you need one?"

"How'd you know he's a demon?" Jon asked Deacon.

The kid wasn't nearly as disturbed by the news as she would have thought.

Deacon tapped his nose. "His scent."

"What about it said demon?" Jon asked.

"You'd have to be a shifter to understand. There are a lot of layers to scent."

"The dogs try to explain it to me."

"They can't, can they?" Deacon asked.

"No," Jon reluctantly agreed. "But that's cause they don't have the words. You do."

"They don't do me any good when it comes to explaining how my body and brain sift through a single scent to analyze it's every component."

"Fine, don't tell me."

Cary rolled her eyes at Jon's sullen tone. Of all the things for him to get upset about at this moment... "Come on," she said, "let's get back to the house."

On the way to the car, though, that feeling of being watched swept a shiver over her shoulders. She looked around the park, trying to pinpoint the source without alerting Deacon or Jon. For a long moment, she stood at the open car door, scanning the park, hunting the tree shadows, studying the people scattered across the open grass to see if anyone was paying any attention to her.

Then the sensation vanished. Whoever had been watching was just...gone.

Damn.

This was really starting to creep her out.

18

Deacon left Jon in the living room watching a movie and joined Cary out on the back porch. She sat on the steps leading down to her grass covered backyard, idly tossing a ball to Fred while Pickles and Buck reclined on the porch next to her. He scooted Buck out of the way—moving Pickles when she was settled was nearly impossible—and sat next to Cary.

The evening had turned chilly but was fortunately still dry. Cary wore a padded flannel shirt over her sweater and jeans. She looked warm enough, but he still had an urge to tuck her under his arm to keep her from the cold.

"You want to talk about it?" he asked. When Fred came bounding back with the ball, he shoved it into Deacon's lap. Deacon took a turn at throwing. There wasn't much light in the yard, but Fred still managed to find the ball and come scampering back at high speed.

"I was just wondering where the hell Jaxer is," Cary said after a moment. "I haven't even gotten a message from him in more than a week. Not since you delivered his last one to the school. I knew he wouldn't want to come around while Jon's here, but…"

"But?" Deacon tossed the ball again without looking at her.

"But I was expecting to hear something by now."

"We'll find out more about Holland."

"It's not just that." She puffed out a breath. "I need him." Her voice dropped to a whisper. "He's my mentor. And I don't know what to do next."

The very slight quaver in her voice nearly broke him. "Cary…"

"After six years, I still feel like I have so much to learn. I don't know how to deal with a demon like Holland. Strategy isn't my strong suit. I've always had Jaxer for that."

She tilted her head to look at Deacon, and he met her gaze, ignoring Fred when the dog tried to shove the ball into his lap again. When Fred got no response, he flopped down on the lower step at Deacon's feet.

"Holland is powerful," Cary said, "wealthy, and has been freed from any demon bonds for a long time, according to your nose. In all those centuries, he's also managed to avoid the demon hunters." She raised her hands in a shrug. "I can stand between him and Jon from now until the end of days and keep Jon safe. But I can't *do* anything about him. I can't make him go away. I… I don't know how."

"It's not your job to make Holland go away," Deacon said. "It's your job to protect Jon."

"But if the demon just keeps coming and coming, what do I do then? You saw how interested that kid was in Holland's job offer. Even if Jon does see through the deception and continues to let me protect him, will I have to keep him here for weeks? Months? Years? As long as I'm around, he won't be hurt, but what if Holland is the persistent type? There's going to come a time when we relax, when we get lazy. When Jon goes somewhere without me." She looked out over the yard again. "Maybe I have someone else I have to protect. Maybe he just goes out on his own one day, and I don't stop him."

"We won't let that happen," Deacon tried to assure her. He had no idea how they could prevent it, but he couldn't stand to see her so frustrated. "We'll figure something out. Holland will give up and leave Jon alone, or we'll find a way to make him go away." He reached out and cupped her cheek. "We'll figure this out."

"That's just it," she said. "Jaxer would know what to do. He always does. He's not limited to a purely defensive power, like I am. He would know what to do. And I want to know why the hell he isn't here to do it."

"Cary…"

She shook her head and stood up. "I want a beer. You want one?"

He nodded and watched her disappear into the kitchen, fisting and relaxing his hands to keep from breaking something. A low growl rose in his throat and he choked it down so he wouldn't scare the dogs. He wanted desperately to help her, to make her see everything would be okay. But his jealousy, an emotion he just couldn't seem to control, kept short circuiting his more tender desires. Damn it, he wanted her to turn to him when she needed help. Not *Jaxer*. And because she was looking to Jaxer, his leopard roared in protest.

He let out a deep breath, pulled in another, and let it out again. His animal half pressed at his skull, making his skin crawl with the leopard's need to get out, to protect his mate. He forced his jaw muscles to relax, counted his breaths to slow them, willed his beast to quiet. None of it worked. His mate was hurting. Every instinct in him screamed to make things right for her.

His control, already tenuous, continued to slip, slowly melting away. There were moments, like that afternoon when they'd faced Holland, when he could barely reason beyond his emotions. He'd wanted to tear the demon to pieces for threatening Cary, and he'd been close to attacking when he shouldn't have, when the situation would have been made worse by a public fight in the middle of the day. He hadn't struggled with his nature like this in years.

He was too dangerous like this.

He had to be more controlled even than other leopards. He was first born to parents who were in turn the first born of first born parents. Birth order and the birth order of one's parents made a difference for leopard shifters. Not just socially. It affected their skills, powers, and the strength of their animal side. He was the result of first borns of first borns tracing back generations. His animal was incredibly powerful even at the best of times, which meant his control had to be absolute.

Meeting his mate had thrown all his discipline into chaos. All those years of self-control laid waste. His leopard could hardly stand to be away from her now. The animal was getting closer and closer to the surface. If Deacon wasn't careful, his animal would subsume his human self.

A disaster not just for him but for all the leopards on this coast.

He needed to convince Cary she *was* his mate. He needed time alone with her, time to…court her. Time to seduce her. Time to prove to her they had a future together. But he wouldn't be able to until Cary no longer needed to protect Jonathon. To finish this business with Holland, she needed Jaxer.

Deacon launched up from the decking, startling Fred and Buck into standing. Pickles raised her head but didn't bother getting up to watch him stalk into the house. Cary was standing at the sink, an unopened bottle of beer on the counter next to her as she stared at the tiled wall.

He stepped up behind her and wrapped his arms around her waist. Touching her helped quiet his angry leopard, and fortunately for him, she didn't seem to mind being touched. He kissed the top of her head when she leaned into him then pressed his cheek against hers.

"I'm going to take off now," he said. "I've got something I need to do. You want donuts again for breakfast?"

She turned in his arms. "You're going so early? What do you need to do on a Saturday night?"

"I know someone who might know more about Holland. But he can only meet me tonight."

"Why didn't you tell me earlier?"

"I didn't think about it." He dropped his mouth to hers because he needed to kiss her more than he needed to breathe.

At first, her lips remained unmoving beneath his. Then she relaxed, opening her mouth to deepen the kiss. God, he loved the way she tasted, the way her scent filled his head, driving him slowly crazy and completing his world at the same time. He wanted nothing more than to carry her off to the bedroom and explore every inch of her.

But he couldn't. Not yet.

He ended the kiss reluctantly and stepped back. "I have to go. I'll be back early. Think of something you might like to do tomorrow. Anything you want."

He left before she could question him more. Picking up his coat and keys, he waved goodnight to Jon and left.

He had a faery to find.

~

DEACON FOUND JAXER SITTING ON A HILL DEEP IN FOREST PARK watching the stars. The faery was dressed in a dark silk shirt and pants, the color making his pale skin glow in the weak moonlight.

"I was wondering how long it would take you to come looking for me," Jaxer said without looking away from the sky.

"Cary needs you, though it pains me to admit it. So where the hell have you been?"

"Sit down, Deacon."

"Answer my question, faery."

"Sit. There's some things you should know." He finally turned his head and looked at Deacon. "My story will explain a lot."

Reluctantly, Deacon lowered himself to the soft grass.

"She really is your mate, isn't she?" Jaxer said. He was staring at the stars again. "I've never seen you so on edge."

On edge was a definite understatement. But since Deacon thought he'd been displaying a remarkable degree of control given the circumstances, Jaxer's comment both pissed him off and annoyed him. "Shit."

"Getting worse?" Jaxer asked.

"Yes."

"Being the mate of a Protector isn't going to be easy, Deacon. Ever."

"Yeah, well that's something we'll have to deal with. She got stuck with an out-of-control leopard."

"Not just any leopard," Jaxer said. "Have you told her yet?"

"No. Later. When I can think straight again, and she's more comfortable with me."

Jaxer nodded. "Fair enough." He blew out a long breath. "I have to say, I am really not happy Cary turned out to be your mate."

"You wanted her for yourself?" Deacon really didn't have to ask. He'd scented Jaxer's attraction to Cary that first morning in her house.

"I thought… In a few months." Jaxer shrugged.

"Why a few months? You've known her for years. Why not hit on her earlier?" The very idea made Deacon's body tight with rage. He ground his teeth together and held on to the last shreds of his control by will alone. He had a feeling he needed to hear this.

"For the last six years, I've been her mentor, she's been my student. I taught her as much as I could about being a Protector. And during all that time, I had to keep my…interest to myself. It's the *rule*." He rolled the word out. "My bosses have been reminding me of this rule a lot. Cary calls them the Nags. It's appropriate."

"You've wanted her from the beginning?" Deacon asked.

"Actually, no. My feelings developed over time. She's a pretty amazing woman. I'm not even sure when I started thinking of her differently. But the feelings have gotten more intense over the years. And in another three weeks and a day, the rule of not getting involved with my student won't apply anymore."

"What happens then?" Deacon clenched his jaw. He hated this conversation. He had to know this stuff, but he didn't like it. Every word made his leopard snarl. And he was afraid the next thing out of Jaxer's mouth was only going to make matters worse.

"My tenure as mentor ends," Jaxer said. "Protectors get six years of mentoring once they begin officially working—"

"Officially working?"

Jaxer paused, frowning a little. "Most future Protectors start their educations early. Then they begin officially working at twenty-one."

"When did Cary start?" The fact that he didn't know, the fact that there was still so much about her he didn't know because they hadn't had enough time alone, only angered his leopard further.

"Twenty-six," Jaxer said. "Her situation wasn't typical. She's not typical."

"You want to explain that?" Deacon growled.

Jaxer ignored the tone. "If she wants to tell you, she will."

"She said she was tricked into it. Something about saving a puppy from a demon."

Jaxer laughed and shook his head. He glanced at Deacon. "I don't know about being tricked, although she loves to pull out that card. She was recruited, so to speak, after she stood up to a demon to protect a dog. Even after she realized she was in over her head, she still faced off against the demon. Bravest damned thing I've ever seen. And the stupidest. But it was a very Cary thing to do. She's perfect for this job. Whether she believes it or not. If not for—"

When he cut himself off, Deacon's instincts jumped with suspicion. "What? If not for what, Jaxer?" Even he was surprised by the deep, gravely sound of his voice.

Jaxer gave him a slight frown, then sighed. "She doesn't even know this."

"Damn it, faery, if you don't start talking I'm going to hurt you. I need to hurt something very badly right now so don't push me."

Jaxer rolled his eyes, not looking even remotely worried. Which wasn't very smart, Deacon thought. When Jaxer still didn't say anything, Deacon snarled. "Talk."

"It's... We're looking into it, okay. But Cary, she's..." Jaxer lifted his hands in a shrug. "Most Protectors have some kind of power. They're not ordinary humans like Cary. They have magic all on their own, usually something they can use offensively. Cary doesn't have that. Without the Protector powers, she's just a vulnerable human who can be killed."

Deacon felt his head spinning. He had to close his eyes to keep from doing violence.

"She knows that part," Jaxer said. "What she doesn't know is... She's not supposed to be getting hurt when she's protecting someone."

Very carefully, with his eyes still closed, Deacon said, "Explain."

"Liruk thought at first it was because Cary wouldn't fully embrace her position as Protector. She still uses that excuse with Cary. But the Nags and I have known for a while now it has to be something else.

Nothing should get through their magic to hurt her while she's protecting someone."

"Your theory?" Deacon spoke through his teeth, his jaw tight. When he felt his hands actually starting to shift to claws, he buried his fingers in the soil beneath him, gripping the earth and rocks like a lifeline to sanity.

"We have no idea," Jaxer said. "As far as we can tell, she doesn't have any powers. The Nags can usually tell."

"Usually?"

"There are a few things they can't pick up, but most of those possibilities have been eliminated over the years."

"Jaxer…"

"All we know is Cary is vulnerable and powerful all at once."

"How is she still powerful?"

"She channels the Nags' magic better than anyone I've ever trained. Which is why her getting hurt is so confusing. Because she doesn't have any other magic, there's nothing getting in the way of the Protector powers. So when she's actually standing between danger and the good guys, as she puts it, she's incredibly strong, impossible to move. She just shouldn't be getting hurt all the time. And when she's not protecting someone, she's too easy to kill."

Deacon let out a slow, deliberate breath. "I can't even begin to tell you how much I hate everything you're saying to me right now." He finally opened his eyes and looked at Jaxer.

Jaxer raised his brows. "Your eyes are glowing. Your leopard is showing."

"Why haven't you told her she's not supposed to be getting hurt?"

"The Nags decided until she got through her seventh year, it was better she didn't know. She's always been a bit of a flight risk. But she'll just keep jumping in front of people to protect them. She'll get killed without the Protector magic. We thought she'd be safer this way. A few cracked ribs are a lot better than death."

Deacon grunted. "Seventh year? Why is that significant?"

Jaxer picked at the grass, not looking at him when he said, "Protectors are set loose in their seventh year. A test of all they've learned. If they survive, their full powers come to the fore."

"And if they don't survive?" Deacon asked.

"Their families are compensated."

Deacon felt something give in his hand. He glanced down to see the gravelly remains of a fist-sized rock dripping from between his clenched fingers. "Does Cary know *this* part?" he forced out.

"No," Jaxer said. "Protectors never do. They have to learn to survive on their own, without the help of their mentors. They have to learn how to solve their own problems. Her powers are already stronger. She's capable of things now that she doesn't even realize. Those powers will continue to develop during the seventh year."

"Will she continue to get hurt?"

Jaxer shrugged. "We don't know."

"So why the hell don't you tell her?" Deacon's anger rolled in his gut.

"She needs to learn about her powers and how to use them on her own. That's what the seventh year is all about." Jaxer fell silent a moment, then quietly, "She'll survive, Deacon. She'll figure everything out."

Deacon couldn't speak. Anger clogged his throat. They were going to throw her to the lions in less than a month, without warning, without telling her all the things she needed to know to survive. She didn't have a clue what was coming. And they were going to leave her to sort it out on her own.

"Were you planning on making your *feelings* clear to her once the seventh year began?" Deacon asked when he could finally speak.

"Yes," Jaxer said. "So I would have stuck around. I wouldn't have been able to help her officially, but I'd still have been there."

"Then why are you abandoning her now? Before the year is up? Why are you pulling back already?"

"I'm supposed to start giving her room to make more decisions. Until you made your claim on her, I hadn't intended to pull back this much. But now… For my sake as well as hers, I think this is for the best."

"For you maybe." Deacon's lip lifted in a snarl. "She's at a loss, hurting and confused, and it's your fault. You're lucky we've known each other so long, or I'd have to rip your throat out for doing this to her."

Jaxer's mouth quirked up at one corner. "That's the only reason I'm still sitting here, leopard."

"Will you go on to mentor another Protector?"

"Eventually. Not right away."

"How long have you been doing this?"

"I've mentored twenty Protectors. I was recruited a hundred and sixty years ago, when I first came to this country."

"How many have survived the seventh year?"

"All but one."

"And that one? What happened?"

Jaxer sighed. "He couldn't control the powers he had, and he lost track of why he had them. He'd been a talented wizard before becoming a Protector. He started going after people during his seventh year—no longer just protecting, but actually killing people who he thought might be a threat someday. He made mistakes. And then he made one deadly one."

"Fuck." Deacon closed his eyes again. "What the hell have you and those Nags gotten Cary into?"

"She chose this life," Jaxer said, "whether she admits it out loud or not. And she's damned good at it. She won't lose track of why she does what she does. Besides, you should be thanking us."

Deacon opened his eyes, incredulous. "Thanking you?"

"Yes, Mr. shapeshifter-future-king-of-the-leopards-going-to-live-another- hundred-and-fifty-years-if-no-one-kills-you-first. Thanks to her Protector powers, Cary's aging has slowed significantly. She'll live much longer than she would have otherwise. I don't know how you can possibly be the mate of a human, but thanks to us, that human will be able to live almost as long as you do."

"If she survives the next year," Deacon pointed out.

"She will," Jaxer said, but he didn't look at Deacon when he said it. "She'll survive. She has to."

"What the hell am I going to tell her?" Deacon murmured after a while.

"About my absence?"

"That. And Holland."

Jaxer turned sharply, staring at Deacon. "Oliver Holland?"

"Yeah. He's the man after Jonathon. Or the demon I should say."

"Oliver Holland is the Boss? Bugger."

Deacon studied Jaxer. "I know he's dangerous as hell, and he smells like death and revenge. What don't I know?"

"I don't know a lot more. He's been untethered for centuries."

Which confirmed what Deacon had already suspected.

"Demon hunters don't bother him," Jaxer continued. "His freeing is something of a legend, though no one seems to know the real story anymore. He's very powerful, rich, and incredibly dangerous."

"All of which we already knew."

"But dangerous as he is," Jaxer ignored the interruption, "he's never made an effort to recruit other supernatural talents before. That was one of the few things that made his existence…survivable. Now, suddenly, he's gathering powers around him? Not good."

"You need to figure out how to take care of this," Deacon said. "Cary's six years aren't up yet."

Jaxer nodded, scanning the dark trees as he thought. "We have to find out what use an animal speaker is to Holland."

"Remember Jon can call animals, too. Even a shapeshifter's animal, against the shifter's will. Someone like Holland is bound to have a use for that."

"The boy couldn't call your leopard fully," Jaxer pointed out. "You resisted. How powerful can he be?"

"Powerful enough the Nags want him protected. Powerful enough that he almost called up my leopard. *Mine.*"

"Fair point," Jaxer admitted, then flowing to his feet.

It was damned fortunate Jaxer was so good at glamour. The way he moved sometimes, he'd never pass as human otherwise.

"I'll go dig into Holland's business," Jaxer said. "Tell Cary I'll be in touch soon with as much as I can find. Tell her I'll send Angie with any information I get."

Deacon released his death grip on the rocky soil and stood. "Anything you need to stop Holland, let me know. I'm not limited to defensive powers."

Jaxer jerked his chin in a short nod. A set of steps materialized next to the faery, leading down inside the hill. When he'd disappeared underground and the stairs vanished, Deacon turned back toward his SUV.

He had some thinking to do. He had to decide just how much of this to tell his mate.

19

When Deacon arrived at her house the next morning, Cary met him at the door frowning.

"What's wrong?" he asked.

"I think you'd better stop bringing donuts over every morning," she said.

"Why?" He slid past her into the house, making sure he brushed against her as he did.

She closed the door. "I had trouble buttoning my jeans this morning," she muttered.

"Maybe they shrunk in the washing machine?"

"They aren't newly washed."

She looked so sad, he had to pull her into his arms. "I think you look beautiful and should eat donuts whenever you like."

"That's nice of you. But it's not just about whether I look good or not—"

"You look good."

His interruption made her smile slightly. "Deacon. I don't mind the extra twenty pounds I carry around because it doesn't interfere with my ability to move fast when I need to. Sometimes I have to run to get between a bad guy and the person I'm protecting. If I put on too much weight, I'll have trouble sprinting. And I put on weight really really easily if I'm eating donuts every morning."

"You want to go running later then? To help work off the donuts?"

She scowled. "I don't run if I don't have to. My Protector powers give me the boost I need when I do have to move fast. I just have to stay fit enough for the powers to work well."

"You don't like running?" he asked. "Even for fun?"

"Fun?" she said, sounding incredulous. "Why on earth would anyone consider running fun? It's what you do when you're trying to get away from bad guys. Or between bad guys and good guys."

"Not always," he said. "Sometimes it's nice to stretch out and just run for the sheer joy of it. To feel your muscles moving, the flex and strain, your blood pumping, your lungs working. The smell of the green earth as you pass between the trees…"

"You're not talking about running on two legs anymore, are you?"

He tilted his head. "No. I guess I'm not."

She dropped her gaze and pulled out of his arms.

"Hey. What's wrong?" A sense of panic shot through him, and he wasn't sure why.

"Deacon… Are you…?"

He took hold of her arms and pulled her closer. "Cary, what's wrong? What did I say?"

"It's just… That's the kind of thing I won't ever be able to share with you. Won't you miss that? Wouldn't you prefer a mate who could go running with you, on four legs?"

"What? No. I mean… *You're* my mate."

"Are you absolutely positive?" she asked. "We both know I shouldn't be. Maybe, if we don't allow things to go any further, maybe you'll find someone else who would be better for you."

"Stop. Where the hell is this coming from?"

"I'm just not…"

"Not what, damn it?"

She scowled. "I'm not sure this thing between us is meant to be. Or that it's even good for us. For you."

"Who says?"

"For one thing, your control says."

"I can deal with my lack of control."

"Like you are now? You do realize I'm going to have bruises, right?"

He dropped his hands instantly and took a step away from her, shock making his heart pound. "Oh god, I'm sorry. Why didn't you tell me I was hurting you?"

"If I was a shifter, would that have hurt?"

"I would never hurt you on purpose. Shifter or not." She was scaring the shit out of him. "What is this about? You don't want me? Is that it? I'm not what you want in a mate."

She laughed, but it wasn't a happy sound. "What woman wouldn't want you? Yes, I want you. But I'm not sure that's enough."

"It's enough."

"Deacon."

He put a finger against her lips to stop her saying any more. "It's enough. Even if you can't run through the woods on four legs. Mates need differences as well as similarities." He risked getting closer. "We just need more time together. Like you said, to get to know each other better. You'll see."

She shook her head.

"Cary." He had to make her understand. "There will never be anyone else for me. You're it. Deal with it."

Her lips twitched under his fingers. Then she sighed, her breath hot against his hand. Reluctantly, he dropped his touch.

"I'm still not sure you know what you're talking about," she said. "But as it happens, I like having you around. Too much really. I suppose I'm willing to deal with your erratic logic."

The pressure constricting his chest loosened, he swallowed the panic that had been about to bubble over. Because he needed to desperately, he pulled her into his arms and kissed her.

"I'm sorry I hurt you," he whispered against her mouth. "I *can* control my strength better."

"It's okay," she said. "I heal fast, remember?"

"Still." He kissed her again, too shaken to do more.

Finally, she pulled back, but she cupped his cheek in one hand, a tender gesture that made him feel infinitely better.

"Let's go eat," she said. "But after this, no more donuts."

He leaned down and picked up the donut bag he'd dropped when she'd started to tear his world apart. Then she took his free hand and led him toward the kitchen.

"Well, maybe every other Sunday we can still have donuts," she said.

"Anything you want," he said. *Everything you want.*

CARY STARED AT HER HAMPER, HALF-LISTENING TO JON COMPLAIN TO Sally about being stuck in the house again. It wasn't even noon yet. They were going to have to do something soon.

"Guess the dirty clothes will have to wait," she said to Fred who was lying attentively at her feet. Having other people living in her house was starting to cramp her schedule. She'd run out of underwear soon if she didn't get some laundry done.

Maybe just one load—underwear, socks, t-shirts—to get her by for a few more days.

Sally knocked on her bedroom door while she was pulling out the single load.

"I'm going to need to do some laundry soon, too," she said, nodding at the pile next to the hamper.

Sally looked tired. Her shift had ended pretty late last night. The fact that she was awake already impressed and horrified Cary. The woman needed to rest some time. She worked six days a week.

"I haven't wanted to ask to use your machine," Sally said. "I figured this would all be finished by now."

"I know. I wish I could tell you when it'll be done."

Sally nodded then edged into the room. "We can't go on like this much longer. I need to live in my own home again. I miss it. And while I appreciate everything you're doing for Jon, he needs to get back to a normal schedule. A normal life. I've worked really hard to make sure he's had as normal a life as a boy like him can have."

"I won't be able to keep him safe if you move out now," Cary said. "And he's still in danger. A lot of danger."

"He told me about that man yesterday, the one offering him a job. He's the one that's been after Jon?"

"Yes." Did she tell Sally the "man" was actually a demon? She was pretty sure Jon hadn't mentioned that part, or Sally wouldn't be talking about giving up Cary's protection. "And he's a very dangerous…man. He's not to be trusted."

"You don't think he's legitimately offering Jon a job?"

"Oh, he may be. But it's not the kind of job a good kid like Jon should consider."

"You know what he wants from my son?"

"No. I just know it won't be good."

Sally sighed and leaned against the wall. "Jon's too young for a job, anyway. He keeps reminding me he'll be sixteen soon. God help me. I don't want him growing up that fast."

"What did you tell him about Holland's offer?"

"That he couldn't take it, no matter how much money the man might offer, because he's not old enough to work legally yet."

"Good," Cary said. "That's good advice. Will he listen?"

"I'm his mother."

Cary smiled. "Will he listen?" she asked again.

Sally gave her a crooked grin. "Maybe. I hope he does. He's a good boy."

"Yeah. He is."

Cary titled her head when she heard Jon's loud, "Isn't there anything to do in this house?" comment floating down the hallway.

"He's also bored," she said.

Sally nodded ruefully. "A trip to the mall might calm him down. Especially if his friend Will can meet us there. I'll go call Mrs. Borosky." She pushed away from the wall. "I could use a trip to the mall, too."

Cary nibbled her lower lip. Great. The mall. A Protector's worst nightmare.

She scooped her pile of clothes up off the floor and headed to the laundry room. At least she'd have clean underwear to come home to. She just had to make sure everyone made it home.

THE MALL PROVED TO BE AS MUCH OF A NIGHTMARE AS CARY THOUGHT it would be. Keeping track of Jon and Will in the multi-storied Lloyd Center proved difficult at best. This time of year, the stores were busy on the weekends, people getting an early start on Christmas shopping. The best Cary could do was keep track of the shops Jon went into. She spent a lot of time standing outside gaming and sports clothes stores, worrying about Holland having spies in the mall.

Sally didn't help matters by going off on her own—she needed a new set of sheets or something. And because Deacon refused to leave Cary's side, the only thing Cary could do was hope no one working for Holland would spot and recognize Sally.

After Sally rejoined them, some of Cary's tension eased. One less person she had to worry about. Unfortunately, Jon then conned them into another hour of "hanging out", so they continued to shadow him around stores Cary had no interest in. Deacon and Sally took turns going into the shops, keeping an eye on the kids while giving them some space. Cary stayed outside, watching the crowded walkways. Waiting for that elusive second shoe.

And when it didn't drop, she wanted to scream.

What was Holland waiting for? What was he up to? Was he taunting them? Maybe he didn't mean Jon harm after all?

Although, if he were harmless, the Nags would never have assigned her to guard the kid. So what was going on?

If she had fingernails, she'd have gnawed them off from the stress. She hated this kind of waiting. Normally, when she protected someone, it just happened. She jumped in front of them and rescued them from something or someone. She'd rarely had to protect anyone for longer than a couple of days.

If Holland continued to *not* do anything, this protection really could go on for months.

When they got home, Cary threw her laundry into the dryer, freeing up the washer for Sally. Then, because she was frustrated, she made an executive decision that they needed pizza for dinner. Jon cheered. Deacon just raised a brow. Sally frowned but one look at Cary and she declined to comment.

"We might even have to have ice cream for dessert," Cary decided.

Deacon leaned close and whispered, "So much for worrying about a few donuts."

She scowled. "Don't start with me," she whispered back, so Sally and Jon wouldn't hear. "I've got dirty clothes to wash, no privacy, and Holland is not making a move. I'm frustrated, annoyed, and I don't know what to do. So I'm eating pizza and ice cream. And maybe opening a bottle of wine."

"You want me to get the ice cream?"

She thought about that a moment, then shook her head. "No. I'll go. I need to get out alone for a few minutes."

"I'm sorry if I'm crowding you," he murmured.

Something in his tone actually brought tears to her eyes. Damn it. She didn't need this right now. It was like being hormonal but *all* the time. Yet she couldn't entirely blame him for her reaction. The fact was she hated the idea of hurting his feelings. Stupidly sentimental, but true.

"It's not you," she sighed. She took his face in her hands and kissed him lightly. "It's not even Sally and Jon. I just need to think. On my own. If Jaxer doesn't find something for me soon, I'm going to have to figure out what to do about Holland on my own. Sally won't stay here much longer. And I can't blame her for wanting to get her life back to normal."

"Jaxer is trying to find answers. He said he'd send news soon."

"I know. But over the course of the day, I've decided I need to figure out how to solve problems like this without Jaxer's constant guidance. I still don't know what to do. I just know I need to stop waiting for him and come up with a strategy on my own."

Deacon smiled but there was something in his expression.

"What?" she asked. "What's that look about?"

"Nothing. Just…" He ran a finger down her cheek. "You're a very good Protector, Cary Redmond."

"Thank you." She hoped he was right.

2 0

Cary stood in front of the freezers at the supermarket for ten minutes trying to decide on a flavor everyone would like. Eventually, she gave up on compromise and got her favorite: chocolate chip cookie dough.

She was halfway to her car, ice cream and chocolate sauce in hand —because you had to have chocolate sauce—when she felt that familiar vibration along her spine that meant someone nearby needed her brand of help.

Following her Protector instincts to the dark alley next to the supermarket, she moved quietly into the shadows, holding her shopping bag in her arms so it wouldn't make any noise. The alley was so dark she had to pause and let her eyes adjust.

Even before they had, she heard the murmur of a low, deep male voice and the whimpering and pleading from a higher, feminine voice. When Cary could finally see, she understood why the woman was whimpering.

Ice cream forgotten, Cary sprinted forward.

"Excuse me," she said, jamming herself between the two bodies, forcing the man to take a step back.

His glowing eyes widened in shock as he stared down at her. Well, that was only to be expected given how hard it was for a mortal to physically move a vampire. Even if he did seem like a pretty young one.

"Hi," Cary said, smiling at his stunned expression. It never hurt to be polite. "Sorry to interrupt, but I'm going to have to break this up. Best be off, now. Thanks very much."

The vampire actually sputtered a bit before saying, "Do you know what you're doing? Do you have any idea what I am?"

His voice was deep and melodic. Under different circumstances, that voice would have had her quivering in her boots.

"I know what you are," she assured him. "The big pointy teeth and glowing yellow eyes give you away." She paused, then said, "Unless you're going to tell me you're the Big Bad Wolf. That would be a surprise."

His eyes narrowed, the glow deepening to an unhealthy jaundiced color. She met his gaze with impunity, something she could only do when protecting. She wouldn't dare look a vampire in the eyes otherwise.

"Listen," she said, "we both know you're a vampire, and you were going to snack on this nice lady. But she wasn't willing, and the deal in this city is they have to be willing." Cary glanced over her shoulder at the woman. "You're not willing to be vampire dinner, right?"

"Right," the woman stuttered.

She was a petit little thing with blond hair, wide blue eyes, and one of those perfect heart-shaped faces. She was the kind of woman that typically made Cary feel like an awkward giant. But the fear in the woman's big blue eyes brought out Cary's sympathies. She patted the woman's shoulder. "Don't worry, you're safe now."

"But...but..."

"What she's trying to say, human," the vampire hissed, "is that you are a fool to think you can stand against one of my power."

Cary tucked her chin and gave him a look. "Please. How old are you? Thirty, forty years? You're a baby. And what makes you think I can't stand against you?"

"Do you know anything about vampires?"

"Yes." She nodded. "I've studied. You suck blood from living creatures to survive. You don't have to kill your food but some vampires still do. You live a really long time until someone kills you." She held up a hand and started ticking points off on her fingers. "You can go out into the sun." Over her shoulder, she said, "That's a myth that they can't." Back to the vampire, she said, "But your powers are really drained in full daylight, and you're extremely photosensitive so most vampires only come out on cloudy days if they come out during the day at all."

To the woman, she said, "That's why we've got so many vampires in the Pacific Northwest. Though not as many as you might think. They're too territorial to clump in very large numbers. Thank god, huh?"

She faced forward. "Let's see, what else? Holy water, crosses, all that religious paraphernalia doesn't hurt a vampire. Oh, unless the vampire came into being in Europe during the middle-ages. Then the Christian holy symbols can kill them. Don't ask me why. Do you know? I've always wondered about that. I mean why not Jewish symbols or Buddhist for that matter. And why the middle-ages? Why not now?"

The vampire made a gesture with his hand, like he was trying to backhand an irritating fly from in front of his face.

Cary continued. "Cutting off a vampire's head works to kill them, but I mean really, that's going to kill just about everything, right? With the obvious exception of certain demon dogs, of course. Setting a vampire on fire, another good way, but the head thing is a lot more of a guarantee. Vampires regenerate from most wounds pretty easily. But if you cut off a limb, say a hand or leg, with a silver blade, it stays cut off."

To the woman, she said, "There are a lot more disabled—I mean physically challenged—vampires than you might expect, too."

The vampire growled and made the hand gesture again.

"Vampires have very strong mental abilities," Cary continued, "and they are excellent at mesmerizing their pray with eye contact. Remember, eye contact with vampires is bad."

He gestured again and then lunged forward, hands toward Cary's throat. He bounced back several feet, repelled by an invisible barrier before he got close enough to touch her.

"They have strong telekenetic powers," she went on. "That's what all the hand gesturing stuff is about. He's trying to knock me out of the way. And when all else fails, they do have superhuman strength. At night, anyway. Have I left anything out?"

The vampire's once attractive face distorted with his increasing rage. His canines grew long and feral-looking, his eyes glowed so yellow the pupils were tiny dots. He lunged at her again, and this time the backlash from Cary's powers sent him flying into the opposite wall. The force of the rebound knocked her back a step, too, and her skin tingled. She brought her arms up behind her to catch her balance and keep the petit woman safe.

"Oh yeah," she said as the vampire pulled himself up off the ground. "Vampires have really bad tempers. And they don't like being disturbed while eating. But I'm afraid unless your meal is willing, and this one's not, I have to put a stop to the feeding."

"You will suffer for this insult, human. How dare you interfere with our hunt?"

"Told you, the deal was willing blood donors only. Sorry. Find someone willing, and I'll leave you alone. But this woman is going home with all ten pints intact."

"How do you know this?" he growled. "How do you know so much about us? You're human. Mortal." He sneered the last word.

"Yeah well, I'm a good study. At least I try to be. And unless you want to go back to your Master and explain how an ordinary human woman got one over on you, I'd suggest just letting this whole thing go. Find one of those willing Goth boys or girls. I'm sure they'd love to have you suck on their necks."

"You know of the Master?" Now the vampire sounded in awe, and just a little afraid under the growling anger still in his voice.

"Gabriel? Yeah, I know of him. Never met him in person." Thank god.

She'd had the dubious honor of meeting the former Master of Portland once, four years ago. Ariel had been one of the scariest things Cary had ever faced since becoming a Protector. The only reason she'd been able to meet Ariel and survive was because Jaxer had gone with her, and she had to protect the faery from vampiric influences. Even Jaxer wasn't strong enough to overcome the powers of a vampire Master. The meeting was instigated by that whole vampire sucking kitten blood thing. Cary just couldn't let him continue draining poor kittens dry. It was rude.

Somewhere in her one and only face-to-face with Ariel, the Master had decided she liked Cary. Was amused by her more like. So they came to an understanding. They'd leave each other completely alone, and Cary would only interfere with a vampire's feeding when it hunted unwilling victims—kittens included.

In some ways, Cary had actually liked Ariel, scary as she was. Ariel understood draining kittens was a bad thing. Though probably for reasons different from Cary's.

She'd been a little sad to hear Ariel had been overthrown and killed by this new Master. She was also terrified of meeting a vampire strong enough to kill Ariel. This pup in front of her was strong. And he would have been pretty scary if she wasn't protecting someone. But he was nothing to a centuries-old Master.

"Listen," she said, "Gabriel made a point of saying he'd uphold Ariel's law—no drinking from the unwilling. He'd be pretty pissed if I had to go and tell him about this little episode." Oh boy, was she bluffing now. "Just call it a night, okay?"

"We will meet again, human," the vampire promised. Then he launched himself toward the alley's entrance and disappeared in the blink of an eye.

"Forgot to say they move at supersonic speeds," Cary muttered to the quiet alley. She turned to face the blonde. "You okay now?"

The woman nodded, her eyes still wide, her skin pale. "How did you do that?"

"Oh, I've just got the knack of dealing with his kind. No biggie. You okay to get home?"

"Y-yes. My cars just in the parking lot."

"Tell you what, let me walk you there. You drive straight home, go into your house, and lock all the doors and windows. That thing about vampires not being able to enter without permission? That's true. Little safeguard for us poor humans. So just don't invite any strangers in, and you'll be fine. Okay?"

Cary picked up her ice cream on the way back to the parking lot. She sighed, knowing it was going to be all melty by the time she got home. On the bright side, that did make it easier to pick out the little chunks of cookie dough.

At the blonde's car, the woman spun around and hugged Cary with surprising strength given her size.

"Thank you," she murmured. "You saved my life." Then she dove into her car and careened out of the parking lot.

Cary winced at the sound of screeching tires and hoped the woman didn't have far to go because she wasn't sure the blonde would be able to hold it together much longer.

She smiled a little as she climbed into her own car. It was nice to have your work appreciated. While being a Protector still irritated Cary sometimes, the job did have its moments.

After pizza, chocolate chip cookie dough ice cream, a bottle of wine split with Sally, laundry, some ABBA, and saving the little blonde, Cary woke Monday morning feeling better and more refreshed than she had in days.

And she had a plan.

The face-off with the vampire, and the memory of her meeting with the former Master of Portland, had given her the idea. She would take Jon, under her protection, to talk with Holland. She'd tell Holland that Jon would listen to his job proposal, say yes or no—no if Cary had any say in the matter—and that would be the end of it. Once Jon's decision was made, Holland wouldn't be allowed to come after the kid again. On Holland's honor, he would have to agree to leave Jon alone.

And why should she trust a demon's honor?

Because the more powerful, the more treacherous the creature, the more likely they were to abide by such an outrageous deal as giving their word to a human.

Ariel had done it out of amusement and had stuck by and enforced her concession to Cary. The former Master considered herself "above" most creatures. Someone with her power took pride in their word, which they so rarely gave it didn't often matter.

Cary had a feeling if she could get Oliver Holland to give his word of honor, he'd probably keep it.

At least that was the possibly-bad-but-it-was-the-only-thing-she-had plan.

Sally would still have to keep an eye on Jon. And there was always the possibility Holland wouldn't give his word to leave the kid alone. But Cary would worry about that if it happened.

For now, she had a plan, a plan that most likely wouldn't get anyone hurt or killed, and it might get Holland to go away.

Her only qualm was whether to tell Sally and Deacon. She didn't want Sally anywhere near Holland if she could avoid it. So far, the demon was leaving her alone. The longer that continued the better. But Sally would be a good, grounding influence on Jon, to keep him from taking the job—the kid had let slip more than once during their mall trip that he could use some money. Unfortunately, given Sally's over-protective nature, she might never let Cary take Jon to meet Holland.

And then there was Deacon.

He'd want to come with her. Would probably insist on it. But with his waning control, he'd be more of a liability than an asset. The last thing she needed was an out-of-control leopard shifter aggravating a proud and powerful demon while she tried to negotiate an end to this standoff.

The idea of not telling Deacon bothered her. It felt like lying, even though it wasn't. And really, it wasn't his business. This was her job. He didn't have any say in the matter. But keeping secrets from him felt wrong.

Which was really annoying.

She rolled out of bed and headed to the bathroom, still working out her strategy. She had to find a way to talk with Jaxer because he'd know where to find Holland.

The fact that she still hadn't heard from her mentor bothered her. Something was wrong. While she'd mostly accepted that she had to figure things out for herself this time, she was worried about her friend.

But she couldn't go out faery-mentor hunting today. It was a school day.

She'd have to call Angie. At the very least, Angie could pass a message to Jaxer. And the woman had connections. She might even know where Holland could be found without going to Jaxer.

As Cary poured herself a cup of coffee—Sally had already put on the pot—she wondered why Holland hadn't left Jon a card or something. Wasn't that the kind of thing big important people did when they wanted you to get back to them? Or did he just assume Jon would be able to ask someone, and they'd know where to find him?

She shook her head, took a sip of coffee, and sighed. Very few things were better first thing in the morning than her first sip of coffee.

True to his word, Deacon didn't bring over donuts again that morning, but he had brought bagels. She could probably afford to eat a bagel, even after her splurge last night. Besides, eating breakfast was important.

She found Deacon and Jon out back throwing the ball to Fred as Pickles and Buck sat on the porch watching. She set her cup down and walked outside to lay a kiss on Deacon's neck.

He shivered and leaned back into her. "You can do that more, if you like," he murmured.

"Good morning." She wrapped her arms around his shoulders. Since she stood on the step above him she was very nearly his height. "Thanks for the bagels."

"You're welcome. Did you sleep well?"

"Very well, actually." Surprising, since she'd been having trouble sleeping for the last couple of weeks. Must have been the chocolate chip cookie dough ice cream. That stuff worked miracles.

"I could have slept better," he whispered so Jon wouldn't hear.

"Hmm..." When her breath brushed across his neck, he shivered again. "What are your plans for the day?"

"I'm going to try going into work for a few hours, if my sister will let me. Then I have a few people to talk to before I meet you and Jon."

"You don't have to come to the school if you have other things to do."

"I thought we had this conversation already."

"All right. Fine. I'll stop trying to talk you out of it." She shook her head. "You know, you're more stubborn than I am."

"Not quite."

"Ha ha."

"You're in a very good mood this morning."

"I enjoyed my night last night." And she had a plan. But since she wasn't going to tell him about the plan until after the fact, she kept that part to herself.

Deacon turned in her arms and hugged her. "I'm glad you had a good night. After yesterday…"

She shrugged. "A little wine and cookie dough ice cream makes Cary a happy woman."

"Is that the only thing that makes you happy?"

The look in his eyes sent heat rushing to all those places on her body where she wanted to feel his hands. And his mouth. Embarrassment had her ducking her head.

"Deacon," she hissed, glancing at Jon. He was far enough away he probably couldn't hear them but still.

"What? I was just asking what else makes you happy?"

The wicked lift of his brow made her groan. "You are a very bad man," she muttered.

He kissed her nose. "And I'm all yours."

Her head spun at the thought, a combination of panic and desire rushing through her system. Part of her wondered why she'd been trying to chase him away yesterday morning. She'd had some pretty valid reasons. Hadn't she? She couldn't imagine what any of them were at the moment.

"Hey, would you guys stop kissing," Jon shouted at them. "I've got to get to school soon." He stomped up the steps, shaking his head. "Get a room."

"Smart ass." Cary swatted at him as he walked past.

He dodged her hand and grinned. "Better than being a dumb ass."

She rolled her eyes. "Everyone's a comedian."

Sally was going to kill her for teaching him that smart ass comeback. She was kind of regretting it herself. She turned to follow him into the kitchen, but Deacon pulled her back.

"If we're going to get accused of kissing anyway," he said, and his mouth dropped to hers.

Her knees were trembling by the time he lifted his head. "You're almost better than coffee, you know that?" she muttered.

"I'm flattered."

"You should be. Speaking of which, my coffee is getting cold. So am I."

He patted her butt, scooting her toward the back door. "Personally, I'm feeling pretty warm."

She groaned. It was hard to walk with her toes curling.

LATER THAT MORNING, AFTER CARY HAD JON SAFELY ENSCONCED IN HIS first period class, she stepped into the hall to ring Angie. Angela Jordan was a green witch and a talented psychic who was paid decently for her skills. In her spare time, she fought the occasional supernatural bad guy and passed messages between Cary and Jaxer. She'd also become one of Cary's best friends over the years.

"Who's this guy Deacon Jones?" Angie said when she picked up the phone.

Cary closed her eyes and shook her head. "Hi Angie. Nice to talk to you, too. You sound just like Lucy."

"Can you blame us? Lucy says this guy claims to be your mate? How is that even possible?"

"I don't know. It's complicated. Can we talk about it later?"

"If you don't get around here soon to discuss him, we will come looking for you. And him. And there might be spells involved."

"Stop!" Cary actually raised her hand to halt her friend's litany, even though they were speaking on the phone. "Personal life later. I promise. First, have you talked to Jaxer?"

"Yes. But what I want to know is why I haven't been talking to you?"

"Work."

"And this Jones guy?"

Cary sighed. "I will go into great detail about him over a bottle of wine some night. I swear. I need to talk about all the mate business with you and Lucy and Marianne anyway. But right now, I have a situation and I need a favor."

"I'm holding you to the full story," Angie said, her voice firm. "I want lots of details. And I mean details."

"Do you have a message for me from Jaxer?"

"Yes, but I'll have to meet you in person because what he's found out will take some explaining. I'm still not sure I understand."

"Meeting you somewhere now is going to be a problem."

"It's okay, I was planning a trip to the school anyway."

"Thanks." Cary glanced through the window in the classroom door to make sure Jon was where he was supposed to be.

"So what's this favor you need?" Angie asked. "You want me to do a reading about your new relationship?"

"No. Not yet anyway." But maybe later. Cary hadn't considered that before. "What I need is an address. Or a phone number. I have to set up a meeting with someone."

"If this is the someone I think it is, you may want to hear Jaxer's news first."

"Oh, yeah, I want to hear what he's found before I do anything. But I still want a phone number or address. Can you get that for me?"

"Sure. I've got a friend in the business, so to speak. He should be able to help."

"You're the best."

"I know. Just remember. Details. I want details."

Cary hung up and went back into the class. Another benefit to settling this situation with Holland would mean she'd have time to have dinner and girl talk with her friends. She needed that and soon.

She spent the morning standing at the back of classrooms, trying to look formidable, and considering the pros and cons of her plan. The biggest con of not telling Deacon was she'd have no back up. At least with Angie knowing what she was doing and where she was going, someone would know where to start if anything went wrong. Though that wasn't entirely reassuring because if something went wrong, it might mean someone had died.

She usually had Jaxer to watch her back, but she couldn't count on him this time. He'd been too elusive lately. Until he told her what was wrong, she knew she couldn't depend on him. A strange and depressing realization since she'd always counted on Jaxer. In fact, she'd relied on him a lot over the years. She had trouble coming to terms with the fact that she couldn't now.

Maybe the news Angie brought would quiet her fears about her mentor. He'd probably just had to work hard to find anything. This was a tricky case. She was just overreacting. There wasn't anything wrong.

Except she knew in her gut there was definitely something wrong.

"So what's Jaxer's message?" Cary asked Angie as soon as she'd slipped out of Jon's math class. This particular period always put her to sleep, so she was glad for the distraction.

"Hello to you, too," Angie teased. She was easily six foot tall, and a striking woman with softly curling brown hair and green eyes fringed by enviably long lashes. She was the kind of beautiful, slim woman who could easily have been a runway model. But she had neither the calling nor the patience for modeling. Witchcraft had called to Angie when she was very young and there'd never been any doubt which direction she'd take.

"Okay," Angie said, launching into business, "Oliver Holland. Outside of gathering a wide range of paranormal talents to work for him, he seems to have some interest in the woods east of the city. He's had people scouting large areas between here and Mount Hood but is concentrating on an area closer to the Multnomah Falls now, between there and the city.

"The only person Jaxer could find who would talk about Holland said he was trying to locate something, but this guy didn't know what—he's too low rung in the organization. He did say whatever it is, Holland is pretty desperate to find it. He's laying out a lot of money in both the search and to keep his activities quiet. All the talents he's hired relate to this search, but Jaxer can't see how as the range is so diverse. Everything from shifters to psychics, witches, shaman, telepaths, and telekenetics. Apparently, he's even hired one vampire, but Jaxer couldn't confirm that." Angie tilted her head to one side and pursed her lips. "Dangerous, though, if he has hired a vampire."

"Why do you say that?" Cary asked. "Outside of the usual reasons."

"Gabriel doesn't like to share. So I've heard, anyway. He keeps a tight rein on the city. He'd consider it tantamount to treason for one of his vampires to hire himself out to anyone, nonetheless a demon."

"Maybe it's an out-of-town vampire?" Cary suggested.

Angie shook her head. "That'd be dangerous, too."

True. "What the hell could Holland want with Jon?" She considered Jaxer's news, absently scanning the surrounding corridor, watching for anyone who might overhear their conversation.

"Jon talks to animals, right?" Angie said.

"He can call them," Cary said. "Even a shifter's animal."

Angie's eyes widened. "Wow. Impressive talent. Must be a lot to deal with for a thirteen-year-old."

"Hard to tell. He's a teenager."

Angie grinned. She had two brothers so she'd dealt with teenage boys before. "Maybe Holland wants him to ask the animals in the woods if they know where this thing is," she suggested.

Cary nibbled her lower lip and finally outlined her plan for Angie.

"Do you think Holland will take no for an answer?" Cary asked when she'd finished.

"You honestly think he'll give his word?"

"I don't know. He seems pretty amused by me. That tends to work in my favor when powerful creatures find me a funny little thing. I don't usually get hurt right away."

Angie dipped her chin to look Cary in the eyes. "Doesn't mean he won't kill you to get what he wants."

"Yeah." Cary sighed. The hole in her scheme in a nutshell. "Could Jon's talent be that important to him?"

"Depends on how desperate he is. And what he thinks Jon can do for him."

"Damn." She ran her hands over her hair, smoothing back the escapees from her ponytail. "I can't keep Jon and his mother living with me indefinitely. Maybe not even as long as it takes Holland to find whatever it is he's looking for."

"I'm not sure it would be so good for him to find it, whatever *it* is, anyway," Angie said.

"Why?" But Cary could guess.

"Anything a demon of Holland's power wants this desperately could only make him more powerful. That can't mean good things for the city. Maybe the world."

Cary released a quiet groan. "What do I do?"

Angie raised her hands, palms up. "Your decision. Glad it's not mine, though."

Cary winced. She wasn't really pleased about the decision being hers either. Unfortunately, she didn't have a lot of options. "I've got to try something. Even if my plan fails, maybe the meeting will tell me more about what Holland wants. Information is always good. Right?"

"Yeah," Angie said, "so long as you survive long enough to use it."

Cary got Holland's phone number from Angie—provided by a demon hunter friend, which Cary found very odd; a demon hunter with a demon's phone number?—just before the end of the period. She promised Angie a girls' night out sometime soon, and Angie agreed to act as backup if Cary met with Holland.

Cary spent the entire next period debating her intended scheme. By the last class, she'd made up her mind. She ducked out with an apologetic nod to Mr. Young. Time to make her phone call.

She wasn't sure what she'd been expecting—something along the lines of a corporate secretary screening calls with, "Mr. Holland's office, how may I help you?" So when the deep, accented voice snapped, "Holland," down the line, Cary froze. For a shaky few moments, she couldn't find her voice.

"Hello?" he barked. "Who the bloody hell is this?"

Before he could hang up, Cary managed to force air through her vocal cords. "Mr. Holland, this is Cary Redmond."

"Ms. Redmond!" His tone changed instantly, both surprised and pleased. "How are you? I wasn't expecting to hear from you so soon."

The fact that he'd been expecting to hear from her at all was more than a little disconcerting. She scowled at the lockers across the corridor and almost backed out.

"What can I do for you?" Holland said, professional and pleasant.

She took a deep breath. Too late to change her mind now. "You can arrange a time to meet with Jon and me. Somewhere neutral. And public."

"Jon is interested in my job offer, then?"

"We're going to sit down and listen to what you have to say. No more, no less."

"I see. And if he decides to take the position?"

"We'll have another meeting with his mother present, so you can explain to her how you're not involving her son in anything dangerous and illegal."

Holland laughed. "We wouldn't want to irritate a mother now, would we?"

"And if Jon says no, outright, at this first meeting?" Cary asked, trying not to hold her breath.

"He says no," Holland answered easily.

Cary inhaled then hurried out her condition. "You'll agree to leave him alone. No more attempts to 'bring' him to a meeting. No more surprise conversations to try and change his mind. No more scare tactics. If he says no, I want your *word* you'll leave him alone."

The pause on the other end of the line was like a lead weight. He knew what she was asking. The fact that he didn't promise immediately, off-handedly, confirmed her suspicions. If he gave his word, Holland would stick to it.

At least, she hoped that was the reason for the silence...

"A concession from you then, Ms. Redmond," he finally said, after what had felt like a long time. "If Jon, and his mother, say yes, you will abide their decision and stop trying to keep him away from me."

"I may continue to serve as his bodyguard while he's under your employ," Cary said. "I won't promise to stop looking after him. But I'll accept whatever decision he and his mother make."

"Your word?" There was an amused lilt to Holland's voice now.

"Do I have yours?" she asked.

"Very well. I give you my word that if I cannot convince Jon and his mother to allow Jon to work for me, I will walk away."

"You'll leave him completely alone?"

"I will make no effort to see him again."

"And your other employees?"

"Will do what I tell them."

"And what will you tell them to do as far as Jon's concerned?"

"You are clever, Ms. Redmond." He laughed. "I will make it clear that no one is to go near the boy once his decision is made. Violation of this will mean facing my displeasure."

Cary shuddered. She didn't envy the poor bastard stupid enough to cross Holland. Did that mean she should be worried about herself?

Probably.

"Do I have your word then, Ms. Redmond?" he asked. "You will not interfere with Jonathon doing his job if he chooses to work for me."

There was a trap in that phrasing. She could taste it. "I give you my word I will accept Jon's decision, whatever it is. But I reserve the right to continue to serve as bodyguard if he and his mother want me to."

"Fair enough," Holland said. "It's a deal then."

Why did she feel like she'd just negotiated a deal with the devil?

They agreed on a meeting time for the next afternoon, after Jon's last class, at an expensive restaurant in the Pearl. "For a late lunch," Holland said.

"Are you paying?"

"Of course. I want to make a good impression on my future employee."

Cary scowled. His smug confidence didn't make her feel any better. But at least the restaurant was a public place. Except, "Don't they closed after lunch and not open again until after five for dinner?"

"They'll open for me."

Great. Maybe not so public after all. But there'd be waiters and staff. That was better than a back alley in Old Town.

She stood in the corridor for a few minutes after ending the call. She'd gotten the thing she'd wanted, Holland's word to leave Jon alone if he said no.

Now, she just had to convince Jon to say no, no matter how glamorous the offer looked, and convince Deacon not to meet them after school tomorrow.

She wasn't sure which of those two things would be harder.

Deacon called her just after the last bell, while she was waiting for the halls to clear.

"I'm sorry," he said. "I can't be there today."

He sounded so upset, she nearly smiled. "It's okay. I'm sure Jon and I can make it home on our own just this once," she teased.

"It may be several days."

Cary resisted the urge to jump up and down in relieved excitement. "What's wrong?"

"Nothing's exactly wrong." He hesitated a beat. "We've just gotten in two tigers confiscated in a raid on an underground…fighting pit."

"A what?" She lowered her voice when Jon and Mr. Young gave her a strange look. "A fighting pit? Really?"

"I'm afraid so."

Her stomach rolled. A part of her had always hoped that kind of blood sport was an urban myth. She should have known better. "Were there a lot of animals?"

"Not left alive."

"Oh god."

"I know," he said. "My team and I are on our way there to pick up the rest now. The tigers are the two biggest exotics, and they're going to need a lot of care and medical attention. But there are dogs, a mountain lion, a few snakes, and two crocodiles left. Those are just the animals we're taking. Animal rescue is looking after the myriad mice, roosters, and rats. They just can't take so many of the bigger animals."

"You can deal with them all?" she asked, trying to ignore another poke in the conscious that she didn't know much about Deacon Jones and his normal life.

"We've got a facility specifically for exotics," he said. "But it's going to take several days to get them settled, get their wounds tended, tract down new homes."

"If you can't find any place to take them, what happens?" She pressed her lips together, afraid to hear his answer. A lot of rescue facilities tried to keep their animals alive until homes were found. But animal rescue and the city pounds couldn't afford to do that. With so many large animals, even most rescue facilities would have a hard time keeping the animals long term.

"Don't worry," he said. "We keep them until homes are found. If no other facility can take them, they become center mascots."

"Thanks," she murmured, though she wasn't sure exactly what she was thanking him for.

"I'll be so busy," he said, "I won't be able to see you." He sounded pained by the admission. "I'm not sure I can stand to stay away, but…"

"The animals need you. And I need you to take care of them."

"I knew you'd understand. Be careful."

"I will. You, too." For some reason, she didn't want to end the call. Stupid. She'd see him in a few days. Not like he was saying goodbye. "I'll see you soon," she forced herself to say. Did she sound upbeat or desperately cheerful? Hard to tell when her chest felt so heavy.

"I'll miss you," he said.

At that, she smiled. "I'll miss you, too. Isn't that strange, though? We haven't even known each other a month."

"It only took me ten minutes to know I'd miss you when you weren't around."

"Yeah, but you have a better sense of smell than I do."

He laughed, the first time during the conversation he'd sounded anything but tired and sad. "I'll call you later."

Jon looked up from his conversation with his friend Will when she ended her call. "Deacon can't come?" he asked.

"He's got some work to do." She didn't even ask how the kid knew she was on the phone with Deacon.

Once they were safely in the car and headed toward her house, she broached the subject of the meeting with Holland. "There's something I need to talk to you about."

Jon turned as far as his seatbelt would allow to face her. "Is it Deacon?"

"No. This is about Holland."

She told him about the phone call and the planned lunch. "We don't have to go if you don't want to, but if you hear him out and then turn down his job offer, he'll leave you alone."

"Why didn't you ask me?" Jon said.

She glanced at him briefly. "Ask you?"

"Why didn't you ask me first before setting up the lunch meeting?" he said. "Maybe I don't want to see Holland in person again."

Cary paused. She hadn't considered Jon might have an opinion one way or the other. She'd just assumed he'd be as happy as his mother to get this mess settled.

"You're right," she said. "I should have asked first. I'm sorry. If you don't want this to happen, I'll call Holland and cancel."

Jon shrugged. "I suppose I could listen to what he has to say."

"I have to tell you, both your mother and I would prefer you turned down his offer. It won't lead to anything good, no matter how attractive he makes it sound, how much money he offers."

"But what if he just wants me to talk to his pets? You know. See why they're not eating or something. I've heard people can make lots of money telling rich people why their pets are depressed."

Cary laughed. "That's true, actually. I always figured it was a scam played on people with more money than sense. In your case, though, you really could tell them what was going on with their animals. Hey, that might not be a bad career choice for you."

"You think?" Jon grinned.

He looked so young. She just couldn't let Holland get his hooks into this kid. "I think that could be a good option. But I doubt that's what Holland wants. He's a bad man, Jon. Nothing he could want you to do for him will be good."

"But if he's paying well, and it's not that bad, Mom could really use the money."

"You think your mom would want money you earned selling drugs or robbing a bank?"

"This isn't the same," he said with a scowl.

"How do you know? Holland is evil. You heard him threaten to kill me. He said it casually."

"He said he didn't want to have to kill you." Jon's voice dropped to a sullen murmur.

"He meant it," she said. "He would try to kill me if I got in his way. Is that the kind of man you want to work for?"

"He couldn't kill you. You're indestructible."

"No, Jon. I'm not. And if anyone could find a way to kill me, it's Holland."

Jon shivered and looked out the side window. "Deacon wouldn't let him."

"That's not the point. The point is Holland is bad. I hope you'll make the right choice tomorrow."

"But it's my choice, right? You're not gonna make me turn down the job?"

"It's not my decision," she said, even if she wanted to make the decision for him. "It's yours."

"Will you stop talking to me if I take his job?"

Cary pulled the car to a stop in her driveway as the garage door rose and turned in her seat to face Jon even though he still wouldn't meet her gaze. "I will continue to be your friend and to protect you for as long as you need me."

He finally looked at her.

"But know this," she said firmly. "If you start doing things that hurt others, I will switch to protecting those others from you in a snap."

"You'd turn on me."

"I won't allow you to hurt anyone. Any more than I'll let Holland hurt you. That's how it is."

Jon was silent for a long moment. She held his gaze, letting him know just how serious she was. Finally, he nodded and climbed out of the car. She wasn't sure where that left them, but at least he was clear on her intentions.

Inside, she brought up the subject of telling Sally about the meeting. "If you're interested in Holland's offer, we can tell her then and arrange for her to meet and talk with him. If we tell her now, she'll just worry."

"I could've told you that," Jon said. "We can keep it quiet until after tomorrow. She might not let me go if she knows anyway."

Cary's gut tightened with discomfort and guilt. She didn't like hiding something like this from his mother. It felt a lot more despicable than hiding the meeting from Deacon, and that felt bad enough. But she really didn't want Sally there giving Holland another vulnerable target. And there was every possibility Holland would manipulate Jon through Sally, if given the chance. The less people Cary had to protect from the demon in one sitting, the better.

"I'm not telling Deacon yet either," she blurted. Then scowled. Geez, the kid didn't need to know about her private dealings with Deacon.

Jon grinned. "He's gonna be pissed when he finds out. I mean, my mom will pitch a fit, but she'll get over it. Deacon's gonna yell."

"No, he won't." His voice would probably drop to that low, dangerous tone that was a lot more terrifying than a yell. "Besides he's got a lot on his mind at the moment."

"What?"

"The sanctuary just got in a lot of exotic animals to take care of." She wasn't about to tell Jon about the blood sports. "Deacon will be busy for days getting them all settled."

"Hey, I could help," he said over his shoulder as he headed for the kitchen. "We could go after the meeting with Holland."

A sweet offer, but Cary wasn't at all sure she wanted Jon to hear what these particular animals had to say. She didn't want to discourage his helpful, generous impulses, though.

"I'll talk to Deacon about it tonight." Then to change the subject and distract him, she said, "That reminds me, what were you and Scratchy talking about the other day?"

Jon poured himself a glass of juice and she made a pot of coffee as he regaled her with the tom cat's stories. They didn't talk about Holland and the impending meeting again.

The restaurant's main floor was quiet and empty of any customers besides Holland's group when Cary and Jon arrived. Sounds from the kitchen assured her there were at least some staff around, but a few cooks and waiters weren't going to help much against a demon. In fact, now that she was here, she realized they just gave her more people she'd have to protect if things went wrong.

The maître de led them past tables covered in pristine white table clothes, set for the upcoming dinner service, to the back of the room where Holland sat alone. The five goons who'd accompanied him to the park on Saturday were sitting at two tables on either side of his with plates of food already in front of them.

Holland's table was empty but for a glass of red wine.

He rose at their approach. "Ms. Redmond, Jonathon, so nice to see you again." He motioned for them to sit.

She shrugged off her beat up brown leather jacket and let it drape over her chair back as she sat. Then she rested her elbows on the table, her chin on her folded hands, and met Holland's sardonic gaze. His lips ticked up at the corners in a subtle grin as he stared back for a long moment.

Finally, he turned to Jon, breaking eye contact first. Cary felt a silly sense of triumph at the small victory. She'd played too many dominance games with her little dog pack—from the beginning, she'd had to make sure Fred knew she was the big dog.

"I haven't ordered yet," Holland said smoothly, his accent rolling the words. He didn't seem the least perturbed by the staring contest outcome. "Please, order whatever you like. It's on me." He smiled. "A business expense."

Jon's eyes lit up as he looked at the menu. "Holy shit, this place is expensive! Even the burger costs twenty bucks."

Cary scowled at Jon for his language.

"But it's an excellent hamburger," Holland said, without missing a beat. "Will you have a glass of wine, Ms. Redmond?"

"No," she said. "I'm driving."

"Surely one glass won't hurt."

"Easier not to have any and know my reflexes will be good." She smiled, showing teeth. "Besides, I'm on duty."

He dipped his head slightly, a silent touché.

Holland chatted easily with Jon while they placed their orders. Cary ordered one of the most expensive dishes on the menu because Holland was paying. A raised eyebrow was his only reaction.

"Not afraid I might've had the food poisoned?" he asked her.

Jon's eyes widened. Poisoned food had obviously never crossed his mind.

Cary shook her head, casually confident. Poisoning her now would be an effort to get her out of the way and allow full access to Jon, so her Protector magic would ensure she wasn't actually effected by it. If she wasn't looking after someone, that was another story. But Holland didn't need to know that.

Beyond poison not effecting her, she'd also be able to taste if anything had been added to their food. She intended to sample everything Jon ate in the demon's company. When she sipped his water once before setting it back in front of him, his eyes got even wider.

She grinned. "You're like royalty. You've got your own taster."

"Cary?"

The tremor in his voice twisted her heart. "Don't worry," she assured. "Nothing will happen to you while I'm around."

Holland said, "There's no need to fear. We're here to discuss a job. I was only…teasing Ms. Redmond."

Cary snorted. "Yeah, that's what you're doing." It was fine by her if Jon was scared of Holland. Less chance he'd take this supposed job.

Rather than take the opening to discuss the business at hand, though, Holland shifted back to amiable small talk and slowly succeeded in wiping the wary suspicion from Jon's expression. She'd give Holland one thing, he was pretty damned charming. For a demon.

When the food arrived, Cary tasted a small bit of everything on Jon's plate, even the side scraps of lettuce she knew he'd never eat. She approved the food and pushed his plate back to him. As she turned to her own meal, she caught Holland studying her. She raised her brows in question.

"A useful skill to have in a bodyguard," Holland said. He picked up his knife and fork. "I didn't realize you'd trained your taste buds to detect drugs."

"Probably good you didn't bother trying to drug him then, isn't it?" She took a bite of her steak, humming at the delicious, un-tampered-with, taste of it melting on her tongue. Then said, "Might have caught you being the bad guy."

He chuckled. "You know, I could use someone with your skills as well, Ms. Redmond. Having a taster would come in handy for a man in my position."

"Thanks but no. I prefer working for myself." Which wasn't technically a lie. She would prefer not to have to jump to the Nags' orders.

"One day, Ms. Redmond," Holland said, "you and I will have to have a long, private chat."

Cary made a noncommittal noise around a mouthful of food. She wasn't having any private chats with a demon if she could help it.

"Are you in love with your leopard, Ms. Redmond?"

She nearly choked on her lunch. Before she could swallow and answer, Jon spoke up.

"She's gonna marry Deacon."

"Is she?" Holland said.

"I am?" she said.

"That's what Deacon told my mom," Jon confirmed. "And the dogs. They approve, by the way. They think he'll make a good pack leader."

"I'm the pack leader. He told the dogs we're getting married?" She wasn't sure how to feel about that. She was a little worried she found his consideration charming. "When did he say that to your mother?"

Holland raised a brow. "Has he told *you* that he intends to marry you?"

"Didn't we come here to discuss a job?" she snapped, her cheeks warm, which was as embarrassing as the conversation. "I don't remember agreeing to a little social visit where we talk about our private lives."

"I did have a point when I brought up the subject of love," Holland said, his smile dropping away.

"And that would be?" she asked.

"It can force you to do extraordinary things."

"Are you telling me love has *ever* forced your hand?" She gave him a look but was extremely glad for the change in topic.

He waved her comment away. "As you say, we came here to discuss a job."

"You have a weird accent," Jon said.

Holland chuckled, and the tension dissipated. "Yes, well, it grows on you."

"If you say so." Jon wrinkled his nose. "Sounds kind of snooty. Like that guy who plays Hannibal Lecter in the movies. When he talks in his normal voice, I mean, not his Lecter voice."

This time Holland laughed so hard the hovering staff and maître de stopped their attempts to look busy and stared at him.

"Quite right," he told Jon and clapped him on the shoulder.

Jon grinned, looking pleased he'd made Holland laugh.

Cary was happier when Jon was scowling suspiciously at the demon.

When Holland stopped chuckling, he wiped his eyes and turned back to his food. "You're a very clever boy, Jonathon. Very clever. But then, I wouldn't be offering you a place in my organization if I didn't think you were."

"And speaking of this job…," Cary said.

"I'd simply like Jonathon to help me find something." Holland turned to Jon. "I'm afraid I can't reveal many details to anyone outside my organization. But I will say that the search is completely legal. A bit like a treasure hunt, eh?"

"Cool," Jon said.

"But what's the treasure?" Cary said. "And if you find this something you're looking for, what do you get out of it?"

"I get satisfaction," Holland said.

"Power?" she asked.

He smiled that barely there smile. "Not the sort you're thinking of."

"What sort then?"

"I'll simply have the triumph of knowing I've uncovered something precious."

"But how could I possibly help?" Jon asked.

He looked curious but suspicious again. Suspicion was good.

"That would be something we'd have to discuss further once you accepted the post," Holland said. "It is one of the details I need to keep to myself for the moment. I can say that you wouldn't be doing anything illegal. Simply using your special gift to aid me in my search."

"What could possibly be so special you'd spend all this money and go to all this trouble for secrecy?" Cary met Holland's gaze. "What could you want so much you'd do all this, yet it won't give you power?"

"One day, Ms. Redmond, one day soon I suspect, you'll realize just how very much a man will do for love." He turned back to a frowning Jon. "I've no intention of pressuring you into this work. I never did. I leave it up to you entirely." He slid a card across the table. "Think it over. Discuss it with your mother. You can assure her I'm not offering anything illegal." He glanced at Cary. "And I do this purely for love."

He shrugged. "Maybe a little obsession, but I can hardly be blamed for that. This is a love search, Ms. Redmond."

From her peripheral vision, Cary saw Jonathon roll his eyes. What did a thirteen-year-old care about Holland's love life? But Cary's stomach tightened as she stared back at Holland. There was something in the way he phrased his words… Very careful and calculated.

"What the hell are you trying to say to me, Holland?" she said. "Just spit it out already."

Holland shook his head. "You really aren't afraid of me, are you?"

"I'm terrified," she said. "I'm shaking in my boots. And you're trying to change the subject."

"Quite."

Just then one of the goons approached their table and leaned over to murmur in Holland's ear. He nodded and motioned the guard away.

Sighing, he said, "I'm afraid I have to cut the meeting short. Please, stay, have dessert. The bill will be taken care of." He rose, dropping his napkin next to his plate. "Jonathon, I don't want you to feel pressured, so I will wait for your answer. If I don't hear from you, I'll assume the answer is no. Ms. Redmond, you can rest assured, Jonathon will not be approached by anyone in or out of my organization regarding this post. The ball is in your court now, young man. So to speak. I hope I'll be hearing from you soon."

With that, Holland and his array of guards filed out of the restaurant. Cary pursed her lips as she watched them go. This hadn't settled matters as she'd hoped. Because Holland hadn't waited for Jon's answer, his promise to leave Jon alone—his word on the matter—didn't come into play yet.

She glanced at the boy. He was studying the dessert menu closely. She drummed her fingers on the table next to her plate. What if Jon didn't say no? What if he said yes?

"I thought you didn't like sweets," she said, tapping the menu once.

"I don't really. But it's free so I should have something. Maybe the apple pie. With ice cream."

"They've got apple pie?" She snatched up her own menu.

"I bet they'll warm it up even," Jon said. "They opened the restaurant for Holland. I bet they'll heat the pie if we ask."

"With ice cream, huh?" Cary murmured.

When the waiter slid up to their table, Cary said, "We'll have two warm slices of apple pie with ice cream."

Jon grinned.

"What?" she asked. "It's free."

JONATHAN SAT ON THE FLOOR IN CARY'S LIVING ROOM NEXT TO THE three sleeping dogs and stared at the business card in his hand. The house was quiet. Last time he'd looked at the clock it was three a.m. In the dim light coming from the window over his head, he could barely see the gold font on white background on the front of the card, but it was the scrawled writing on back that kept him from sleeping.

He angled the card to catch the light. Black ink, elegant handwriting. It reminded him of those fancy cards people wrote to one another in the British historical films his mom liked to watch.

"Starting Salary: $250,000/year."

Two hundred and fifty thousand big ones. A year. Just to start! He'd only have to work a year and he could pay off all his mom's loans and debts. A second year and he could buy her a house like Cary's with a backyard and everything. Then they could have dogs and cats and maybe even some birds and a guinea pig.

That much money would solve all their problems.

He turned the card around and around in his hands.

He hadn't talked to his mom about the job yet, and Cary hadn't said anything either. He'd made her promise to let him tell his mom.

Two hundred and fifty thousand dollars.

He reached out and tunneled his fingers through the thick fur on Fred's neck.

Fred stretched out and sighed, opening his eyes only long enough to say, "Hi. Scratching is good." Then he drifted back to sleep, content with his place in the pack.

Jon envied Fred. All Cary's dogs. They had a good life. With Cary, they never had to worry about food or love.

Or money.

Jon looked at the card again. Two hundred and fifty thousand dollars could fix an awful lot of things.

2 4

$\mathcal{T}$hursday morning, while standing in the kitchen waiting for the coffee to finish brewing, Sally brought up Thanksgiving. "I want to take Jon to my parents for the long weekend. They live in Olympia."

Cary blinked then nodded. She hadn't thought much about Thanksgiving outside of canceling her trip to New York to visit her sister and her sister's family. Her parents were going on a cruise with her mom's sister and her husband—something they did now that they were retired so her mom didn't feel the need to cook. Cary hadn't considered she might have to spend the day with strangers. Granted, they were Sally's parents, and Cary and Sally had developed something of a friendship. But still...

She sighed.

Sally reached out and patted her hand. "I'm not expecting you to come with us."

Cary opened her mouth, but Sally squeezed her hand, cutting her off.

"I'm not inviting you," she said more firmly. "This isn't because I don't like you. I can't tell you how grateful I am for what you've done for Jon. But we need some family time. Alone."

Should she be relieved or offended that Sally didn't want her around?

"And you need to spend some alone time with Deacon," Sally added. "I notice he hasn't been around for a few days."

"He's been busy with work." Cary couldn't begin to consider how she felt about Deacon's absence, or the fact that she did miss him even though she really shouldn't after only a few days. Thinking about Deacon was a distraction when they still had a demon to worry about.

"You should be with your family," Sally said.

"That wasn't going to happen this year anyway." A niggling of worry curled in Cary's stomach. She didn't want to let Jon out of her protection yet, not when things with Holland weren't finalized. "Are you sure?"

"Jon told me about the job offer," Sally said. "He said he'd call Mr. Holland and refuse. He also said Mr. Holland gave you his word to leave Jon alone if Jon said no to the job."

Cary blinked. Jon hadn't told her he'd spoken to his mother about all this yet.

"Do you believe he'll keep his word?" Sally shuffled away to get mugs, not meeting Cary's gaze.

"Actually, I do," Cary said.

Sally's shoulders sagged as she let out a pent up breath. "Good. That's good."

"If you're still worried, I can keep protecting Jon for a while longer. I wouldn't have to interfere in your family time. I could just camp outside in my car, keep an eye out for—"

Sally raised a hand to interrupt. "I would never ask that of you. Jon will be safe as soon as he turns down Mr. Holland's job. You said so yourself." She flashed a crooked smile as she poured coffee into the two mugs. "Look on the bright side. You're about to be rid of us. That hunky boyfriend of yours can spend the night again."

Heat rushed across Cary's face. She gulped at the coffee Sally handed her so she wouldn't have to say anything. The burnt tongue was worth it.

CARY'S CELLPHONE RANG JUST AFTER MIDNIGHT, PULLING HER FROM A deep sleep. She scrambled for it, silencing the ring before the noise woke Sally or Jon. "Hello?"

"I'm five minutes away. Meet me at your front door," Deacon said and disconnected.

She blinked at the phone. He'd sounded so…intense. What was wrong now?

Scrambling out of bed, she pulled on a pair of sweats and hurried to the front door, opening it when she heard his car door close.

She barely recognized the man stalking toward her. His hair was mussed, his shirt unbuttoned, and a fine sweat covered his chest. His eyes looked like they were glowing in the dim light from the street lamp.

She sucked in a breath and took an involuntary step back.

Then he was on her, sweeping her into his arms and burying his face against her neck. His big body trembled and shuddered. The muscles in his arms flexed. He gripped her shirt, bunching the material up in his fists.

For a heartbeat, she couldn't move. When the shock eased, she wrapped her arms around his neck and hugged him. She didn't know what else to do.

"Cary," he whispered, his voice a hoarse croak.

"Shhh. It's okay. Everything's fine." She couldn't say where the need to comfort came from, but seeing such a strong man so upset stunned her. "What's wrong? How can I help?"

"Don't let go," he choked.

He held her so tight she had trouble taking a deep breath, but she didn't ask him to loosen his grip. Even when she heard the material of her shirt tear.

Eventually, his body stopped shaking and his muscles relaxed. Cary eased back enough to see his face. "Better?"

His laugh sounded strained. "A bit."

"What happened? What's going on?" She kept her voice low as she ushered him inside and closed the door.

"My control… I shouldn't have stayed away from you for so long. I thought I could handle it, that my control couldn't get this bad. But I nearly shifted in front of some of my staff tonight when one of the tigers challenged me." He shook his head. "I wouldn't have even acknowledged the challenge before, but…"

He pulled her close again and rested his forehead on hers. "I've been snapping at everyone, nearly took the head off one of the volunteer vets, literally. It's just lucky there haven't been other leopards around. My sister threatened to tranquilize me if I didn't come see you."

Despite the seriousness of the situation, Cary grinned. "I can't wait to meet your sister. Caitlin, right?"

"She's looking forward to meeting you, too." He took a deep breath and let it out slowly. "I hope I didn't wake Sally and Jon."

"I doubt it. Sally would have come out to see what was wrong."

"Can I… I need to stay with you for a little while. Please."

The please did her in. He sounded so desperate, and she had a feeling that didn't normally happen to him. Ever. "You can stay." She cupped his cheek. "You look tired."

"Haven't had much sleep this week."

"Work?"

He shook his head.

She didn't ask more. She wasn't sure she wanted the truth yet. "I'm tired, too," she said instead. "Let's go lay down."

"Sally'll kill you if she finds out."

But he didn't resist when Cary took his hand and led him toward her bedroom. "She'll just have to get over it."

She closed the door and climbed into bed, taking Deacon with her. He paused long enough to toe off his shoes. When he stretched out next to her, he pulled her close, wrapping her in heat and the delicious male scent of him.

The need to comfort was so overwhelming she wasn't even self-conscious about having him in her bed. She had no idea where her feelings came from, but she couldn't have turned him away even if she'd wanted to.

"I won't stay long," he said. "I just have to be with you for a few minutes."

"You can stay as long as you need to."

"Sally will be scandalized." The tension eased from his voice and body. He still sounded hoarse but not nearly as desperate.

"She won't mind when I tell her it was an emergency." After a moment, she said, "But we'd better be quiet. Just in case."

He tugged at her ripped t-shirt. "Sorry."

"I have others. Although, if you're going to treat my clothes like this all the time, I'm gonna make you pay for replacements."

"Gladly." He sighed. "I'm not used to this. I've never, *never* even come close to losing my control before. My thoughts don't seem like my own—when I can think at all. I feel the animal just beneath my skin, and I'm not sure how much longer I can keep it from taking over."

Cary stroked his hair away from his face. "I'm sorry."

He frowned. "For what?"

"For what you're going through. For not being able to help. For—"

He cut her off with a sharp growl. "You're helping. Right now."

"Yeah, but I'm not proving to be a very good mate, am I?"

"Yes, you are. You're perfect."

She ducked her chin and gave him a look. "If I was a perfect mate, you wouldn't be on the edge of losing it."

"How do you know?"

"Deacon." She sighed. "We both know if I was a shifter—"

"You'd probably be doing this to me on purpose to guarantee I was your real mate," he said, cutting her off. "My sister's been telling me stories." He gave an exaggerated shudder. "Honestly, I'm pretty damned grateful you're not a leopard."

She snorted.

"I'm not trying to rush you, Cary. That's not why I'm here, and that's not what I want. I need you to know that."

"Your self-control is saying other things," she pointed out. "Dangerous things."

"And that's my problem to deal with. Not yours. It's obvious to everyone around me who knows about these things that I've found my mate. That means forever in our world."

He kept his gaze on her shoulder as he said that last, and she frowned even as her pulse pounded with a panicked shot of adrenaline at the thought of forever.

"And to get forever right," he went on, "we need time. You need time." He shrugged. "We need to go on a date at least."

She chuckled softly. "I was thinking that recently. Sally thinks you're my boyfriend and we haven't even had a real date. I'm not sure playing football at the park and facing off against a demon counts."

"It could under the right circumstances. But I was hoping for something a little more romantic."

She buried her face in his neck to muffle her laugh. His deep breath and the slow stroke of his hand along her back reminded her there was still a lot of tension and chemistry between them, even if the trust and friendship was still building.

"So what do we do?" she asked, meeting his gaze again. "I still need more time. You seem to be running out."

"No. I'll be okay, so long as I don't stay away from you for such long periods of time. I can manage."

"Would Caitlin agree with that?"

He grunted. "She'll tranquilize me if I get too bad."

"I'm really really looking forward to meeting her." She studied his face, pushing a strand of hair off his forehead. "I do have some good news. Sally and Jon are moving out soon. They're going to Sally's parents for Thanksgiving."

"You'll go with them?"

"No."

She told him everything then, about her lunch with Holland, how she'd gotten him to give his word, how Jon intended to call Holland tomorrow to turn down the job.

"Why didn't you tell me you were meeting with him?" Deacon asked.

"Because I was afraid you'd want to go with us. And no offence, big guy, but your moods…"

He let out a huff that sounded both irritated and resigned. She tensed, preparing for a fight.

Instead, he said, "You're right. I hate it. But you're right. The state I'm in, I would have been a liability."

Her eyebrows popped up. That had gone a lot more smoothly than she'd been expecting.

"So when do Jon and Sally move out?" he asked.

"Sunday. We decided it was best to stick to Jon's routine for the rest of the school week. I want a few days after Jon calls Holland to make sure the demon keeps his word, too."

"You think he will?"

"Yeah. Funny as that sounds. But I don't trust him not to try… something. He's probably already found a loophole in the promises I made him give me."

"What's Jaxer say?"

She shrugged. "He doesn't know about any of this. We haven't talked. He left one message with Angie, but that's it." She would have liked to have discussed her strategy and the results with her mentor, but that was tough to do when he wasn't around.

"And the Nags?" Deacon asked.

"They leave the protecting to me most of the time. Once I'm on a job, they let things run their course without interfering."

"Jaxer will probably make an appearance once Jon leaves."

Cary hummed under her breath. "I don't know. Something's wrong. I wish he'd talk to me about it." She levered up on her elbow. "Has he said anything to you? Do you know what's wrong?"

Deacon stared up at the ceiling for a long, quite moment, very obviously not meeting her gaze.

"What?" she asked, turning his chin so he had to look at her.

He sighed. "I think it's best if he tells you. If he hasn't said anything to you in a couple of weeks, I'll tell you everything I know."

"A couple of weeks? What makes you think my curiosity will let me wait that long?"

He reached up and tunneled his fingers through her hair. "I'm sure he'll talk to you soon. You have beautiful hair. You should wear it loose more often."

"You're changing the subject."

"Yes. I don't feel like talking about Jaxer while I'm in bed with my mate. If you don't mind."

"Don't think this lets you off the hook. I fully intend on grilling you about this subject at a later date."

"But you're willing to be distracted?"

She rolled her head against his hand. "I suppose I could be persuaded to talk about something else."

"And if I don't want to talk?"

"Then we really will scandalize Sally."

"Sally. Right." His gaze traveled over her face. "When are they moving out again?"

"Sunday."

"What time?"

She chuckled. "I don't know."

"Call me the minute they leave. I'll be waiting in the car around the block."

"Deacon!" She slapped his chest lightly and bit her lip to hold in her laugh.

"I meant for our long overdue date." He feigned innocence.

"Right." She didn't believe that look even a little bit. "Tell me about the animals," she said, because his hand playing with her hair was doing things to her pulse and she needed a new topic of conversation now. "How are they recovering?"

"Now look whose changing the subject."

"Your idea. How are the animals?"

"Better. Some of them still think the next fight is coming, though. They don't know they're safe yet."

"I know I discouraged the idea, but maybe you should ask Jon to talk to them. At least tell them they're going to be okay."

He frowned. "I may have to with the tigers. I think they've decided I'm the next combatant."

"I'm surprised your sister is still letting you near them."

"She's not now." He ran a finger down Cary's cheek. "But she has shown infinite patience with my current sorry state." His questing finger moved across her jaw and down her neck.

Cary blinked against the distraction of his touch. She cleared her throat. "So. Animals are okay, then?"

"They will be." He smiled.

"I thought you were tired."

"Not anymore."

"Sally…" Her voice trailed off as he pulled her face close to his and touched his lips gently to hers.

Cary's stomach clenched. She let out a soft sound somewhere between hesitance and surrender. And Deacon deepened the kiss.

The barest ounce of sense returned when his hand closed over her breast. The feeling was so exquisite, it stole her breath. She arched into his palm, moaned softly, and realized she was on the verge of rushing things she wasn't ready to rush.

Reluctantly, she eased back. "This isn't going to work."

He raised a brow. "I thought this was working just fine."

The wicked glint in his eyes made her groan. "Sally," she reminded him, her voice a harsh whisper. Desire clogged her throat.

"Maybe I should go."

"You don't have to go yet," she hurried to assure him. Did that sound desperate? Probably, since she was.

She was surprised to realize she didn't want him to leave so soon. She hadn't recognized how much she'd missed him until just that moment. Phone calls were nice but not the same as having a big, warm Deacon next to her.

"I mean…" she muttered over her embarrassment, "maybe if I turn around. Might be easier to sleep that way." Less temptation to look at.

He made a noncommittal sound and loosened his hold so she could roll over. She settled her back to his front and realized immediately this had been a mistake. Now she could feel the hard press of his erection against her butt. He had better access to her neck too and took advantage, nuzzling her hair aside to place hot little kisses along her pulse.

Nope, this wasn't helping at all.

25

"Tell me something I don't know about you," Cary croaked. Sally and Jon are still in the house, she repeated to herself over and over. Remember Sally and Jon.

Deacon's teeth scraped the skin high on her neck near her ear. *Sally, who?*

"What would you like to know?" he asked.

His breath was hot against her skin, sending a shiver across her shoulders. "Don't do that," she said. Her efforts to sound firm failed miserably. She made the command sound more like a plea to continue. Damn.

"I remember telling you the same thing the first night we met," he said.

"You did?"

He hugged her tighter to his chest. For some reason, the gesture made her feel well-loved and cosseted. A very strange sensation, but she liked it.

A little too much.

"You breathed on my neck while examining the binding ring," he said.

"Oh, yeah." She'd been busy trying not to notice how yummy he smelled. Sucking in a lungful of air, she let that same scent infuse her senses now.

"I've never been so uncomfortable being naked before," he said. "I sure as hell didn't want this strange woman Jaxer had sent to rescue me to know I had a hard-on just because she breathed on me."

"Strange, am I?"

"Beautiful and mysterious."

She snorted.

"Fortunately for me, you were very careful to keep your focus on my face."

"I did peak," she confessed without a hint of guilt. "At least from the waist up."

"So did I."

She turned her head toward him. "What did you peak at? I was fully dressed."

"Your shirt gaped open, giving me a very nice view of your cleavage." He cupped her breast. "I had a hard time keeping my hands to myself, despite the danger of the situation."

She felt her eyes rolling back in her head. "Deacon, you're not trying very hard to make this easier."

"I'm not, am I?" He nuzzled her neck again. "I'd never had such an immediate reaction to a woman before," he said. "It pissed me off, at first."

She managed a shaky laugh despite the heat clawing through her body. "Why?"

She felt his smile against her shoulder.

"I didn't want my hormones going crazy when I still had to get out of that apartment. And at first, I thought you were doing it on purpose. Some great joke to drive me insane."

"Who would play that kind of joke?"

"Jaxer."

"Yeah, well." She swallowed and tried to steady her voice. "Jaxer has a weird sense of humor." She reflexively pressed her butt back against his hips, and he growled in reaction.

Distraction. They needed a distraction. "How would I affect your hormones on purpose?"

Well, that wasn't much of a distraction. But the part of her brain still functioning was curious. How did one go about turning a reluctant man on against his will?

"I thought you were a witch and you'd cast a spell on me."

"Could have just been chemistry," she said.

"But it had never happened to me before. I didn't like it."

"No?" She wasn't sure why that bothered her. What was wrong with being attracted to her just because? She conveniently ignored the fact that she hadn't wanted to be attracted to him either.

"I hate being out of control," he said. "If you haven't noticed, it's dangerous. And I had no control over my reaction to you."

"Oh." Okay, she could understand that. She'd felt the exact same way so she could hardly complain. Except she wasn't dangerous when she was out of control. She just acted like an idiot.

"Once I'd had a chance to analyze your scent," he said, "I realized why I responded to you the way I did."

"Yeah, that scent thing again," she muttered under her breath.

She couldn't seem to get past the fact that they were here because pheromones were driving them. Chemistry and instinct. That was what they had. And that was all well and good for a fling. But "mates" were supposed to be more than temporary among leopards. He'd said as much just a few minutes ago.

She still had no idea how this could have happen between her and Deacon and had a hard time trusting it. But if this *was* a mate bond, then they might be together not because they actually liked each other but because some primal chemistry was driving them. It seemed so… superficial. So impersonal. She could be absolutely anyone, and Deacon would still be acting this way with her because she was, supposedly, his mate.

Did mates ever hate each other? Did they end up resenting the bond?

If he'd met her while his sense of smell was impaired and he didn't recognize her as his mate, would he still be attracted to her? Would he have even taken the time to get to know her? Would she have gone so lust-crazy for him that she completely ignored six years of hard won lessons about preternatural sex gods? If not for this mate thing, would they have even seen each other again after Halloween night?

She had significantly more questions than she had answers at this stage.

"What's wrong?" Deacon murmured against her neck.

"Nothing."

He propped himself up on his elbow and turned her chin up so he could look at her. "Talk to me."

God, he was sexy. She blinked to clear her head. Speaking of chemistry. "Nothing's wrong," she insisted. "I was just thinking."

"Oh, oh."

"Hey." But she smiled at his teasing tone. She took a deep breath and asked a question she wasn't sure she wanted an answer to. "Have you ever been in love before?" There, it was out there.

He shook his head.

"Never?" She narrowed her eyes. "Come on. Not even once?"

"No."

"I don't believe you."

"Why not?"

"Because you're... Well, I'm sure there've been enough opportunities."

"I have had lovers. I've just never been in love before."

For some reason, that was worse than hearing he had been in love with another woman.

"How about you?" he asked.

"What? Oh. Yes. Once." She smiled a little at the memory. "First love. He was a nice boy."

"How old were you?"

"Eighteen. First year of college. We had a sweet six months together then broke up with no hard feelings."

"How was that possible if you were in love with him?"

Cary frowned a little at his tone. It was hard to tell because they were talking so quietly, but she'd swear she heard a new tension in his voice. "We knew from the beginning we'd only have a limited time together. He was on his way to Europe and a job in the diplomatic core. And neither one of us wanted to do the long distance thing."

"How did you know you loved him?"

She shrugged. "I just knew. It was a simple kind of love, I guess. Not fireworks and inner turmoil. Not the Romeo and Juliet 'I'll die for you' kind. Gentle. Nice. A good first experience. But not the kind of love that lasts forever."

"If you met him now?"

"I'd expect to see pictures of his wife and three kids, and I'd be happy to hear what he's been doing for the last fourteen years."

"He's married?" Deacon asked. "You've kept in touch?"

"I'm just guessing," she said. "He was the type to get married and have kids. But I haven't talked to him since we broke up."

"You wouldn't want him back? He was your first love."

Ah. There was the reason for that strained note in his voice. "I wouldn't want him back," she said. "I haven't been in love with him for a long time."

"But you don't think it would come back?"

"Of course not. I knew then he wasn't the one for forever. I wish him all the best, but I sure as hell wouldn't want to go out with him again."

"I don't understand that," Deacon said.

"Do you want any of your former lovers still?" Another question she really didn't want answered. She bit her tongue to keep from taking it back.

He shrugged. "I was never in love with any of them."

Which didn't exactly answer her question, but it did beg the follow-up: just how many former girlfriends had there been? She really really didn't want to know that, so instead, she said, "Maybe we just have a different definition of what constitutes love."

He frowned and turned his gaze toward the room's darkened shadows. He didn't seem to like her observation.

She wasn't so happy with it either.

"How did we get onto this topic, anyway?" she said, trying to lighten the mood. They'd only known each other a few weeks, and still had to get to that first date. It was way too soon to be worried about love and whether they'd ever feel it for each other or not.

He shook his head, as if to clear it, and smiled. "I blame you. You were trying to distract me."

"Did it work?" She waggled her eyebrows playfully.

He gripped her hip in one hand and pressed her back against him so she could feel his still very aroused cock.

"What do you think?" he murmured.

"I think we're not going to get much sleep tonight."

"A man can hope."

Oh boy. "Sally. Remember Sally."

"Sally will be gone on Sunday."

He brushed his lips over hers, a gentle caress that made her tingle everywhere.

"Are you busy Monday?" he murmured.

Monday? "Not yet."

"How about Tuesday?"

"Nothing so far," she said slowly.

"Good."

"Why?"

"Because I intend to spend as much time with you as I can after Sally leaves. We'll have that date finally. More than one if you'll agree to it. And I will make every effort to seduce you. The less you have to do next week, the better."

She swallowed. Hard. Probably she should argue with him, or at least put up a token resistance. She wasn't going to, but she should. "What kind of date did you have in mind?" Her toes curled when he kissed her neck.

"Dinner. Caitlin tells me feeding a woman is a good way to get a second date."

Cary chuckled. In her case, that was probably true. "Then?"

"A romantic walk. A lot of kissing."

Mmm…

When his big hand slid around to rest low on her stomach, Cary thought her head might explode.

He nudged her over onto her side and spooned up behind her, wrapping her in his arms. "Try to get some sleep," he murmured.

"Right." That would happen tonight.

ary woke the next morning, gritty-eyed and irritable, to find Deacon had already left. She turned her head to see the clock. Probably good. Sally would be up any minute.

Over breakfast, she asked Jon how his phone call to Holland had gone. He'd planned to call first thing that morning.

"Fine," he said, shoving a spoonful of cereal into his mouth.

She raised her brows. "Fine? Just fine? What did he say?"

Jon shrugged. "Thanks for calling. Sorry you won't be working with us. That kind of thing."

"He wasn't mad?"

"Nope." Jon spooned in more cereal.

Cary pursed her lips, studying him.

"What?" he asked then filled his mouth again.

She shook off her unease. "Nothing." Lifting her coffee mug, she said, "Good coffee this morning. Thanks. I'm going to miss having you around to help keep the pot full."

He shrugged and stuck his face closer to his bowl. "Gonna miss you, too," he muttered to the milk.

"You can still visit sometime if you want. Talk to the dogs. They like you."

He popped his head up, his grin gross with mashed up Wheaties. "Yeah? Cool. I like the dogs, too. And maybe Deacon and I can throw the football around?"

"Sure. Bet he'd like that." She thought about asking Jon if he'd be willing to talk to Deacon's tigers but decided she'd leave that decision to Deacon.

As she watched Jon slurp up the last of his milk, her heart tightened. She was gonna miss him, too. She'd never had a little brother, and her nieces and nephew lived too far away for her to have a close relationship with them. It was amazing how quickly she'd gotten used to having Jon around.

"Want to go to the park tomorrow, if the weather holds?" she asked as he dumped his bowl into the dish washer. They were having an unusually warm bit of weather this week, and no rain. If it lasted, the weekend would be gorgeous.

"Yeah," Jon said. "That'd be great."

She watched him saunter out of the kitchen—he'd been trying to imitate Deacon's way of moving for a few days now—and smiled at his back. He was a good kid.

Her smile dropped. She hoped he stayed that way.

THAT NIGHT, BY THE TIME SALLY AND JON WERE MOSTLY PACKED, Deacon had arrived with pizza and wine.

She kissed him on the cheek in greeting. "Thanks for bringing dinner."

"You're welcome."

His golden gaze held such heat she lost her breath. She blinked and looked away before she embarrassed herself by jumping him right then and there. Sally would not be amused.

Although, when she caught Sally's gaze a moment later, the woman didn't look disapproving. In fact, she was giving Cary a downright wicked smile. Great. She had no doubt what Sally assumed would be happening tomorrow between her and Deacon. They were supposed to be a couple so of course the minute they got alone time they'd land into bed. That wasn't the plan yet. The plan was a date, but still… Knowing exactly what Sally was thinking was embarrassing.

Cary took her warming cheeks off to the kitchen to hide the blush and get glasses for the wine. Wine was definitely called for tonight.

Deacon followed her, backed her against the counter and braced his hands on either side of her hips, imprisoning her. "Hi," he said, leaning close without actually touching her. "How was your day?"

"Great. We went to the park. What are you doing?"

"Holding on to my shredded control. What did you do in the park?"

"This might be a safer conversation if we were in the living room with our chaperones."

"Probably, but I need a minute alone with you. Now, quick, tell me about your day before I strip you naked and fuck you right here against the counter."

Cary's entire body spasmed at the thought. When her lungs started to burn, she had to remind herself to breathe. How were they going to get through a single date, nonetheless several dates, when their chemistry was so off the charts? Damn.

She focused on breathing. "My day. Right." What had she done all day? Oh yeah. "We went to the park. Took the dogs. Tried to throw the football around. I'm getting better. I only got hit in the stomach twice and only once on my hip."

"Good job." His gaze dropped to her body. "Any bruises I should worry about."

"They'll be gone by tomorrow."

He nodded but he continued to stare at her breasts, watching them rise and fall as she breathed. Which only made her breathe harder.

"What else did you do?" His voice rasped out now.

She shivered. "Fred chased the ball around some. Pickles and Buck joined the games for a while then slept while Jon tried to wear Fred out."

"Did he succeed?"

"Of course not. Then we ate lunch."

"What did you have?"

"Sandwiches. Potato salad…" Her voice trailed off when Deacon leaned even closer and his scent hit her hard, making her dizzy.

"Potato salad and what else?" he asked.

"Huh?" What was he talking about? And why couldn't she seem to think anymore?

His head dipped lower and he nuzzled her neck. Cary swore she saw sparkles dancing in front of her eyes.

The sound of something cracking startled her back to reality. She looked down to see an actual dent crushed into the edge of her marble countertop. There was a matching dent in the counter on the other side of her hip. Whoa. She blinked up at him. She knew he was strong, but…

Whoa.

"Sorry," he said, stepping away from her and grimacing. "I'll pay to have it fixed."

She waved his offer away, but frowned. "How am I going to explain that to Sally and Jon?"

He winced and took another step away.

When she started to follow him, she panicked. They needed to get out of this kitchen immediately. She picked up the wine glasses. "We'll just get Sally drunk and hope she doesn't notice."

Cary snapped awake Sunday morning to an unexpected phone call. From her mother.

"Darling! We're coming for Thanksgiving."

Cary shot up in bed. "What? What happened to the cruise?"

"Your uncle has the flu and you know how your aunt is, can't let the poor man take care of himself. She's such a fuss. Anyway, we canceled this year and your sister tells me you had to cancel your trip to New York so that means we can come to your place for Thanksgiving instead!"

Cary blinked at the wall, a new kind of panic creeping over her. She loved her parents. Truly she did. But a Thanksgiving visit was…

inconvenient timing. "Why aren't you going on the cruise alone? Just you and dad?"

"It's not as much fun. And I miss you. It's been ages since we've visited."

"True." Cary tried to force a smile. "When are you arriving?"

"Today! Isn't that wonderful. Your dad wanted to surprise you but I told him we had to call ahead. What if you had to work? Or had company."

Cary pressed her lips together at the mention of company. Deacon had planned to arrive right after Sally left to take Cary on their long delayed date.

Oh god, what if her parents had shown up at the same time Deacon had? How would she have explained him? She could hardly tell her mother she was seeing someone and hadn't mentioned it yet.

"That sounds great," she told her mother, hoping she sounded excited and not disappointed. "How long are you going to stay?"

"You have us for an entire week and a half," her mother chirped.

"Yay."

Oh boy.

"I'm so sorry," Cary said over the phone to Deacon. She'd called him the minute she hung up with her mother. "I know we made plans and everything. And I know you're... Well, I understand this is inconvenient."

There was silence on the other end of the phone, long enough Cary wasn't sure how to interpret it. Was he angry? Frustrated? Hurt?

Should she be this worried about how he felt?

"Okay," he said, though he sounded strained. "It's just another week and a half, right?"

"Right." Unless the Nags came up with another job for her in the meantime. "Are you...okay?" she asked.

"I will be. Though..." More heavy silence she couldn't interpret.

"Would you…" He cleared his throat. "Would you object to me coming over for visits while your parents were there?"

Her eyes widened at the thought. "I really wouldn't know what to tell them about you. And I'm not…not ready for that yet."

"In that case, I might have to, uh, leave town for the duration."

"What? Why?" And why the hell was she panicking at the thought? What the hell was wrong with her?

"I won't be able to stay in control…and in my human form for an entire week and a half without spending any time at all with you. I've barely been able to keep my leopard at bay the last few days, and we've been together during that time. I need to be somewhere I can shift regularly and run."

"Deacon…" She wasn't sure what she meant with her sigh, but he seemed to know.

"Please don't tell me we're a bad idea again," he said, his tone harsh. "Just don't. You're my mate. I will do what I have to to make this work."

"Even if it means torturing yourself?"

"Even if."

"My life…it's not ever getting less complicated, you know. Family, friends, my work, all of it will keep popping up and taking my time. The Nags are notorious for just showing up in my living room. I will drop everything to help my girlfriends if they need me. I'll change plans to accommodate my parents or my sister. This is my life. Are you really sure you want to deal with all that?"

"Damn it, Cary, of course I do. I've made that abundantly clear. Please stop trying to push me away."

She closed her eyes briefly. "I just want you to know what you're getting into with me."

"You don't know what you're getting into with me yet, either," he snapped.

"What does that mean?"

Another silence. Then, "It means we have a lot to learn about each other, and how this relationship will work. And we have time to do that."

"Are you sure?" she asked. "You have to leave town because your control is so on edge. And this is just an ordinary month in my life. This is how my life always is. There's a reason I've only slept with two men in the last six years."

There was a pause before he said, "I'm trying to decide if I'm happy to hear that or jealous. I'll figure it out when my leopard stops hissing in my head. In the meantime, just know that I'm willing to deal with all this. It's life."

She huffed out a sound halfway between a laugh and a groan. "My life anyway." She wanted to ask him if he was sure again, but she was tired of arguing. "Where will you go?" she asked instead.

"I'll go visit my family. They'll know how to deal with me."

She smiled a little. "Tranquilizers?"

He chuckled and some of the pressure in her gut eased.

"Probably," he said. "How long are your parents staying?"

"A week and a half. Until Wednesday morning. And then, unless the Nags come calling, I'm free."

"A week and a half, then," he said, his tone slipping into that deep, sexy tenor that made her toes curl. "A week from Wednesday night. Dinner. A romantic walk. And lots of kissing."

She hummed under her breath as her stomach danced in anticipation. "It's a date."

27

*S*ally and Jon left just after eleven that morning. Sally with a hint of sadness but mostly an obvious relief. Jon with a lot more reluctance.

"Come visit the dogs after you get back from your grandparents' house," Cary told him.

"'Kay."

He gave her a tight hug, startling a smile out of her, then turned away to watch his mom loading her suitcase into the trunk of her old, well-cared-for Corolla. Cary studied the side of his face, but turned away and pretended not to see his sniffle and the way he wiped his eyes with his jacket sleeve. Something nagged at her, a worry she couldn't quite place her finger on, and she glanced back at him. She was reluctant to let him out of her protection. And yet eager to have her home to herself again—at least for a few hours before her parents showed up. There was guilt mixed into her feelings too, though she wasn't sure why. But mostly there was worry. Something just not quite right…

Given the already chaotic morning she'd had, she figured it was just her overstressed nerves. After all, she had a house to clean before her parents arrived.

Sally came back and rested her hand on Jon's shoulder. She had to reach up. "Come on, kiddo," she said. "We need to get home. The place'll need airing out after this long."

They exchanged final goodbyes, Sally thanked Cary again, and Cary stood in the doorway watching them drive away, still with a niggling sense of unease.

She knew she couldn't keep them here forever. But was she hurrying them out? Had she rushed things with Holland?

Ultimately, it had been Sally's decision to go. And probably everything would be fine. Jon had called Holland, Holland had agreed to leave Jon alone. That was that. Just her overactive sense of responsibility plaguing her, she was sure.

She wished she could discuss all this with Jaxer.

Sighing, she closed the door and headed for the guest room so she could change the sheets and start getting things in order for her parents' visit. The house seemed strangely silent even with three dogs underfoot.

"What do you think, guys?" she said to them as they followed her. "You think I made the right decision letting Jon and Sally leave?"

They stared up at her with loving expressions lacking any judgment —or any helpful answers. She sighed.

What did she expect?

THE VISIT WITH HER PARENTS WENT AS WELL AS CARY COULD HAVE hoped. Better really since the Nags stayed away. Her mother even compromised and let her eat nachos instead of turkey for Thanksgiving since Cary wasn't crazy about turkey. They went shopping on Black Friday—which Cary would *not* have done without her mother's urgings. Her mother reorganized the kitchen to "be more efficient." And her father kept the dogs entertained while telling Cary stories about their last trip to Yellowstone.

And for a solid week and a half, Cary worried.

About Deacon. How was he doing? What was he doing? Was he

managing to maintain some semblance of control?

About Jon. Did he settle back into school okay without her? Was he safe? Had Holland broken his promise or were things still quiet?

About Holland. Had he found whatever it was he was looking for? Was he still out there somewhere gathering supernatural powers to his search? Could she afford to ignore the potential threat he posed? Was it any of her business now that he wasn't a threat to Jon?

About Jaxer. Where the hell was he? What had he told Deacon that Deacon was still keeping to himself? Why had he vanished?

Her father noticed her distraction, but when he asked and she excused it as work related, he let it go. He was a good dad.

She never heard from Deacon—he'd warned he wouldn't call because he wasn't likely to spend much time in human form while he was away. She didn't hear from Jaxer either, and the silence had her as pissed off as it worried her.

She did, however, hear from Angie on Monday, demanding a girls' night and gossip on Tuesday. An opportunity—with her parents' permission, no less—Cary just couldn't resist. It might be the only way she made it to Wednesday night...

And her impending date with Deacon.

WITHOUT CARY'S CONSTANT PRESENCE, JON COULDN'T FIND MUCH motivation to stay in school after Thanksgiving. He made it through the entire day Monday, but only as far as second period on Tuesday, then he took off.

Too bad he didn't have Mr. Young earlier in the day. He liked Mr. Young's class. But not enough to deal with all the boring teachers in between. Especially math. Even Cary had trouble staying awake during math. Borrrrring.

He got off the bus close to home and ambled up the street, stopping at the spot where Cary had saved him from the dragon shifter. A little shiver raced up his neck. He looked around, half expecting to see the big black car pulling up to the curb.

But of course it didn't. No one from Mr. Holland's group had come anywhere near him.

Jon fingered the card in his pocket but didn't take it out.

When he got home, he checked the mailbox and shuffled through the envelopes as he climbed the stairs to the apartment. Two letters jumped out at him. One was an expensive looking tan envelope from Malory, Smith & McTierney, Attorneys at Law. The other was stamped in big red letters, "Final Notice."

He frowned at them. They didn't look like junk mail. The return address on the final notice letter was from his mom's bank.

He locked the apartment door behind him, dropped most of the mail on the rickety table in the entryway, let his backpack slide to the floor, and headed for the kitchen with the two letters.

Setting them on the counter, he considered them as he poured himself a glass of juice. He never took his gaze off the envelopes, even when he returned the carton to the fridge.

He shouldn't open them. His mom would know. She'd get really pissed if she knew he opened her mail. He could probably get away with one, say he thought it was junk. But he'd never get away with opening both. There was a way, though, wasn't there? So no one would know. Steaming. Did that work in real life?

He put a pan of water on the stove to boil then went to find his mom's checkbook. She never took it with her. Said it'd only encourage her to buy stuff. She kept it in a drawer and used it to pay bills. The rest of the time she used cash. She didn't even have a credit card. Too much temptation, she said.

Would she have the balance recorded? He'd watched her while she wrote out checks for the bills, the way her brow crinkled and her mouth tightened into a thin line. Her eyes got all scrunchy, too. Her worried look. The look she gave him when she found out he was ditching school.

He opened the checkbook. His mom recorded every penny. There was $25.19 left in her account and payday was the end of this week.

He closed the checkbook, put it back exactly the way he'd found it, right down to the overdue phone bill angled across it's corner.

The pot of water was boiling when he got back to the kitchen. He burned his fingers the first time he tried to hold one of the envelopes over the steam. Using tongs worked better.

He started with the "Final Notice". The seal buckled under the moisture, and he opened it easily. By the time he'd read the contents, he didn't care if he could close the envelope again.

They were gonna lose the car.

Mom owed four back-payments with interest and penalties, and the number at the bottom of the angry letter was a lot higher than $25.19. He didn't know how much his mom's paycheck was, but he knew what his tuition cost and that was due next month for the spring term.

They were gonna lose the car.

He didn't bother steaming open the letter from the law firm. Ripping through the expensive paper, he pulled out a single sheet. The words were terse, dense, and stuffy sounding. But he understood the important point. The landlord was "initiating eviction proceedings" next month.

Jon grabbed his keys and left the house, carefully locking the door behind him.

"Jonathon," a smooth, accented voice said. "What an unexpected surprise. What brings you here?"

Jon blinked up at the older man. "Mr. Holland," he greeted without any enthusiasm. He was too depressed for enthusiasm. He hadn't known what to do after opening the letters from the bank and the lawyers, so he'd gone to the mall. But even the gaming store depressed him. He'd been sitting on a bench, staring at the floor long enough for his butt to hurt.

"Jonathon? What's wrong? You look down."

Jon kicked his feet against the bench and shrugged. "Car company's gonna repo mom's car, and we're getting evicted from our apartment. She pays too much for that stupid private school I'm in. Don't know where we'll live. Grandma and grandpa's maybe. But she'll lose her job here and then what?"

"I'm very sorry to hear this." Holland sat on the bench next to him. "What about your father? Can't he help at all?"

"Don't know where he is. Ran off when I was a baby. Mom says he was a deadbeat anyway."

"It can be very difficult to grow up without a father."

"You didn't know your dad either?" Jon asked.

"Oh no. I knew him. I knew the bastard very well."

The bite in Holland's voice made Jon look up.

Holland smiled faintly. "Sometimes you're better off not knowing your father."

Jon pondered that in silence, pursing his lips as he continued to swing his feet. A lot of people walked by as they sat quietly. A woman with a baby stroller and three trailing toddlers. Two old ladies with their heads together walking like they were in a hurry to get somewhere. An older couple holding hands. A group of high school kids shouting at each other from two feet away and taking up most of the walkway. Jon didn't see Holland's bodyguards anywhere. That was weird. Did they get days off?

"You know, Jon," Holland said after a while, "my job offer still stands. I know you never rang, which was your way of telling me you didn't want the position, but… Well, I'd still love to have you work for me. I promise, despite what your friends and mother think, I don't want you to do anything illegal. I'd just like you to…call someone for me. That's all."

Jon frowned. "Call someone?"

"As only you can."

"I can't call humans like that," Jon said.

"Ah, but she isn't human."

"She?" He cocked his head. Holland wasn't gonna start all that love talk again, was he?

"Someone I care very much about," Holland said.

"Like your girlfriend or wife?"

"We haven't managed to get to the husband and wife point. But you could call her my girlfriend."

"Why do you need me to call her?"

"We had a…fight. She's not speaking to me."

Jon narrowed his eyes in an expression he'd seen Cary use. "You're not gonna hurt her are you?"

"No. Of course not." Holland waved off the idea. "I just need to talk to her, to make things right between us."

"Sounds like a lot of trouble for a girl."

"Believe me, one day you'll understand."

Jon nodded, not at all convinced.

"I need your help, Jonathon. To get back the woman I love."

Ugh. The love thing again. He liked girls and all. But all this talk about old people in love was just gross. "What if she won't come when I call? If she's so pissed at you she won't even talk to you, I might not be able to help?"

"Well, perhaps you could reach some of her family, call them out? If I could talk with them, convince them to take me to her, I could explain everything. You know," Holland paused, tilting his head, "I imagine you'd like their city. It's very beautiful, I understand. Full of riches."

"Oh yeah?" He perked up. "Where is it?"

"Ah, there's the rub. If I could find the city, I would already be camped on Nira's doorstep trying to make her see reason."

"You don't know where her city is?"

"Not specifically. Generally. But without an escort, no one can find the entrance. That's why I need Nira to come to me, or one of her relatives. Someone who can lead me to the city."

"Maybe she doesn't want you there."

Holland's eyes narrowed slightly, but his smile widened. "Well, she is upset with me. But I know she'll see reason. I just need to convince her to speak to me again."

"I don't know…" Jon made a face and glanced past Holland's shoulder. It all sounded kind of weird. Holland might be old, but he was rich. There had to be other girls he could get.

"Outside of the payment I'll provide for your service," Holland said quietly, "I'm sure her family will offer up some of those riches I mentioned. They're a very generous people."

"Yeah?" His legs swung faster, and he straightened his shoulders. "They might give me something worth something?"

"Worth more than you can imagine."

But no one gave away valuable things for free. "Why?" There had to be a catch.

"It's the way they are. Once we enter the city, once we're led to it, I'm sure they'll be more than willing to give you whatever you want." Holland's smile gleamed. "And of course there's the salary I'll pay you, which if you remember, was quite generous." His voice dropped. "More than enough to buy your mother a new car. Plenty to afford a better apartment. Even a house."

Jon nibbled his lower lip. He could use the money for his mom. She worked so hard. He could finally give her something back. A house. With a backyard. All the bills paid on time. She'd stop getting up in the middle of the night to pace in the living room. She wouldn't sit in the dark and cry anymore.

And Holland made this mysterious city sound really cool. Jon would like to get a look at those riches.

"You're sure no one will get hurt?" he asked after a moment.

Holland looked him square in the eyes. "No one will get hurt."

"If she's not human, and I can call her, then what is she?"

"She's a Naga."

Jon gaped. "Hey, they're like snake shifters sort of, aren't they?"

"In a way."

"Cool." He'd like to meet a Naga.

"So you'll help me, then, Jon?"

He bit his thumbnail and studied Holland. The guy wasn't so bad for a demon. And he did say no one would get hurt. Two hundred and fifty grand would be really nice, too.

He rubbed his hand on his pants leg then held it out to Holland. "It's a deal."

Holland smiled, his big hand engulfed Jon's, and he shook it firmly. "Deal."

Cary found parking right in front of Angie's cute little cottage-style house, a stroke of luck that helped raise her mood. The worries had only gotten worse as the week started. No word from Jaxer, Holland, Jon or Sally left her wondering if things really were settled, and she was just fretting over nothing. But she had this nagging sense that the second shoe still hadn't dropped and it kept her sleep restless.

Well, that and thinking about Deacon. Dreaming about him. And waking up to worry that she couldn't stop thinking about him.

She really needed this girls' night, even if just to vent to the three people who knew her best. And if more than one bottle of wine was consumed, well, she had a taxi company's number already in her cell's contact list.

Cary climbed out of the car just as Angie opened the front door and stepped out onto her large wooden porch. She waited for Cary at the top of the short flight of stairs right next to the hand carved, wooden sign that advertised her hours of business for tarot and palm readings. She had one front parlor set aside for work, all decked out in the typical psychic trappings of black and purple silks and velvet, candles, incense and sparkling beadwork.

The rest of the light and airy house she kept off-limits. The earthy, southwestern decor of the little cottage fit Angie's personality so much better than the dark and moody parlor.

"Dinner is ordered," Angie called. "Thai food. Marianne will be here soon. Lucy is running late after her last class, but is on her way."

"Perfect," Cary said as she straightened her skirt. They were staying in, but they'd decided to dress up a little since they hadn't had a chance to get together in a few weeks. Cary had picked comfortable dress up clothes—a flowy skirt, a fitted but stretchy blouse, and sparkly flats—but for her anything that wasn't jeans and boots was dressing up. Angie wore a long, fitted tan skirt with a slit up one thigh and a red sweater. She'd foregone shoes, which was typical Angie.

Cary was halfway up the walk when she noticed Angie's frown. Almost at the same instant a tingle of warning crept across her shoulders. Before she could turn completely in the direction Angie was frowning, a bright green ball of electricity sizzled past her, missing her by mere inches. She screamed and lunged toward the porch just as another flash of green hit the bricks where she'd been standing. The smell of burnt ozone clogged her nose.

Angie moved down the two steps to her lawn, her hands twisting in a pattern Cary vaguely recognized. As Cary tripped up the stairs past her, Angie flung her hands out, palms forward, facing the threat. The gesture stopped another electricity bolt two feet from Cary's head. It spun in the air like an angry Telsa ball, spikes of green shooting in all directions within a tight, invisible sphere.

Angie's voice rolled out, deep and powerful, as she chanted an incantation in what Cary thought might be Latin, though she was too freaked out to be certain. The ball of electricity exploded, temporarily blinding Cary with the bright flash of white and green light. When she could see again, she scanned the street, waiting for the next attack.

Nothing happened for long minutes. Angie jerked her hands down in a deliberate gesture and murmured a short phrase under her breath. Cary sensed something different but because she wasn't protecting anyone, she had no idea what her friend had just done.

"What was that?" she asked, her knees shaking from the adrenaline rush. She leaned against the porch railing to keep her feet under her.

"I think someone just tried to kill you," Angie said.

"Shit."

"Any guesses who it might have been?"

Cary gave her a look. "You want the whole list of people who want to kill me or just the most recent options?"

Angie raised her brows. "You have been going around town for the last few weeks pissing off a demon."

"But Jon isn't with me anymore. I stopped pissing Holland off more than a week ago."

"Maybe he holds a grudge."

"Shit," Cary said again, her legs trembled so much she was grateful she was wearing flats. If she'd had heals on, she'd probably be sitting on Angie's porch now, not leaning against a post. If Holland had decided to come after her, just her without any other agenda, without trying to get through her to someone else, she was in serious trouble.

She let out a breath, trying to slow her heartbeat, and looked at her friend. "What did you do?"

"That was magic being thrown at you," Angie said, "so I shielded against the initial attack. Then I activated the circle around my house. I'll have to come out and let Lucy and Marianne through when they get here."

Angie had admitted to Cary once a few years back that she maintained a sacred circle around her home, in the soil out of casual sight, set with salt and activated by a spell when Angie felt she needed it. If she crossed the barrier and broke the circle, she inactivated its protection. But so long as they stayed within it, they'd be safe from magic. And demons.

Cary hoped.

"Come on inside," Angie said. "I'll cancel the Thai order until I'm sure the wizard throwing those kill spells is gone. Lucy and Marianne can handle this weirdness. A poor delivery guy shouldn't have to."

Cary swallowed at the words "kill spells." Plenty of people had tried to kill her before but almost always while she was protecting someone and so was safe. This time, whoever that had been, they weren't aiming at Angie or even trying to get around Cary to get to Angie. Cary was the target. Angie wasn't in danger. So the Protector magic hadn't been there to keep Cary alive.

She was more than a little terrified to think that whoever had just attacked knew what she was and had known exactly how to get around her defenses. The fact that so few people could figure out exactly what she was had typically been her saving grace over the years.

Had Holland figured it out? Was he trying to get her out of the way now just because she *might* be able to stop him from doing...whatever it was he was doing? She had no plans to go anywhere near the demon again if she could possible avoid it. But maybe Holland didn't want to take any chances?

She could feel someone watching them, and realized it was the same feeling she'd been getting a lot recently, that spine shivering certainty that someone was staring at her. She'd assumed that had to do with Jon, though. Maybe she'd been wrong.

Would the wizard out there leave now that he knew Angie's magic could keep them safe? Or would he just wait for her to leave and attack again?

Shit shit shit.

"You'll be able to tell when whoever's out there is gone?" she asked and was appalled to hear her voice shook.

Angie pulled her into a hug. "I'll know. Wizards can't hide from me once they've used their magic."

"Is he...is he testing your circle?"

"He tried once and stopped. A gentle, elegant try, though. Whoever he is, he's powerful, and in full control of that power."

Great. A powerful wizard was trying to kill her. For some reason, she thought of Sheldon, whose body had disappeared the morning after Halloween before Jaxer could get to him. Sheldon, who'd tried to steal Deacon's body.

Sheldon, who'd known exactly what Cary was, what Protectors were.

Was he alive? Could this be him? But Angie said this wizard was in control of his power, and Cary had had the impression that, though he was powerful, Sheldon wasn't necessarily a gentle and elegant wielder of magic.

Still, he had known what she was. If he was still alive…

She flexed her fists a few times to try and control the panic crawling over her skin. "Feels weird to be the one being protected," she muttered. "I hate when people try to kill me."

Angie hugged her tighter. "I've got the makings for some really disgusting nachos in the house to make up for no Thai food."

"Nachos are good." As if she hadn't had enough to worry about, now someone was trying to kill her. "I could really use a drink." She sighed as Angie turned her toward the house. She wobbled because her knees were still too shaky to support her. "It's been a weird few weeks."

"Death threats, demons, and new boyfriends will do that. I'll break out the Tequila to go with the nachos."

Cary let the tension in her shoulders relax when Angie closed her front door. "That's the reason we're such good friends."

THE NEXT MORNING, CARY SAT IN AN EXTRA WARM BATH contemplating her hangover. Not much of one at this point. Like all other injuries and illnesses, she got over self-inflicted pain quickly, too. She'd actually slept through the worst of it, except when she woke around four a.m. with a rolling tummy and the room spinning around her bed.

Wine hangovers were the worst. The Tequila probably hadn't helped. She didn't envy Angie this morning. Which was why she was soaking in a tub instead of collecting her car, which she'd left behind in wise favor of a taxi. No point going to Ang's until noon at the earliest. She supposed she could have collected her car without waking her but that might cause her friend to worry given what had happened after she'd arrived last night.

Cary had crawled out of bed long enough to wish her parents goodbye, pretending she wasn't hungover—though she suspected her father realized she was hurting—and wish them a safe drive back to their home on the coast. The three hour drive ensured her parents were close enough for occasional visits, but far enough away Cary mostly had privacy. It was a good arrangement.

She'd gone back to bed and slept another hour before she woke up and couldn't get back to sleep because she'd started to worry again. At that stage, she gave in to the inevitable and made coffee.

Swirling her hands in the warm water, the last of her hangover fading, she mulled over a plan to alleviate some of those worries. Later, she intended to do a little research, try to figure out who was after her. Angie had promised to look into it since the attacker was a wizard. Jaxer might know something, too, especially if this did, by freak chance, have to do with Sheldon. Provided she ever managed to talk to her ass of a mentor again.

She picked herself up out of the tub and dried off. But first, before anything else, she had to pay the bills.

And then that night, she had a date. Her tummy danced at the thought. A date with Deacon. She was both looking forward to it and a little nervous. More than a little now that she didn't have a hangover to dampen the jitters. After spending weeks with him hanging around, she wasn't sure why her nerves were jumping. It wasn't like a real first date when you had to figure out what to talk about. Anticipating his goodnight kiss might inhibit her ability to hold a conversation, though. That would be…interesting.

She'd just finished paying her phone bill online when the front doorbell rang. She glanced at the computer clock. Twelve. Too early for Deacon. He was supposed to pick her up at five—early for a dinner date, but he'd said he wouldn't be able to wait longer than that after a week and a half without seeing her. She wasn't expecting anyone else.

With a frown, she went to the door. She never got Jehovah's Witnesses, missionaries, or salesmen coming to her house thanks to the glamour. She wasn't expecting a delivery and the mailman left packages by the front door anyway. Angie, Lucy, and Marianne were all probably still unconscious. Chris, Cary's computer guru, was out of town. She hadn't heard from Jon and Sally since just before Thanksgiving.

She was almost to the door when the bell started buzzing nonstop, as if someone held a finger to the button. She only knew one person who was that rude.

"Jaxer," she snarled as she threw open the door. "Where the hell have you been?"

The gorgeous blond faery lounged against her doorframe, grinning. "Good to see you again too, sweetie."

He leaned in and kissed her on the mouth before she could blink, ran a finger down her cheek, then walked past her into the house without waiting for permission.

"Jaxer?" She followed him. "What's going on? Where have you been? Do you have any idea what I've had to go through in the last few weeks?"

"That's why I'm here," he said. "We have some things to talk about."

She studied his serious expression, the slight creases on his forehead from his frown. Jaxer never let himself look anything but flawless, yet she could see the strain in his jaw, the lines bracketing his eyes.

"Yeah," she said, "I think we do."

"I've done this many times in the past," he said after a quite minute. "I was actually looking forward to it this time." He shrugged. "Until Deacon showed up."

"What does Deacon have to do with anything?" she asked.

"Side issue. Will we sit?"

Still frowning, she dropped onto the couch, turning to face him when he sat next to her. "This is pretty serious news?"

"Serious enough," he said. "How are thing between you and Deacon, anyway?"

"You're stalling."

"A bit. So?"

"So," she said. "I don't know. We have a date tonight, our first. That'll be interesting since his control is so…iffy."

"Haven't slept with him yet, then?" Jaxer grinned.

"None of your business. And don't look so pleased about that."

His smile grew. "He's suffering. I'm amused."

"I thought you two were friends."

"We are. To a point."

"What point?"

He shook his head. "We'll get to that later."

"You're the one who wanted to discuss this," she said. "What gives?"

Jaxer gave one of his elegant shrugs. "Let's just say, knowing you aren't falling into Deacon's arms makes my day."

"I think you two have some issues to work out."

"Just one."

He held her gaze for a long moment. When she couldn't stand the suspense any longer, she said, "What?"

"You know, Cary, mates…don't always…work out."

She narrowed her eyes. "Meaning?"

What the hell didn't she know? She was sure Deacon hadn't told her everything about the mate business. Maybe Jaxer would.

"I've known couples bound by the mate bond who ended up miserable and hating each other," Jaxer said. "Being mates is no guarantee of a happy future."

"So what are you telling me?"

"Just be careful. I don't want to see you hurt."

"You think Deacon will hurt me?" she asked quietly.

He shook his head. "That's not what I came here to talk about. I've stalled long enough. There's something we need to discuss."

"Okay." Though she fully intended to get back to the previous topic soon.

"You're a week away from entering your seventh year as a Protector."

She nodded. "Something special about this particular anniversary?"

"Very." He reached out and ran a finger along her jaw then rested his hand on the side of her neck. "All Protectors have to spend their seventh year on their own. No more help from their mentors. No more help period. You have to prove you can survive on your own. And if you do… You get the full use of your powers."

Her eyes widened with each word. When he fell silent, she had so many questions pummeling to get out she didn't know where to start. "What…? How…?"

He leaned in and kissed her again, on the mouth, a lingering touch that made her frown deepen. That was a pretty serious kiss for a friendly, calming gesture. She pulled back to glare at him.

"All Protectors have to go through this," he said, his voice low. He tunneled his fingers into her hair and tugged gently. "And we aren't allowed to tell you about it ahead of time. But I've trained you well. You won't have any trouble."

"Alone? You… You won't be around at all? For a year?"

"I'll be around." He cupped her cheek and rubbed his thumb over her cheekbone. "I always intended to stay near. I could never leave you completely alone."

"But if you're not supposed to help…" Her head spun so badly she actually missed her hangover.

"No, you're right," he said. "I won't be able to help. Not really. Not obviously. But do you really think I could stay away from you for a year?"

She shook her head, to dislodge his touch more than to answer his question. "Jaxer, I don't understand. What happens this year? Can the Nags still send me out on assignments, or do I just protect whoever I come across? Will my house still be safe, or do I lose the glamour? Are they going to keep paying me? If you're not supposed to help me, how can you still be around? Is this why you've been acting so weird lately?"

"Weird?" His eyebrows rose.

She rolled her eyes. "You know what I mean. You disappeared and left me to handle Oliver Holland all on my own."

"You were never alone. I've been around the entire time. But you had to know you could be a Protector without my constant supervision."

She leaned back in the couch. "You guys could have warned me?"

"I wanted to," he said. "Believe me. But it's against the rules. You're a damned good Protector, Cary. Amazing really. The others, they have years to adjust, to learn, to develop before they enter their apprenticeships, the six years you've just gone through. You started so late, with nothing but the powers the Nags gave you. And you've been brilliant. One of the best Protectors I've ever trained." He leaned closer, cupping her face with his hand again.

"Jaxer?" She frowned.

"Cary, there's more… I—"

The doorbell rang, cutting off whatever he'd intended to say. She jumped off the couch. Now what?

Whoever was ringing her bell started pounding on the door. Then she heard Sally's voice through the knocking. "Cary? Are you there? Cary, please. I need your help."

She opened the door to a frantic-looking Sally.

"He's gone," she said. "Jon's gone."

ary ushered the panicked mother inside. "Slow down, Sally. Tell me everything."

"He's gone," Sally said, rapid and breathless. "He left a note. He's gone. He took the job. I can't find him anywhere."

"He's gone off with Holland?" Cary asked slowly.

"Yes! He said he'd call me tonight. I don't think he expected me to find the note until later, but I took a few hours off work and came home early."

"What did his note say?"

Sally took a deep breath, letting her gaze travel the room. When she noticed Jaxer, still sitting on the couch, she gasped. "Who are you?"

"A friend of Cary's," Jaxer said, his voice calm and assuring—a tone Cary rarely heard from him. "I help her in her job," he finished.

Cary blinked at her mentor. He looked less…stunning than usual. More like an ordinarily handsome man. The impression made him a lot less intimidating and much more approachable. He must have adjusted his glamour so as not to frighten Sally more. A bit of kindness Cary wouldn't have expected from him.

"It's okay," Cary said to Sally. "You can speak freely in front of him. He knows everything. He can help."

Sally took another deep breath. "Okay. Okay. I got home early from work. I've been worried about Jon since we got back from my parents'. He's been quiet. And last night…I could barely get two words from him. I thought maybe he was having trouble adjusting to…to living normally again. You know, without all the attention." Sally swayed on her feet.

Cary jumped forward and caught her by the shoulders to keep her upright. "You'd better sit down." She led the woman to a chair, plopped her into it then dropped onto the couch next to Jaxer again.

"I got home from work," Sally continued, "and I found this note. Before I even read it, I noticed something beneath it. Two letters. A bill… A final notice. For my car. I… I haven't been able to make the last few payments so they were going to repossess it. The second was from a lawyer. But that was just… I'm having an argument with my landlord. He can't really evict us. I do pay rent. But I haven't told Jon about any of this. I didn't want him to worry."

She ran a hand through her short curls, mussing her already tangled style. "I think…" She paused and swallowed visibly. "I think Jon found the letters and… I don't know. Panicked. If he'd talked to me, I could have explained. I could have told him I have a backup plan. I can get to work on the bus. It wasn't a big deal. I was willing to do without a car if it meant I could send him to college without needing huge loans. And the threatened eviction was a scare tactic, nothing more. I could have explained everything. But he didn't give me a chance."

"What did his note say?" Cary asked.

"That he'd called Holland and taken the job. He said not to worry, and that it was enough money to pay for the car, for the apartment, for everything." Sally's bottom lip shook as she sucked back emotion. "Cary, he's working for a man who tried to kidnap him. You have to go after him. You have to bring him back."

"Did he say where he'd gone? What sort of work Holland wanted him to do?"

Sally shook her head. "He said he'd call. So I know he has his cellphone with him. I tried calling before I came here, but it goes right to voicemail."

"Did you leave him one?"

"Yes! I told him to call me, and I'll come pick him up, wherever he is. His note said he'd be out of town. Out of town! Cary, what am I going to do? Holland could have taken him anywhere."

Cary jerked when she felt Jaxer's hand on her arm.

"I might have an idea where they've gone. Holland's..." He glanced at Sally, then turned back to Cary. "Holland's research center. In the woods to the east of the city, a few miles from the river. Angie told you about it?"

"Research center?" Sally's voice rose to a near scream. "He's going to study my son?"

"No, no, Sally. Calm down." Cary raised her hands, palms out. "Just breathe. That's it. Breathe. Holland isn't studying people. He's looking for something in the woods. We think he wanted Jon's skill to help him find this whatever it is he's looking for."

"You have to go after him, Cary. You have to bring my baby back."

"I will." Cary turned to Jaxer. "My car's at Angie's."

"I'll drive you," Sally said.

"No," Cary said. "You have to stay near home in case Jon calls or comes back. I'll have my cell so you can contact me if he gets in touch."

"Deacon?" Jaxer said.

"He should be back in town by now." Cary nodded. "Do you know where this facility of Holland's is?"

"Tell Deacon to take 184 east." He gave directions to the exit and the following turns. "After about ten miles, you'll see a small logging road to the right. Take that. Twenty miles after that, you'll come to the main body of Holland's workers. His search is focused four miles to the north of that, but you'll have to go over ground to reach the site without being seen. I'll meet you there."

Jaxer had his own way of getting around. She didn't bother questioning it anymore. "Thanks."

He grinned, a charming expression that lacked any hint of glamour. He was out the door even as she picked up the phone to call Deacon.

~

CARY STARED THROUGH THE TREES AT THE SMALL ARMY OF preternatural beings. They were easy enough to see, despite the dark, moonless night, thanks to a series of storm lights surrounding the clearing.

"Great," she whispered. "Just great."

"You knew there'd be a few of them," Deacon said.

He spoke into her ear to keep from being overheard, but the hot brush of his breath made her tummy clench. She shook her head against a wash of desire, annoyed by the reaction she didn't seem to have any control over. No time for that now. She had a kid to save.

"Jon is smack in the middle of them all, though," she said.

She scanned the crowd and noticed the three witches she'd confronted at the beginning of the month weren't there. Neither was Tom the leprechaun. For some reason, that made the situation seem a little better. But not much.

She looked back to Jon. "What's he doing?"

Deacon was silent a moment. Then said, "I think he's calling."

"What?"

"He's using his power. He's calling something."

"How can you tell?"

"Because he's calling so strongly it's pulling at my own animal. Anyone with less control in the area will be shifting and heading this way."

"Oh good," she said. "That's what we need. More shapeshifters. What about the shifters already here?"

"Watch." Deacon nodded to the group. "They're having trouble not changing. That one…the dragon, he's young and less controlled. He's not going to hold out much longer."

Cary's eyes widened. The dragon shifter was the same one who'd tried to kidnap Jonathon off the street all those weeks ago. For some reason, she'd assumed Holland had killed him for his failure. Maybe the demon still had a use for him. Or maybe Holland wasn't strong enough to kill him.

As they watched, she saw the man start to change. A flash of fire shot from his mouth, singeing the ground near a woman who screeched and jumped out of the way. Then his body started to spasm, and he roared, a sound that echoed through the trees like death.

"Holy shit," Cary murmured. "That kid's got some skill."

"But can he control a dragon shifter and still continue to call whatever he's calling?"

She flicked a quick, horrified glance at Deacon as she realized the possible threat, then she turned back to Jon. She had to get to him, distract him. There had to be some way to stop him before all hell broke loose.

Again.

She was getting really tired of hell breaking loose all over her warm summer nights. The fact that it was summertime warm in late November was a little disturbing, but not the most disturbing thing she had to deal with at the moment. As the dragon struggled to regain control of his shape, Cary felt sweat trickle down her back. She could have left her jacket at home. Deacon, in his long black coat, must be sweltering.

"What's with this heat?" she asked.

He shook his head, a movement that brushed his hair against her cheek. "Something to do with the thing Holland is looking for?"

"Can you tell what Jon's trying to call?"

The dragon had settled back down into human shape, but his body continued to jerk at intervals and another stream of fire burst from his mouth.

"No," Deacon said. "Whatever it is, it's resisting. And has been for some time. Jon is wearing out."

Deacon was right. The kid swayed on his feet even as she watched. Holland stood just beside him, staring intently into the trees ahead. The demon reached out a hand to steady Jon, but he didn't take his gaze from the forest.

"Okay, I have a plan," Cary whispered. "You let me protect you, and we'll dodge into the middle of all those scary creatures, scoop Jon up, and run away. Very fast."

"Some of those 'scary creatures' are going to attack you and ignore me if we do that," he pointed out. "You'll be vulnerable."

"I'll be rushing to protect Jon."

"They aren't attacking Jon. They're using him, but he came with them of his own free will. He's doing the job Holland gave him. He's not in danger here. You are."

"He's just a kid, Deacon. He doesn't know what he's doing."

"We need a better plan."

"I'm open to suggestions. Do you want to risk Jon being successful in calling whatever the hell it is he's calling? It'll be something strong, and probably scary, and then I'll have to protect stupid dragon shifters and whatever the hell else is in there from this scary thing."

"Why would you have to protect Holland's soldiers?"

She scowled and rolled her eyes. "Because it's what I do. I never said I liked the job, did I? Seem to recall mentioning being tricked into it." When she heard a soft, suspicious sound from behind her, she turned to glare. "Are you laughing?"

"Of course not."

But even in the dark, she could see his grin. "We'll talk about *that* later," she said. "Now—"

Movement from trees to their left caught her attention. She strained to see into the darkness beyond the storm lamps. The sound of something scraping over dried twigs and pine needles made her skin prickle. The hissing sound made the hair on her nap stand up. Beside her, Deacon growled so quietly it was hard to hear.

What the…?

And then from the trees emerged a creature Cary had assumed was a legend. Its long, scale-covered body slithered along the uneven ground, its forked tongue flickering out, tasting the air as it wound toward Jon. The huge snake's movements were sharp and jerky, like the dragon's had been. Cary spared the dragon a quick glance. He seemed completely in control again.

"Jon's powers are focused on the Naga now," Deacon said, answering her unspoken question. "His call isn't tugging at all of us anymore."

"A Naga?" she breathed. "It's really a Naga?"

The mythical snake people from India were so elusive, Jaxer told her that most thought them extinct. Others claimed the Nagas' underground cities remained, but the Nagas themselves rarely mixed with outsiders. Their cities existed in a realm just offset from this dimension, similar to the way Faery existed in another part of time and space. This helped protected the Nagas and made their cities impossible to find. Without being led to an entrance, where the city linked with this realm, no one could get to them.

For a heartbeat, Cary was tempted to believe the slithering, blue-green creature was nothing more than an ordinary snake. But even as she watched, the Naga's head rose, its body following in a swaying motion. It continued to rise, higher and higher until only the last foot of its tail remained on the ground. The rest of the long, slim body undulated in the air, its black eyes focused on Jon.

Then it started to shift. The snake body contorted and twisted until arms and legs appeared. The body turned and thrashed, emerging as a female human form beneath a snake's head. Finally, the head followed, finishing the full transformation.

When the change was complete, a stunning woman stood at the edge of the clearing. Her hair was dark and thick, hanging down to her knees. Her skin was also a deep shade of brown over bones that looked fine and delicate in the harsh light from the storm lamps. Her face was angular, her eyes dark. A large red ruby rested between her arched brows. She seemed completely unaware of her nudity as she stood before the gaping crowd. Her gaze was for the boy who'd called her and for him alone.

"Now what?" Jon asked. His voice was ragged and gravelly, and he swayed on his feet again even as he stared back at the Naga.

"Ask her how we enter the city, Jonathon," Holland said.

"But I thought you wanted to talk to her?"

"I do. But first I must have the city's location. Then I will try to reason with my lady love."

Cary had to bite back a growl. *Lady love, my ass.*

Bits and pieces of that strange conversation with Holland over lunch came floating back to her. When he'd claimed a man would do a lot for love. Holland was certainly staring at the Naga with a kind of coiled intensity. But if this was the extent he would go to, forcing the woman to come to him against her will, Cary didn't think Holland's feelings qualified as love.

Knowing he wanted entrance to the Naga city also strongly argued against love as a motivational factor here.

"How do we get to the city?" Jon asked the woman.

Her head jerked from side to side, but her gaze remained firmly on his. Finally, she said, "Follow the path I have left."

Her voice sounded hollow and monotone, any personality washed away beneath the force of her compulsion.

"Where is the entrance?" Jon asked.

"Two miles from here," she said.

"And when we reached the entrance?" Holland urged.

"How do we get into the city?" Jon asked.

A tear trickled down the woman's smooth cheek. She bit her bottom lip. Even from a distance, Cary could see blood drip over her narrow chin. The woman's hands clenched and unclenched and her body trembled visibly.

"She's fighting Jon's power," Deacon murmured.

"This has gone on long enough." Outrage nearly choked Cary. The poor woman. Well, now she definitely had someone to protect, and she intended to do it.

She was going to box Jon's ears for this.

As quietly as her human feet would carry her, she eased around the edge of the tree line so she would be closer to the Naga. She stopped suddenly when Deacon's hand landed on her shoulder.

He leaned in close to her ear and whispered, "I have to come in from the opposite direction. The breeze is carrying my scent to the other shifters. The werewolf there in particular. The one closest to us."

Cary looked at Holland's little army again. One man seemed to be darting glances in their direction. "Won't he smell me, too?"

"He'll recognize you as human and not consider you a threat."

Oh good. "Be careful," she said. "I'll meet you in the middle."

Because she could, because in that moment she needed to, she pressed a brief, hard kiss on his lips. Then she moved off again, stepping with care over the dry pine needles.

3 0

As Cary moved, she kept darting glances at the Naga. Holland had moved closer to her and was caressing her cheek, wiping away a tear. His voice was too low to hear, even in the silent forest, but tears continued to stream down the woman's face. Her gaze remained locked with Jon's, but her lips were pressed firmly shut. Still fighting the compulsion. Strong woman.

Cary had an awful feeling the only reason the woman could fight, though, was because Jonathon was exhausted. He'd dropped to his knees and was still swaying under the effort to control her. Scary to think how much power that kid had. When he trained it fully, when he got through puberty and gained the full extent of his powers, Jonathon Webber would be a force to reckon with. She only hoped, by that time, he'd have decided to be one of the good guys.

At that moment, though, Cary was damned glad not to be a shapeshifter.

Through the dark, Holland's voice reached her. She was close enough now to hear even his quite words. "Nira, my love, please don't struggle. It's pointless to fight me, now. I don't like seeing you hurt."

"Bastard," she hissed, then clamped her mouth shut again.

"I still love you, Nira. I want you for my queen. I always have."

Through her teeth, she said, "I will not give you my city."

"Please," Jon said, his voice so rough it sounded an octave deeper. "Just tell him what he wants."

She shook her head, but her gaze remained locked to the boy's.

Cary got as near to the woman as she could while still inside the tree cover. She took a deep breath, spared a quick glance at Holland's soldiers—several were staring in her direction and frowning now—and charged forward with all the speed she could muster. Since she was rushing to protect someone, the speed was significant for a human.

She knocked the Naga to the ground, covering the woman's body as a flash of fire shot over her head. Damned dragon shifter.

She looked into the Naga's wide eyes. "Are you okay?"

The woman nodded, and Cary had a sharp *déjà vu* memory of rescuing Jonathon from the dragon's flames. She smiled at the woman, Nira, and Nira smiled back, though her mouth quivered with the effort.

When the fire died down, Cary looked up, her skin tingling in the aftermath of the attack. The dragon lay in a steaming heap, blood welling from the hole in his chest. Eew. So much for Holland not being able to kill him.

"Such lack of self-control," Holland said into the silence. He turned to stare down at her. "Ms. Redmond. Fancy meeting you here."

She grinned without humor. "I bet you're just thrilled."

"You could have had better timing," he said. "This is a private matter between me and the lady I love."

"Don't give me that crap. You weren't grilling her about her feelings a minute ago. You want her city. Even I know what the Naga cities are supposed to be like. Wealth beyond imagining. Power so mysterious even the myths won't name its nature. Impossible to enter without a guide."

"Yes. I do have an interest in this city."

"Greedy bastard. You're already rich." She glanced at the dead dragon. "And powerful."

"Not rich enough," Holland said. "Never powerful enough. Not to prevent..." He tilted his head to one side. "With the wealth of a Naga city backing me, I can command legions."

"Oh, that's something I'm looking forward to."

"Your sarcasm aside, Ms. Redmond, you're meddling in a matter that doesn't concern you. I will not be chained again. Especially by my own father. I *need* the city." He sucked in a breath between his teeth. "But never mind. I believe I have enough information now to get there. Good thing, too."

He glanced over his shoulder, and Cary followed his gaze. Jonathon lay in a crumbled heap on the ground, looking like a small, wounded animal just run over by a truck. His eyes were closed. And he didn't seem to be breathing.

"No," she whispered.

"Backlash, I imagine," Holland said. "From your…shield? He was straining his powers to get this far. Poor boy. Shame. He'd have been quite a valuable force one day."

Cary glanced at Nira. "Shift and leave, quickly. Go warn your city." Then she scrambled to the fallen boy without waiting to see if the Naga followed her instructions. "Jonathon? Jon?" She sat on the ground and scooped him up into her lap. "Answer me, kid. Come on." She shook him gently then pressed her fingers to his neck. Still had a pulse. She leaned close enough to feel his faint breath on her cheek. "That's it, kid. You're still alive. I just need you to wake up for me."

"Why bother, Ms. Redmond? He's as good as dead. You've killed him."

"Shut up." Cary glared at Holland. "You did this. You brought him here. If not for you, he'd be safe at home in his bed right now. Don't you dare try to pass this off on me."

But guilt still washed through her. She'd rushed Jon out of her house and her protection, she'd let him go and left him vulnerable. She should have called him. She should have gone to see him before he turned to the demon. Damn it, she was supposed to keep people safe.

"My powers didn't kill him," Holland murmured. "Yours did."

"No, they didn't." She blinked back tears. "Come on, Jon. Wake up." Where the hell was Deacon? She shook Jon's inert body again. "Please, kid. Please." When he groaned, she nearly choked on her relief. "That's it. Open your eyes. Good boy."

"I'm not a boy," Jon said in a barely audible wheeze.

"No." Cary grinned as his eyes fluttered and opened. Her throat was so tight she could barely speak. "No, you're not a boy. But you are an idiot."

He tried to smile, but the expression fell away. "I'm sorry, Cary. I didn't mean to hurt anyone. But I was, wasn't I? That's why you had to protect the Naga."

"Yeah. But everything's okay now."

"Are you mad at me?"

She sputtered out a sound that might have been a laugh on a better day, when it wasn't mixed with tears. "No. But your mom's gonna be pissed." She rocked him gently in her arms, fighting back the ill-timed urge to weep.

"We don't have to tell her, do we?" Jon asked.

Cary snorted. "Maybe not all of it."

A heavy sigh brought Cary's attention back to Holland. And she realized Nira hadn't left.

When she met Holland's gaze again, he said, "I can control her now that she's here. I just couldn't get her out of the city."

"Don't do this, Holland," Cary said. "You said you love her. Let her go."

He smiled, a look that sent a chill down Cary's spine. He flicked a glance at the soldiers, all those scary beasties surrounding them, pointed to her and Jonathon and said, "Kill them."

Cary barely had time to register Holland's order before a barrage of powers rained down on her. Fireballs, energy bolts, rocks and twigs swirling up from powerful spells, all pounded the air around her. She curved her body over Jon's and squeezed her eyes shut against the glare of color and light. Sulfur and acid burned the air, singeing her sinuses.

She could feel the power, the strength of so many different magics beating against her skin, making her hair stand up and her pulse race. The strength of all that power was unlike anything she'd had to deal with before, and the pressure of holding it off built under her skin until she felt like her body would break apart. The usual tingles that coursed over her when protecting against magic turned into full blown pain, like her nerves were burning from the inside.

A sound beyond the racket of those spells echoed in her ears. It took her a minute to realize the sound was her, roaring against the attack. In her arms, she could feel Jonathon screaming, but she couldn't hear him anymore.

And then, as suddenly as it had begun, the attack stopped.

Cary blinked in the sudden silence. Spots danced in front of her eyes, and every inch of her skin stung like she'd gotten a severe sunburn. She heaved in a breath over her raw throat and tried to swallow. Then she glanced down at Jon. His eyes were huge, his skin more pale than when he'd been unconscious.

"You hurt anywhere?" she asked.

"N-no." He shook his head and glanced at the surrounding monsters. "But I nearly peed my pants."

"Me, too," she said, not joking.

She continued to keep her body wrapped around Jon's as best she could while she studied the small army circling them. Most were breathing hard, some looked confused, a werewolf and two people she suspected were sorcerers looked really pissed. The wolf was growling and snarling. He wouldn't hold out long before shifting.

Beyond the immediate circle, she saw a few bodies on the ground, a booted foot here, a sprawled hand there. No doubt backlash from her protections. She had a brief thought for whether it was their own power that had got them or the spells of one of the other attackers. It didn't matter either way. Each body meant one less person trying to kill her.

In the darkness beyond the circle of monsters, she caught a glimpse of pale skin and a tall, skinny form moving into the trees. She gasped. Sheldon? But the person she thought she saw was lost in darkness and blocked by other monsters before she could be sure if she'd actually seen anyone at all.

Spots still interfered with her vision. Maybe it was just another skinny teenager and she'd only imagined he looked like Sheldon. She sure as hell hoped so.

There were too many shadows dancing in the uneven light from the storm lamps for her to see the surrounding monsters clearly, and she didn't trust her still blurry vision, but she didn't need sight to feel the waves of menace rolling over her.

This situation was very very bad.

What the hell had happened to Deacon? And Jaxer for that matter? The faery was supposed to have met them but there'd been no sign of him when they arrived. Her heart clenched with a sudden terror—had they already been captured? Or worse?

The sound of clapping startled her back to her surroundings. All eyes turned to the demon. Holland stood over Nira, smiling at Cary. The expression made her stomach roll.

"Ms. Redmond," he said. "I am impressed. And, unusually for me, surprised. You're a Protector. I haven't come across one of your kind in years."

Cary's heart rate tripled and suddenly she couldn't breathe. Holland had been around a long time. If he knew her vulnerability, she was a dead woman.

But to kill her, he was going to have to let Jon and Nira go. Freely and with no intention of going after them once Cary was dead. Protector powers were a tricky thing—fortunately for her. Unfortunately, if anyone could get around her magic, Holland could.

Though by his admission, he hadn't realized what she was before this. So he wasn't likely the one who'd attacked her at Angie's house. Or if he had ordered that attack, it wasn't because he'd realized that Cary was a Protector. She wasn't sure if that was good news or not. If Holland hadn't been responsible for that attack, there was still someone beyond this group of monster who wanted her dead.

She'd have to deal with that later. If she survived this.

She kept her gaze locked on Holland's, her body hunched over Jon, and waited. She refused to confirm or deny his assertion, but they both knew he'd uncovered her secret.

"The problem with Protectors," Holland finally said in a low, quiet tone, "is that they spend all their energy protecting. They come to think they're invincible. And no one is invincible, Ms. Redmond."

Since she didn't consider herself invincible, she couldn't really argue with him. But that meant he wasn't invincible either. She tilted her head to one side as she realized his unintentional meaning.

"Glad to hear it," she said.

He blinked slowly, then turned one hand to examine his nails. "Besides over-confidence—a trait you have in abundance, and which should have given your true powers away earlier—Protectors share a few, very important vulnerabilities."

Oh shit. Here it was. He knew, and he'd figured out a way to use that knowledge to kill her. Her heart hammered and her breathing came in short bursts. She hunched closer to Jon, hoping whatever Holland had in mind for her wouldn't hurt the boy.

"The most important vulnerability as far as I'm concerned," Holland said, his voice even lower now, "is your compassion."

Cary's eyebrows popped up in surprise. What was he getting at?

"Compassion is the thing that makes a Protector. Without it… Well, you'd do something else, wouldn't you? But that great well of empathy for mankind, that drive to keep innocents safe from harm… That weakness is your undoing, Ms. Redmond."

Holland's hand began to glow red and little sparks of power jumped like lightning between his fingertips. She tried to swallow but didn't have any spit left.

"You see, my dear, deluded girl." Holland's smug smile dropped away, leaving stone and ice behind. "The problem you have is that you can't save everyone."

Power shot from his hand and slammed into Nira's chest, making the woman's small body convulse. Her scream rent the night air.

31

"No!" Cary lunged toward Nira to help, despite knowing it was too late. Before she could get up, though, the attack on her and Jon started again.

She had just enough time to see Holland turn into the woods, following Nira's path back to the city, before the battering magics took all her focus. She curled around Jon as the assault beat down on her, unable to see or hear beyond the attack now. Her heart felt like it would burst in her chest. And one or two of the powerful spells got close enough to send small electrical shocks down her spine.

She screamed against the terror and pain of failure, the possibility that she would fail again, and Jon would die. Her body shook with the effort to keep him safe, to do this one thing right. She had no idea how much time passed as she huddled on the forest floor and hoped against hope she'd be able to keep Jon alive.

After a while, she realized the attack was lessening, the number of powers battering her decreasing. Her own shields seemed to rebound as the attack waned, and she could no longer feel the strain so acutely. She heaved in two long, deep breathes and opened her eyes…

In time to see the four remaining soldiers cut down by gunfire. She jerked at the sharp, loud crack of the semi-automatic gun.

And then she saw Deacon moving from the trees, his long coat flowing out from his body like a cloak, his handsome face set in such unflinchingly vicious lines, she actually gasped. His eyes glowed a golden yellow. Before she could take in the fury and bloodlust that had filled his expression, he was beside her, kneeling on the ground and cupping her cheeks in his hands.

"Cary? Cary, are you okay?"

She shook her head. "What…? You have a gun?"

"For situations like this. Trick my mother taught me."

Cary couldn't begin to process that. "Huh?"

His lips lifted, not quite a smile. "Most preternatural creatures forget to protect themselves from mundane weapons during a magical battle. And no one expects a shapeshifter to use something as ordinary as a gun most of the time."

"I'm not sure I'd call an Uzi ordinary."

He brushed his lips over hers, ignoring her exaggerated evaluation of his weapon. Then he glanced at Jon. "You okay?"

"Holland…" Jon gulp in a shaky breath. "He killed her."

Cary's throat closed at the catch in his voice, the terror trembling through the kid's words, and her own failure rose like bile to choke her. She passed Jon to the safety of Deacon's arms and scrambled on her hands and knees to the fallen Naga.

Her beautiful face was motionless, her dark eyes fogged and blank, and a line of red ran from her mouth down her chin and cheek to the leaf-strewn ground. Cary sobbed as she forced herself to look at the wound in the woman's chest, a blackened circle the size of a volleyball carved an inch deep into skin and bone. The stink of burned flesh caused the bile to rise in Cary's throat again. Tears streamed down her cheeks, but she ignored them.

Carefully, she lifted Nira's head to her lap and smoothed her dark hair back from her face. The ruby between her eyebrows winked in the ugly lamplight.

"I'm sorry," she murmured, her voice thick. "I'm so sorry." She rocked against the ache in her own chest, hunched over the woman's head, and let her tears flow.

The feel of a firm hand on her shoulder made her stop rocking. Her body shuddered in one violent jerk, but the warm grip remained in place.

"I couldn't save her," she said. "I tried. But…"

"You've never lost anyone before?" Deacon's voice was quiet and even.

Her tears kept streaming. "I've been terrified of this since becoming a Protector. That I wouldn't be good enough. That I'd fail and someone would die. Now I have."

"Cary."

The sound of Jaxer's voice snapped her head up. The faery stood in front of her, across Nira's body. He tilted his head to one side and sighed. Unable to speak, she looked away, and noticed the others for the first time.

Ten, maybe fifteen men and women surrounded her, most sporting a precious gem of varying sizes between their brows. On the ground, near the dead woman's feet, a giant snake lay in a tall coil. Its forked tongue flickered out to touch Nira's toes. Cary didn't have to ask who the newcomers were.

"They caught me circling back to you," Deacon murmured. "They wouldn't believe I wasn't with Holland until Jaxer arrived and convinced them."

One of the men stepped closer. Something about the shape of his eyes, the curve of his lips looked familiar.

"He's a shifter," the man said. "The demon hired many such creatures to find us."

"Why did you believe Jaxer?" Cary frowned at the harshness of her own voice. She barely recognized the sound.

"Fae are of the earth, like Nagas."

Not much of an explanation. But it didn't matter. She glanced down at the woman still cradled in her lap. They'd all been too late to save her. She sucked in a breath when she realized where she'd seen the man's eyes before. "She was a relative?"

"My sister." He sounded almost emotionless, but she heard the suppressed rage. He held his body carefully still, and his breathing was harsh.

"I'm sorry I couldn't save her," Cary said.

Jaxer knelt beside her, resting a hand on her shoulder, opposite Deacon. "You are a wonderful Protector. But you can't save everyone."

Jaxer's words echoed Holland's, roaring through her head like a ricocheting bullet. She bit her lip and jerked her head in denial. What good was being a Protector if she couldn't save this strong, loyal woman, a woman willing to die to protect her people? What use was all her power if she was powerless to help?

She looked up and locked gazes with Nira's brother. She might not be able to save everyone. But she could damned well try.

"Can you get me to the city entrance before the demon?" she asked. "A short cut?"

"Why?" He frowned, his gaze moving between her and his sister's body.

"Cary, no." Deacon's voice crackled in the quiet clearing. "Jaxer, don't let her try this."

Cary kept her gaze locked with Nira's brother, ignoring Deacon's protest even when his grip on her shoulder tightened. "If I can get between his army and the city," she said, "I can... I can stall them long enough for you to seal the city, to destroy or barricade the entrance. Can you do that? Seal the city off from his entry?"

"We can erect defenses. The leaders might already be preparing for attack after..." His gaze darted down to his sister again, then quickly away. "We can't cut our city off from this realm without forming another link to another location. That takes time and power. But we can make getting through this entrance difficult while we do that."

"Cary, damn it," Deacon said.

"How long do you need?" Cary asked, ignoring Deacon. "Have you started setting up another entrance already?"

Deacon dropped to his knees beside her, took her face in his hands and forced her to look at him. "You can't protect an entire city from an army. You'll be killed."

"She died trying to save her city." Cary glanced down at Nira, then back at Deacon. Past him, in the dim light, she could see Jon swaying unsteadily, his gaze riveted on them. She dropped her voice. "I failed her once. I have to try." She cupped his cheek. "I have to do this."

"No."

"Cary," Jaxer said, "it's never been done before, not by any Protector. You're human. You won't be able to channel power long enough. It will kill you."

Another tear tracked down her cheek, but it was her last one. Anger, determination, sheer stubborn will blanketed her grief. She knew deep in her soul she could hold the army off. At least for a little while. She could give the Nagas time. She *would* give them the time they needed.

"Holland will not get through me." She said each word slowly, distinctly for everyone to hear. Then she shook off all the restraining hands, laid Nira's head gently on the ground and rose.

Deacon launched to his feet and gripped her shoulders. "I can't lose you," he whispered harshly.

"Holland will not enter that city," she said. "If you want to keep me alive, help me."

"How?"

She glanced at Nira's brother. "Can you get Deacon and Jaxer inside the city?"

"Why?" the Naga asked.

She turned back to Deacon. "Help them set up defenses at this entrance while they work to build the new one. They need as much help and power as they can get." She looked at the other Nagas. "We'll split up. I'll go with Nira's brother, you go with the others. Take Jon. We can circle the arm and not give them an easy target before we get there."

"I'm staying with you," Deacon said. "Jaxer can help the Nagas."

"What if Holland uses you against me?" she said. "The way he used Jon. I don't want to lose you either." She held his gaze even as he cursed in frustration. Gripping his forearms, she squeezed. "I'll be stronger knowing you're in the city. I need you and Jaxer to keep Jon with you and protect him. I *need* you to keep Jon safe. So I can concentrate. If I'm afraid for you or him..."

When he shook his head and looked away, she gripped his arms tighter until he looked back at her.

"I have to stand alone, with no distraction. I can do this, Deacon." She leaned closer and dropped her voice. "I will do this."

He stared at her for a long, quiet moment. She knew this went against his every instinct. Following her plan would mean allowing the possibility of her death, and for those few silent seconds, she feared he wouldn't have it in him to let her take the risk.

Then, with a sudden jerk, he pulled her close, kissed her hard and pushed her away again. "Go. Before I change my mind."

She managed a slight, wobbly smile, and turned to follow Nira's brother and one other Naga male.

"Cary."

Deacon's voice stopped her at the edge of the tree line. She glanced over her shoulder. He stood with his hands on Jon's shoulders. Beside him, Jaxer rose slowly to his feet. All three men looked…worried.

"Don't die," Deacon said.

She nodded then plunged into the trees.

3 2

The journey through the forest was dark and difficult for an ordinary human woman, but Cary kept up with the two Nagas as best she could. Her jacket caught on branches, a stray limb tore a slit in her jeans, and her boots felt heavier with each step. She ignored all the discomforts and concentrated on jogging after her guides.

At one point, they stopped and Nira's brother raised his hand for silence. She gulped in air as quietly as she could. His head wove from side to side and his tongue—forked even in human form—flickered out to taste the air. The other Naga remained silent, waiting. Then Nira's brother motioned them in a new direction.

They came out of the trees at the edge of a large river bed. A steady stream of water, no more than a foot deep and two feet wide flowed down the middle of the bed. The Nagas led her into the water, then turned to walk upstream. Nira's brother held her wrist to keep her close.

Her boots squelched. Her socks and the lower part of her jeans clung wetly to her calves and feet. But at least the water was cool, and the stream easier to traverse than the thick trees and underbrush.

She turned her wrist so she could squeeze her guide's hand. Without slowing, he looked over his shoulder.

Her foot slipped on a slick stone. She regained her balance and whispered, "Why are we walking through water? To throw off the scent?"

He shook his head and gestured toward the woods bracketing the river bed.

She gasped. Running along the bank, just inside the tree line, were two large wolves. They stopped and stared right at the spot where Cary and the two Nagas were standing. Sniffing the air, they turned their heads, looking up and down the river. Then the front wolf made a soft whining noise and shook its head. Both animals ran back into the trees.

"They saw us?" Cary murmured, her heart pounding.

"No," Nira's brother said and continued upstream.

"No?"

"We are not visible as long as we remain in the water."

Wow. Cool trick.

Several more members of Holland's army crossed their path, but the Naga's magic held and they were never spotted. She wondered if Deacon and his escort were doing the same thing to avoid the army.

Finally, after a long pause to taste the air, Nira's brother led her out of the water and back into the trees. They picked up the pace, stretching out into a loping jog with Nira's brother in front and the other Naga taking up the rear. Cary focused on the ground and tried not to trip. One more tree branch caught her as they ran, slashing a thin line across her cheek. She fingered the blood and sighed. Chances were good this wouldn't be the only blood she shed tonight.

The Nagas stopped suddenly and she bounced off Nira's brother's back. She had to catch herself on a tree to keep from falling.

"Sorry," she muttered. "Are we here?"

He pointed to a rocky out-cropping which looked like a dozen others they'd passed. "This is it."

The second Naga male who hadn't spoken during the entire journey had shifted to his snake form while she wasn't paying attention. He slithered past her, into the rocks, disappearing into the mounds. She couldn't see any cracks to indicate an actual entrance, though.

"Which direction does the city spread from the entrance?" she asked, still frowning at the rocks.

Nira's brother traced an arch with one arm.

"So between this entrance and the direction Holland's coming from, there's no part of the city?"

"No. Is that important?"

She shook her head. "I just like visualizing what I'm protecting. It helps me focus while I'm channeling the power." She shrugged her jacket off and wiped a hand down her face. "Why the hell is it so hot?" she muttered to herself.

"That's caused by our defenses," the Naga supplied. "And the power we're exerting to establish another link to this realm."

"You said you can't close this entrance before doing that. Why?" So much of Naga lore was conjecture and uncertain, she wasn't sure if anything she knew about them, the few facts she had, were even true.

"Without some link to this realm," he said, "our city will die. We need the earth, water, and energy we get from this realm to maintain our position outside of it."

"And it takes a lot of time to form the new link?" she asked.

"And a lot of our energy. Between that and the defense against the demon's army, we have been using a lot of magic. The demon has been probing the area for many weeks now. His sorcerers and wizards have dried the skies and forced the rivers to run low."

That explained the unseasonably dry weather the last couple of weeks.

"We require the water for our magic," he continued. "So without it, we're at risk. But we couldn't let the demon find our city. To remain hidden, we had to tap into ancient rituals from our place of origin."

Cary frowned. "And that's causing this heat?"

He almost smiled, though the expression didn't convey much amusement. "India magic is hot magic."

She didn't really understand, but there wasn't enough time to question him further. Instead, she asked, "What's your name?"

"Zakin."

"Zakin, thank you for your help." She glanced at the entrance again. "Can you tell if Deacon and the others have come this way yet?"

"They are inside." When she frowned, he said, "The other Naga with us confirmed this after he went in." At her continued frown, he added, "We have a form of communication that isn't audible to humans, more to do with vibration and taste than actual sound."

"Ah." That sort of made sense. Knowing Deacon, Jon, and Jaxer were safe inside the city eased some of her worry.

She glanced at the trees, in the direction she knew Holland was coming from. "You'd better get inside, too," she said. "The army will be here soon." She could almost hear them now, though she suspected Zakin had an even better sense of where the invaders were. She glanced back to see him staring at her.

"Why are you doing this?" he asked.

"It's what I do." More quietly and without meeting his gaze, she said, "And I owe this to Nira because I couldn't stop Holland from killing her."

Without another word, Zakin shifted to a giant, green and black-scaled snake. The creature hovered a moment, his body upright and swaying in the air. The ruby between his brow ridges winked in the darkness from a light of its own. His clothes hadn't ripped away, like Deacon's did if he shifted while fully dressed. Zakin's clothes had changed with him, blending into the snake's scaly hide. Deacon would be jealous of that skill.

The snake swung away and disappeared into the rocky out-cropping with a whispered hiss of scales across stone. Cary barely had time to watch his tail disappear through a fissure in the rocks when she heard movement in the woods behind her. She placed herself between the entrance and the sound of tramping feet and waited.

She didn't have to wait long.

Light from more storm lamps accompanied the small army. Holland emerged from the midst of the group and glared.

"Persistent little bitch, aren't you, Ms. Redmond?" he said.

Her answering smile was more of a snarl. "You have no idea."

"This would be much less painful for you if you simply stepped aside."

"Not gonna happen. You're not welcome here."

"The city is mine."

"You're going to have to get through me first." She spoke in a matter-of-fact tone that made Holland growl.

"Fair enough," he said.

He motioned sharply with his left hand, and a man Cary hadn't seen before stepped from the shadows.

The man was beautiful, so perfectly sculpted he looked unreal. His hair was a dark fall of silk, his eyes a blazing green, his lips generous and red against his pale skin. High cheekbones, a straight nose, all combined to create a creature of such unflawed masculine beauty, he could be only one thing.

A vampire.

A wave of nausea rolled through her stomach. Deliberately, she met his gaze. "Gabriel's gonna be pissed when he finds out you're working for a demon," she said.

The creature chuckled, a low vibration that hummed over her skin, making the hair at her nap prickle.

"You know the Master of Portland?" he asked.

"By reputation only," she allowed.

"A significant reputation, I understand."

Odd phrasing. "It would have to be to overthrow Ariel. Her, I did meet."

"And survived?"

Cary shrugged, holding her ground as the vampire sauntered closer. "Ariel and I had an understanding," she said. Another thick hit of nausea punched her. She swallowed, kept her jaw clenched against the feeling, and watched the creature as he neared.

"Indeed," he said. "As I'm sure you and I can come to an understanding."

"I don't deal with underlings."

His eyes flared yellow for a brief moment then settled into that sparkling green again. Cary's stomach turned.

"I am no underling," he said. "I am Antonio."

A faint scent of rotting meat brushed past Cary. She gagged. "If that's supposed to mean something to me, I'm sorry but it doesn't. Don't really follow vampire society. But, Antonio, you're working for a demon. That would appear to qualify you as an underling."

"I do not work *for* anyone." He stepped to within a foot of her, near enough that one lunge would close the distance. "I work only for myself."

She raised a brow and darted a glance at Holland. "Seems like you're just following orders."

"I have allies, of course. Wise men do. And Holland recognizes the advantages of an alliance with one such as myself."

"Yeah, like what? Calling down the wrath of the Master of the Portland?"

Antonio laughed softly, and Cary felt like bugs were crawling under her skin. She took in a long, slow breath. What the hell was wrong? The vampire shouldn't have been able to affect her with his powers. But her nausea, the itching skin, the difficulty she had holding his gaze weren't normal. Not with an ordinary vampire.

"Gabriel's wrath means little to me," he said. He stretched out one pale hand toward her cheek.

When he was a few inches from touching her, his fingers began to smoke and a bright white circle of light cupped his hand. Cary gagged again, nearly doubling over as her stomach rebelled. Antonio continued to reach toward her for a second longer, then snatched his hand back with a snarl.

Her stomach settled somewhat, but she still felt like she might throw up. She settled her hands on her hips and concentrated on breathing. Antonio surged closer but hit the invisible barrier that protected her and was forced back a step. Cary pressed a palm to her stomach and clenched her jaw.

Through her teeth, she said, "You might want to stop that before I barf on your shiny black loafers."

He snarled and reached for her again. This time both his hands burst into flame. Cary watched in fascination as he put distance between them and shook the flames out.

"Wow," she said. That was a stronger reaction than most vampires got when they came up against her Protector magic. Usually, they just got flung backward. But flames after so brief a contact with her shield? Flames only happened with sustained contact. Or if the vampire was extraordinarily powerful. Which meant… "You're a Master," she said, finally catching on.

Antonio sketched an ironic bow, then studied his hands with a frown. As she watched, the pale flesh healed, restoring his hands to their former glory.

"What the hell are you doing here?" she asked without really expecting an answer. And she wasn't disappointed.

"Antonio," Holland stepped forward again, "I thank you for your efforts. But before she burns you more severely, perhaps we should try a different method."

Antonio glared at her. Then slowly, he smiled, revealing viciously pointed canines. "Some other time, Ms. Redmond. If you manage to survive."

Oh great. That's what she needed, a Master vampire with a pride-grudge against her. But, as he said, she'd have to survive this stand-off first.

"Heaven forbid," Holland said, chuckling as the vampire disappeared into the shadows. A few of Holland's other soldiers glanced nervously at each other.

She'd make a bet they weren't nervous about her.

She faced Holland again. Suddenly, and without warning, a bolt of blue-white electricity shot from his hand and slammed against her barrier. The shot ricocheted into the army and one small, skinny man who looked vaguely mole-like didn't move fast enough to avoid it. The ball of energy hit him in the chest. He screamed and blew apart, scattering bloody chunks across the nearby trees and those soldiers unlucky enough to be standing too close.

Cary swallowed hard and looked away. "That was really gross."

She wasn't sure how she felt about her powers ricocheting an attack back on an innocent bystander like that. Granted, the guy was in this group, so he probably wasn't so innocent. But usually her powers either absorbed an attack or bounced it back on the attacker.

Knowing the skinny little man would have tried to kill her given the chance only made her feel a little better about the fact that he was now scattered in pieces on the forest floor.

"You channel power well, Cary," Holland said.

She blinked in surprise. He'd dropped the formality of calling her Ms. Redmond. That couldn't be good.

"The few others like you I've met couldn't keep channeling their protective magic for long," he continued, "not while using their offensive skills." He tilted his head. "You don't try to strike back, though. You just—" he gestured vaguely in her direction, "—stand there."

She didn't know what to say to that, so she kept her mouth shut. She knew she was unique among Protectors for being so fundamentally normal, but she never considered how her sheer ordinariness would affect the way her magic worked.

She wanted to ask what had happened between Holland and these other Protectors but was afraid of the answer.

"The others all died," Holland said, as if reading her mind. "As will you."

"Well, yeah, eventually," she said. "Us mortal-types always do after a while. It's called aging."

"Do you suppose you're being funny?" he asked.

She shrugged. "I'm entertained by me."

"I'm glad you're so amused only moments before your death."

"Yeah." She grinned without humor. "Me, too. But it's gonna take my death to get at this city. Oliver."

He raised a single brow. "As you wish."

3 3

*P*ower slammed at Cary, first from Holland, then one by one, the sorcerers and wizards joined him. Cary lifted a hand to shield her eyes from the glare of light created by the spells. She gasped when a large, hairy shape bounced off her barrier just to the left. From the corner of her eye, she watched the werewolf shake itself then lunge again.

Another blast of fire fountained off her shield and she realized with a start there was another dragon shifter in the group. Given how rare they were, that stunned her.

The powerful magics combine with the lunging physical attacks from shifters and other creatures she couldn't quite see battered at her. She could feel every jolt and hit, dully so they didn't hurt much, but with enough force to steal her breath. One volley hit so hard, she was forced backward a few steps.

She steady herself by sheer will, braced her legs farther apart, and ducked her head, leaning into the pressure of the attack as it continued in ever increasing intensity. She flung her hands out to the side, balancing herself as best she could.

Panting, she realized with a start that she could feel her Protector barrier more distinctly than ever before. Usually, she accepted its presence and strength on faith and practice. It was just there. She'd felt the rebound of power and the tingling along her skin after the magic had worked. She'd been hurt through the protections, which according to Liruk was somehow Cary's fault. She'd even seen the shield visibly flaring to meet certain attacks. But in six years, she'd never actually felt the barrier *itself*.

With the feel of the shield, she became aware of the power channeling through her, the vibrations of it in the soles of her feet, tingling up her fingertips, bubbling in her blood like carbonation.

She gasped.

The attack's intensity increased. She could practically see her shield moving closer now, leaving less and less space between her vulnerable human body and the barrage of weapons hammering her. She dropped to one knee, ducking her head. The air around her crackled and blazed. Breathing got harder, as if the magic sucked away all available oxygen. The stink of sulfur and roasting hair and flesh mixed with the sweet scent of burnt pine needles.

Through the din, she heard Holland's voice. "More. She's faltering."

Cary gulped in what little air she could. And her barrier moved closer.

She was going to fail. Again. There were too many of them, with too much power, and they wanted the city too badly.

Gritting her teeth, she flexed her muscles and willed herself to hold on, hold out just a little longer. Give the Nagas time to secure the city. She had to protect them, as long as she could. She *had* to.

The tingling in her system that she now recognized as her magic swirled and heaved. Without thought, she focused on the power she knew came from outside herself and yet was as much a part of her now as her own blood and bones. She drew on the power, heaved in a breath, and on the exhale forced her barrier out an inch. Another breath, another exhale, another willed inch.

She squeezed her eyes shut and focused on the shield. If she could just force it back another few inches, she'd be able to breathe, she'd be able to hold out for a few more minutes.

Another push, another two inches. Better. The attack felt more like mid-sized rocks than boulders pummeling her now. She concentrated on gaining another few inches and the rocks became pebbles. With a groan, she forced herself back to her feet, and gained another few inches. Splaying her hands, arms stretched out to the side, she heaved—

And gained a foot.

The pebbles became sand.

Cary took a deep breath and blinked open her eyes. Holland's eyes blazed red in the darkness. His hands crackled with preternatural fire. When he pointed that fire at her, the shock of impact against her barrier knocked her backward a step.

She planted her feet, clenched her jaw, and let the power bubbling in her blood rise. From the distance, she thought she heard someone shouting her name.

Her gaze locked on Holland, she sucked in a deep lungful of air and held it as the Protector magic flowed through her faster and faster, feeding her barrier in a stream of effervescent energy. She couldn't feel the attack any more, but then she couldn't feel much of anything beyond the power flowing through her veins.

A few inches more. Another foot. And she could hold out as long as it took. Pulling on all the energy rolling through her, flooding her shield, she gave one, huge shove.

Heat and light exploded forward, carried by a shockwave of energy. The pale purple pulse spread like an expanding bubble but with the battering force of a moving mountain. Those of Holland's army still standing were leveled, cut down like so much grass. The screams stopped abruptly when the power flowed over them. Cary shook as the bubble expanded, farther into the woods, running over the few soldiers who tried to escape.

And then, suddenly, the bubble burst, spilling power and light into the soil like water.

As the light dimmed, the only sound in the forest was Cary's harsh breathing.

Very slowly, she sank to her knees. Exhaustion like she'd never felt dragged her limbs down until she thought maybe gravity had doubled while she wasn't looking. She blinked away the spots in her eyes but couldn't find the energy to turn her head when she felt a warm body settle on the ground beside her.

"Cary?"

Firm hands cupped her cheeks and provided the power for head movement. Deacon stared at her with wide, golden eyes.

She smiled. Or at least tried to. "Hi," she said.

"Hi." Without another word, he pulled her into his arms, hugging her tight.

She snuggled against him with a contented sigh. "Did you demolish your clothes again?" She rubbed her cheek against his bare chest.

Kissing the top of her head, he said, "No. I was stripping so I could shift and come help you. Jaxer stopped me."

She nodded but couldn't think clearly enough to decide if it was good or bad Jaxer had stopped him. She pressed her lips to his chest, wrapped her heavy arms around his waist and hugged him close, or at least tried to with limbs that felt like rubber.

"Cary?" he asked.

"Hmm?"

"What did you do?"

"No idea." She waved vaguely toward the flattened soldiers. "Not even sure if they're dead or alive. Pretty good trick though, huh?" Her brain was so clouded with exhaustion she thought she might pass out soon. She had a hard time keeping her eyes open. Part of her did wonder what she'd done, but she was simply too tired to think about it now. She'd wonder about it more later.

"Since you're still alive?" Deacon said. "Yes, it was a good trick."

She closed her eyes and let him rock her, vaguely aware of the sound of shuffling feet and the hiss of scales moving over the ground behind her. She only forced her eyes open when she felt Deacon tense.

Jaxer stood over them, but his gaze was turned to the downed army. She glanced in the same direction, noted the Nagas moving over and between the bodies, then looked up at Jaxer again.

"Are they dead?" she asked.

"Some," he said. "Not all."

"Holland?"

Jaxer turned his attention to Zakin bending over Holland's inert body.

"He's still alive," Zakin said.

The hint of satisfaction Cary heard in his voice made her turn away. That tone did not bode well for Oliver Holland. A dark shape threw a shadow across her face, and she looked up to see Zakin standing over her.

They locked gazes for a long moment. Then the Naga blinked, a slow, careful flick of the lids. He dipped his head. "Nira would be grateful for all you did to help our city. You have our thanks. And our debt."

Without waiting for her response, which she was really too tired to make anyway, he returned to Holland's body where several other Nagas hovered and talked too quietly to be heard.

"Jaxer, what the hell did I do?" she murmured.

Her mentor frowned down at his feet before meeting her gaze. "I have no idea. No other Protector in the history of Protectors has ever managed something like that, not using Protector magic or even their own powers while still channeling Protector shields. And you don't have anything else but Protector magic—which doesn't work offensively. At least, not like this." He nodded to the downed army.

"Meaning?" she asked.

"You shouldn't be able to tap into Protector magic directly and use it like a weapon."

"I did that?"

He gestured at the fallen army again. "What else would you call this?"

"But how?"

"I don't know."

If she'd had the energy, she'd have rubbed her forehead. "But…"

"Maybe we should find a more comfortable place to discuss this," Deacon said. "Sally will want to know Jon is safe."

Jon must have decided that was his cue. He appeared from nowhere and threw himself at Cary, burying his face against her shoulder and hugging her tight.

Between Deacon's arms and Jon's, she felt enveloped in relief. She wrapped one arm around Jon and patted his back.

"I'll help the Nagas clean up," Jaxer said, "then meet you back at Cary's place." He dropped a gentle hand on her head, held her gaze for a long moment, then walked into the forest with the Nagas.

ONCE THEY GOT JON HOME, IT TOOK A GOOD TEN MINUTES TO TALK HIM into letting Cary go. He held her hand even as he lunged into his mother's arms. Cary spent another ten minutes convincing Sally and Jon they were safe now. Finally, mother and son allowed her to leave. Once Sally had her son all to herself, Cary figured it would be a while before either could let go. She left them to their tearful reunion and let Deacon drive her home.

The dogs launched themselves at her as soon as she opened the door, almost as if they knew she'd been in trouble. Buck and Pickles probably had. She dropped to her knees, hugging and kissing them all, even letting them take a few licks at her face.

"Good to be back," she murmured into Buck's thick, golden fur. Fred stuck his head in her lap. And Pickles let loose a bone deep, "Woof."

As Deacon helped her to her feet, she asked the question she'd been afraid to voice in the forest. "What do you think the Nagas will do with Holland?"

"Nothing nice, I'm sure," Deacon said. "But nothing he doesn't deserve." He settled onto the couch and pulled her onto his lap.

Leaning close, she drew in the warm scent of him and closed her eyes. "I don't feel the slightest urge to try and protect Holland from the Nagas, even if they torture him. Is that bad?"

"No."

She smiled at the complete lack of hesitance in his voice. Then, "I killed a lot of people…creatures…people tonight."

"None of them were good people. They committed suicide by being there. You didn't kill them."

"This isn't like the other times when people got killed by the backlash of their own powers." She spared a brief thought for Sheldon who might have actually survived his backlash. Then shoved that problem away for another day. "A few tonight did that," she said. "Or maybe they were caught in the backlash of someone else's power. But I did something. I don't even know how I did it…"

Deacon cupped her cheek and lifted, raising her gaze to his. "You were still protecting, and they still, essentially, killed themselves. By being there with Holland and attacking you without mercy." He swiped a tear as it rolled down her cheek. "Besides, if you hadn't killed them, I would have."

She smiled at his admission. "So what do you think I actually did do?"

He shrugged. "Don't ask me. I'm just glad you're alive." He kissed her lightly, then kissed her again, deeper.

The last remaining dregs of tension ease from her bones.

She surfaced with a contented sigh, then she settled her head on his shoulder and let her eyes drift shut again. "Not exactly the plan for our first date, was it?"

He chuckled. "We'll get it right one of these days."

"Whatever I did tonight," she said quietly, "I'm not sure I could do it again. I don't really remember *how* I did it. And I'm so bone weary now, I could sleep for a week."

"I'm sure Jaxer will figure it out."

"But what if he can't? Or what if he's not supposed to find the answer because of this stupid seventh year thing?"

Deacon made a small sound and rubbed a hand down her spine. "He told you finally."

She sat up. "You knew about this. When you said you'd explain what was wrong with Jaxer in a few weeks… You knew I was about to be cut loose?"

He didn't answer, but he didn't have to. She could see it in his slight frown and the creases on his brow.

She slumped. "What am I going to do? On my own, without his help, without anyone…"

"I'll be with you," Deacon said. "No matter what. I'm not going anywhere. You'll never be on your own."

Cary stared for a long, unblinking minute into his beautiful golden eyes. Then she leaned close and kissed him.

Who knew rescuing a black cat on Halloween would lead to all this? But she could imagine a lot worse things than having Deacon Jones standing beside her.

"By the way," he murmured against her mouth. "My mother invited us to come stay with them for New Years. She's very intrigued and really wants to meet you. I told her I'd try to talk you into the trip."

Cary's eyes widened, but before she could say anything, he kissed her again.

Meet Deacon's mother?

Oh boy.

I hope you enjoyed the first novel in the Cary Redmond series! There's plenty more adventures with Cary and Deacon ahead. Also, don't miss the short stories about how Cary met some of the important people (and pets!) in her life. Watch out for those throughout the coming year. For release updates and the occasional free read, you can join my newsletter here: http://eepurl.com/OxQQL. In the meantime, please keep reading for an excerpt from book 2, The Trouble with Ghouls and Serial Killers.

Thank you!

~Kat

THE TROUBLE WITH GHOULS AND SERIAL KILLERS

A CARY REDMOND NOVEL, BOOK 2
EXCERPT

1

$\mathcal{C}$ary Redmond stretched, blinked her eyes open, and frowned up at the faces of her three best friends and her smallest dog Fred hovering over her. Fred woofed and licked her face.

"Ugh, Fred." She wiped her cheek. "You know you're not allowed up here."

Fred barked happily and jumped away.

"You're awake," Lucy cooed in her little girl voice.

"Finally," Marianne said, shaking her head.

"You had us worried," Angie added, her deep voice tinged with relief.

Cary sat up, looking around. "What the hell happened?"

She was in her own bedroom, lying on her own bed—she glanced down—wearing her own pajamas. Nothing seemed out of order except for her friends all being there. Her Labrador, Buck, and her basset hound, Pickles, were sitting at either side of her bedroom door, just inside the room, guarding the entrance as only a demon dog and a foo lion could. Fred plopped down next to Pickles, his tongue lolling out to one side.

She frowned at her little dog pack. They didn't usually sleep in her bedroom, even if they were guarding her.

She tunneled her fingers through her hair, encountering tangles and a loosened hair band about to fall out. She didn't precisely remember going to bed, but she felt wonderful. Fully rested. She double checked… Nope, no sore spots, aches, or pains. That was unusual. She tried thinking back to the last thing she remembered.

"You've been asleep for a little over three days," Marianne said, as if reading Cary's mind.

Which was unusual since Angie was the psychic, and Marianne made magic clothes.

"Three days!" Cary groaned. "Three days?" No wonder she felt so well rested. "What time is it?"

"Four in the afternoon," Lucy said.

"What day?" Cary asked.

"Sunday," Marianne said.

Cary gaped at her friends. "How long have you all been hovering over me?"

"Jaxer didn't tell us you were hurt until last night," Lucy said, her tone accusatory, but in her high, soft voice it just sounded like a cute little pout.

Lucy was petite, red-headed, had dark brown eyes, pale freckled skin, and was a multi-blackbelt wielding marshal artist who could fell men more than twice her size—often several of them at once. Most people mistook her voice as a sign she was a push over. They were always wrong.

Marianne sat at the edge of the bed next to Cary. Her expression soft and understanding as she patted Cary's hand. But there were creases around her dark eyes and bracketing her mouth, marring her normally smooth dark skin.

"You're okay now," Marianne said quietly. "We're here to look after you."

"Okay, someone needs to tell me what's going on," Cary said. "Marianne is being too calm and sweet."

That made the seamstress grin. "Well at least we know you're feeling more yourself," she said.

"When wasn't I?" Cary asked, rubbing her forehead. "I can't

remember coming to bed, nonetheless sleeping so long. Shouldn't I feel, I don't know, stiff or something?"

"It was a healing sleep," Angie said. The tall, lithe, super powerful witch was currently straightening up the few pieces of dirty clothes scattered across Cary's floor. "Jaxer didn't call us after that thing with the demon or we would have been here sooner to look after you," she added.

"Thing with a demon?" Cary frowned. Oh! Right. Oliver Holland. Everything came flooding back, including the fact that she'd used her powers in a way that wasn't supposed to be possible.

Being a Protector wasn't something that just came naturally to a person, and it most certainly hadn't been part of Cary's life plan. She'd been a perfectly ordinary human until six years ago. Then she'd saved a puppy from a demon and somehow ended up working for a group of North American Fae, whom she'd nicknamed the Nags because they were.

They imbued Protectors with their powers, powers that were purely defensive, and helped to keep innocents safe. Cary could now jump in between a bad guy and a good guy and the magic the Nags had given her kept the bad guys from hurting the good guys. She was like a walking, talking Kevlar vest. Which was handy when a rogue demon kept sending scary people after the kid she'd been protecting.

But Protectors couldn't *use* that power. The magic just happened, Protectors channeled it, and everything was good.

Except she'd somehow managed to do more than just channel it.

"Did Jaxer explain what happened?" she asked, sitting up a little higher in bed. Jaxer was her faery mentor, the person she'd most relied on since becoming a Protector, even if she did occasionally want to kill him.

"Not much," Marianne said. "Just that you did something impressive, and it knocked you out. Took too much out of you to handle the power the way you did."

"Damn." Cary had been awake after the face off with Holland. She remembered coming home, and... "Deacon!" He'd been with her.

Deacon Jones was a leopard shifter who had gotten it into his head that they were mates, even though it wasn't supposed to be possible and she still wasn't sure he knew what he was talking about. He was also Greek-god-gorgeous, and sexy, and occasionally scary, but mostly she kind of liked him. Which went against every self-preservation instinct she had and everything she'd learned about preternatural sex gods in the last six years.

"We were supposed to go on our first date." Cary huffed. The incident with Holland had interrupted that. "He was here when I came home. Did you meet him?" She looked up at her friends.

All three women made faces ranging from annoyed to frustrated. It would have been comic if Cary wasn't still trying to piece together the last few days.

"Jaxer was here when we got here," Lucy said. "Apparently, Deacon got called away on family business yesterday afternoon and didn't want to leave you alone, so Jaxer called in the cavalry."

"Us," Marianne said with a cheeky grin.

"Thanks," Cary said, smiling back. "So Deacon was here then? The whole time?" She could still smell him faintly in the room. The fact that they hadn't been on a date yet—or slept together—but her room smelled like him was…a lot more comforting that it should have been. She scowled at that. It was supposed to be irritating and disturbing. Damned man had wormed his way into her life and she was getting too used to him.

"Deacon and Jaxer both apparently," Angie said, coming back to the bed and sitting opposite Marianne.

Lucy jumped up on the edge of the bed, sitting on her knees like it was natural. Which for Lucy it was. "Neither of them saw fit to call us sooner, or we would have been here too," she assured.

Cary grinned. She had very good friends. With a sigh, she glanced around. "Three days." It was the longest healing sleep she'd ever had. "Well, I probably shouldn't do that with my powers again, huh? Whatever the hell I did."

"Don't remember?" Angie asked.

"Nope." Something else of the day came back to her and she groaned, dropping back against her pillow and putting her hands to her eyes. "Did Jaxer mention this seventh year business to any of you?" she asked, peaking at them from between her fingers.

The pointed silence made her drop her hands and stare at them. Maybe she didn't have such good friends after all.

Angie raised a hand. "Not before yesterday," she said, calming Cary's fears. "I would have warned you if I'd known. Especially after that wizard tried to kill you. Just before the demon did." Angie scowled. "You might have too many people trying to kill you."

"I agree," Cary said adamantly. "What did Jaxer say about the seventh year?"

"That you were gonna be on your own," Lucy said. "But you won't be. You've got us."

"And we sure as hell won't leave you out to dry like those Nags," Marianne added. "I've already started some new clothes for you, with the extra good magic in them." She grinned and wagged her eyebrows.

Cary launched up and hugged Marianne. Which started a group hug as her girlfriends surrounded her. From the door, Pickles let loose a deep, reverberating woof that Cary interpreted as happiness.

When the friends parted, Angie ducked her chin and met Cary's gaze. "Seriously, though, how do you feel?"

Cary shrugged. "Great. Better than I usually feel after a big job and almost getting killed."

Unusually for her, this particular job hadn't involved any trips to the ER, and that was always a bonus. She hated trying to explain her weird injuries to the hospital staff, because they were never what they should have been when one was, say, shot or broke their toe kicking a vampire.

"No sore muscles?" Lucy asked.

"Headaches? Tingling in strange places?" Angie asked.

Cary chuckled at that. "Nope, no tingling." Mostly because Deacon wasn't around.

"Nothing else bothering you?" Marianne asked.

"No. I'm good. Hungry." Actually now she thought about it, she was starving.

"Deacon left some bagels in the fridge," Lucy said with a grin.

"Apparently, he left donuts too," Marianne said, "but Jaxer ate them all."

"Bastard," Cary said.

"Right?" Marianne said in obvious agreement. She and Cary shared a similarly eager sweet tooth.

"That was nice of Deacon, though," Angie said, looking at Cary expectantly.

"He does that a lot actually," Cary said. "He brought me bagels and donuts every morning for most of last month."

"He's feeding you," Marianne said in approval. "Must be serious."

"We'll see." Cary wasn't sure how to feel about this thing with Deacon yet. But she did like the bagels and donuts. "We should probably go out on an actual date first, though."

"Demon hunting doesn't count," Marianne agreed.

"It could, under the right circumstances," Lucy said.

Cary laughed. Then she sighed. "I'm so glad you guys are here. I had a rough week last week." She frowned. "Actually, a rough day. And a lot of sleep." She shrugged. "But it's good to have you here."

"Come on," Angie said, patting her leg. "Let's feed you and get you cleaned up. Then we'll get you out of the house for a little fun. You've earned it."

"What do you have in mind?" Cary asked as she rolled out of bed.

"Dancing!" Lucy and Marianne said in unison.

Marianne's girlfriend owned a small but popular nightclub in Old Town. On a Sunday night, when Cary might have expected it to be quiet and half empty, the place was packed to the rafters for 80s night. A mix of 80s pop favorites blared from the speakers and people of all ages crowded the dance floor in the middle of the club's first level. The upper area was little more than a circling gallery with tables and seats scattered around, and a great view of the people below.

Cary hadn't been to the club in ages. At least it felt like ages. She'd been working a lot. And that meant less time spent just hanging out with her friends. But if the Nags were throwing her to the wolves this year, she intended to spend more time doing fun things. Life was too short to not go dancing.

And given the fact that she wasn't entirely sure she'd be able to survive her seventh year as a Protector, *her* life might just be even shorter.

In an attempt to ignore the worry of what she faced this year, she pushed through the crowd to the long wooden bar with Lucy in tow to get the next round of beers. She was joking with Lucy about her dance moves, enjoying the energetic beat of the B52's Love Shack blasting through the club, when her cellphone buzzed in her back pocket.

Frowning, worry tightening her gut—because that seemed to be her default these days—she looked at the text.

Deacon: *where are you?*

Cary: *Dance club with friends. Where are you? They said you had a family emergency? Everyone OK?*

As soon as she hit send, she felt a little guilty she hadn't texted him earlier. Between him looking after her for days and then only leaving because of an emergency, she really should have thought to check on him. Oops.

Deacon: *where are you exactly? need to talk to you.*

Since he lost his mind and control when he wasn't with her for long periods of time, she assumed he just need a few minutes in her company to settle his leopard down. She texted him her location and put her phone away.

The mate thing had left him on edge and holding onto his control by a thread until—according to his *mother* (ahhh!)—they had sex. A lot of sex.

He wasn't rushing her, though, which was good because the entire thing had her more than a little freaked out. It was a weird and intimidating responsibility, knowing Deacon could lose control of his animal side just because she wasn't around. She didn't particularly like the idea. Or the responsibility for that matter. And she didn't trust the mate bond thing. Not even a little. So she was happy to take things slow with him.

At least as slow as her own hormones would allow. She was having an embarrassingly hard time resisting the man.

"Who was it?" Lucy shouted over the music.

"Deacon," Cary shouted back.

"Aw," Lucy cooed.

Cary rolled her eyes.

"What did he want?" Lucy asked.

"I think he was worried about me," Cary hedged with a shrug. "He wanted to know where we were so he could come see me."

"Is that stalker-y or sweet?" Lucy asked.

Cary laughed. "He's not stalking me. It's the mate bond thing."

"So long as you're safe?"

Cary didn't miss the question in Lucy's tone, even in the loud club. "I'm safe from him. He wouldn't hurt me," she assured.

"Good." Lucy flashed a wicked grin. "He must really like you. Not even waiting till tomorrow."

Cary made a face. "I'm still not sure, Luce."

"You don't think he's serious about you? He's been bringing you food for a month."

"Yeah, but that might just be the mate-chemistry. Wait till you see him. I'm not exactly in his league."

"If you mean," Lucy said very seriously, "that he's not good enough for you, I'll agree with you on that."

Cary grinned. "You're so loyal."

"Bet your ass."

"I love when you say 'ass' in your cute little voice."

"Well, for that crack, this round is on you."

"Deal." Cary handed over her credit card and set up a tab. Given how much support her friends were giving her, and how much she was going to need them over the next year, she figured she owed them a few rounds.

And since she wasn't entirely sure if the Nags were going to continue paying her during her seventh year, she wanted to get the payback drinks in while she could still afford them.

They were on the dance floor when a commotion near the door

caught Cary's attention. She knew exactly who it was before she saw him—the mate thing apparently affected her too on some level.

She faced the direction of his approach as the crowd cleared and some of the noise around them quieted. Deacon emerged like a mythical being, all sexy intensity and heat. The colorful strobe lights did nothing to disguise his exquisite male perfection. Dark hair, golden eyes, the body of a god inside fitted jeans and a black t-shirt. Quite a few of the women, and a number of men, gaped as he passed. One woman fanned herself. Another placed a hand over hear heart. All eyes followed him as he strode toward Cary. Cary couldn't blame them. She couldn't seem to look away either.

And his full attention was zeroed in on her.

From behind her, she heard someone whistle, and Lucy muttered, "Holy hell."

~

Don't miss
The Trouble with Ghouls and Serial Kills
Book 2 in the Cary Redmond series
Coming soon!

BOOKS BY KAT SIMONS

The Cary Redmond Series

1 - The Trouble with Black Cats and Demons

2 - The Trouble with Ghouls and Serial Killers

Tiger Shifters Series

1 - Once Upon a Tiger

2 - Along Came a Tiger

3 - Here There Be Tigers

4 - Her Tiger To Take

5 - To Tempt a Tiger

6 - Down Will Come Tiger

7 - To Catch a Tiger

8 - What a Tiger Wants

9 - Taming Her Tiger

Tiger Shifters Series Vol 1 (Books 1 - 3)

Tiger Shifters Series Vol 2 (Books 4 - 6)

ABOUT THE AUTHOR

Kat Simons earned her Ph.D in animal behavior, working with animals as diverse as dolphins and deer. She brought her experience and knowledge of biology to her paranormal romance fiction, where she delights in taking nature and turning it on its ear. After traveling the world, she now lives in New York City with her family. Kat is a stay-at-home mom and a full time writer. The first book in her newest urban fantasy series, The Trouble with Black Cats and Demons, is out now.

For more on Kat and her future books:

Website: http://www.katsimons.com
Newsletter: http://eepurl.com/OxQQL